URCHIN

URCHIN

by

KATE STORY

TABLE OF CONTENTS

Every plague needs an abomination.

How fitting! I am one.

This particular plague arrived in New York in August. The Norwegian vessel *Bergensfjord* wired ahead: ten passengers had taken ill, and three had died at sea. The boat was met at the pier by ambulances and health officers, and the afflicted were placed in isolation.

That didn't stop the thing. Nearly thirty thousand in the city have died: four hundred spirits a day. And they are hard deaths. Patients gasp for breath as their lungs fill with bloody fluid and froth, drowning in a bouillon made by their own bodies. Influenza, they call it, from the Latin for *influence*: the old belief that sickness is caused by a misalignment of the planets.

Boy Scouts distribute warnings for violation of the Sanitary Code to those caught spitting in public. Armies of volunteers have arisen to cook and carry. There's a lovely camaraderie in the church brigade kitchens. We share recipes, cook endless meals, crack jokes, cry on each other's shoulders when needed—and of late, oh, how it is needed. I am prized for my uncanny driving skills; I transport the meals we prepare to the terrified sick in quarantine. I've always loved driving, but I've never been able to afford my own car. We all agree it is a time when, more than ever, it is good to cultivate gratitude for small rewards from unexpected quarters.

I pass. I dress like the rest of them. Nobody suspects what I really am. If we weren't in the middle of all this, it would be almost funny. The police are very polite to me, now:

I, who have been jailed for public indecency, and any number of trumped-up charges.

When the others in the kitchens—where I toil alongside them—speak of husbands and children, I am sympathetic. Oh, yes, this sickness has a sense of humour. It overwhelmingly spares the weak. The young and healthy are its preferred sacrifices.

On my rounds I pass a billboard advertisement for Formamint: *The Germ-Killing Throat Tablet. Why catch their influenza? Attack the germs before they attack you!* Coughing people waver behind a woman in an enormous beribboned hat, stealthily opening a tin of the useless mints with her gloved hand.

There's not a jar of Vic's VapoRub to be found; panicky purchasing wiped out druggists' stocks weeks ago.

You and I joked about it, gallows humour, until you, too, fell ill.

We were both in denial at first. *It's just a headache.*

You felt unwell. *Who doesn't feel unwell, these days?*

Now you are feverish, and gasping for breath.

The thing runs its course in two or three days. Two or three days will tell us whether you survive, or—

If I could make that dash as long as all infinity—

We are in quarantine now. It is better than hospital: cases crammed into cots, the dead stacked all around like cordwood. I sit vigil, and I hope.

You asked me to write down this tale.

I don't know if I can do it. My mind is on you, and inside me is a great, aching longing for the capacity to pray. But I was not brought up to it; and there is the little matter of my abomination. I have no god to appeal to. There is only broth, lemon juice, wet cloths on your hot, dry forehead, and watching. Endless watching.

Whenever you hear my typewriter fall silent, you begin to fret. *Write the story! You promised.*

But you already know all this stuff.

Write it anyway, you tell me. *Write it for the others, the ones who don't know. And then, when I am better, you can read it aloud to me.* You smile. *I'll let you know where you go wrong.* That gets a laugh out of me. And when still I hesitate, protesting I am no memoirist, you take my hand. *I love it when you read to me.*

They said my family was cursed.

That's a good beginning, you say. *A grand first line. Start with that.*

So when I am not attending you, my fingers pound the keys like one possessed.

I can do this for a few more days. If it keeps you with me, I can do anything.

SPARK AND ENERGY

They said my family was cursed.

I was a Southsider born and bred. But the north side of St. John's had its advantages. Over here, I wasn't instantly recognizable as my mother's horrifying, disappointing daughter. Here, I was just some ill-bred urchin running down Prescott Street on a mild December day, dirty coat a-flapping, another school day over. Freedom!

A great grand tilt of a hill it was, like the hand of God was trying to tip the rubbish off into the harbour. Momentum took over. I nearly smacked into a woman with an enormous old-fashioned bustle, decked out in a cruel mess of jewellery. She shrieked—her gentleman companion struck at me with his umbrella—I licked out my tongue and rattled on.

Brat though I was, the city was younger than I. Three fires had burned through it—catastrophic, ravenous, feverish conflagrations. All good things come in threes. Within a year of the latest inferno, row upon row of wooden houses had been flung up: flat-roofed, bracket-eaved affairs, leaning on each other like friends, aboard each other like bad neighbours. The glavauning homeless hordes needed roofs over their heads, and to build out of brick or stone would take too much time. Besides, why dwell on past mistakes?

There were some who muttered that the Great Fires had all of them provided the merchants with tidy insurance payments, but they were not much listened to. The city built flesh on the old rames, like Bram Stoker's Dracula enlivening himself with blood. Commercial buildings—by decree built of stone and brick—clustered around the harbour. Residential dwellings— evidently less crucial to the success of the Dominion—climbed the hill, rank upon rank of tinder waiting dumbly for the next person to boil a pot of glue, or smoke a pipe in a stable.

It had been storming for days, but this morning the gale had blown itself out and the city had emerged with a scrubbed and effervescent clarity. I came up short at Duckworth Street, waiting to cross through the busy traffic.

Signal Hill hulked at the mouth of the harbour, topped by the brand-new Cabot Tower, erected to mark Queen Victoria's Diamond Jubilee and the turn into a new century. Near Fort Amherst an unseasonal iceberg gleamed turquoise and white. A wall of colourless fog hovered outside the Narrows, a soft and deceptive beast. By night it would engulf the city.

Across the harbour crouched the massive Southside Hills. I could pick out wharves and premises along the south side of the waterfront, and the houses, none of them alike, a ragged processional climbing the Hill. There, just east of the others and a little above them, my own home huddled. Innocuous enough from this distance, tiny as a child's toy.

My great-great-grandfather—a captain, and a builder of ships—had caused our house to be made so that it swayed in high winds. During storms I thought I could hear the rote of the sea, beating against the cliffs outside the Narrows while the walls shifted and creaked around me. All night long I'd dreamt that the house was far out on the ocean, a two-masted passenger ship, pitching and yawing, racing furiously before the wind. Sailors called out: *Ho, one! Ho, two! Ho, belay! Larboard, clap on! Belay!* Waves towered over the vessel. She toiled up the face of each liquid mountain, only to slide down the other side into a churning chasm. Passengers cried out in fear and sickness. All but one: a slender man, just above average height, but I could not see his face. It was his energy that pulled me—taut, he was, like the rigging of the ship. He turned toward me, and in the dream I saw that his face was covered with a glittering, crawling, heaving mass. What *were* They, so full of spark and energy? The Things bore into him, yammering and crying. They hated him. They were the cause of the storm. He was on his way from England to Newfoundland. And They did not want him to arrive. His gaze was on me, although I could not see his eyes. I felt, rather than saw, his look, and I suddenly felt, too, the attention of the Things pass to me, as if They were trying to send a signal of some kind, one I could not understand. What did They want from me? Did They want me to prevent the man from coming to our shores? The signals became confused, shaping into dazzling patterns. A thousand high-pitched voices wailed in a chorus. The man passed his hand over his face, but before it could be revealed to me there was a pause, the ship suspended at the top of an enormous wave. And then the ship slid down and down, and the glittering yammering Things came together in a vortex and launched themselves at me, straight into my face.

I'd awoken screaming a tight, high scream.

Remembering it now brought a chill over me, twinned with enervating excitement. It had a peculiar force, that dream. I stood like a block of wood on the corner, oblivious to passersby, staring out the Narrows.

Just then a crow came cawing over me. It lit on one of the street lamps, a single white feather on each of his wings—yes! My heart leapt. He was back!

This snappy-looking bird had befriended me a few months ago. I'd been snivelling under a tree in Bannerman Park, hiding from a meanness of girls, when he'd flown into the branches over my head. I didn't pay him much mind at first, but he'd kept hopping from branch to branch, perching ever closer, making a noise in his throat like rolling marbles. It was strangely tender, that noise. I'd wiped my snotty face on my pinafore, fumbled in my pocket for a crust of bread, and tossed it up to him—he'd caught it from the air in his beak. From that day on, I always looked for him. He'd show up a scattered time. I fed him if I had anything, but even if I didn't he'd walk around me or perch overhead, never close enough to touch, but close enough for companionability. He'd make that tender sound in his throat.

I had no name for him. I sensed he had a name, and that it wasn't for me to know. Not yet.

Cawing again, he rendered a tight circle over my head before soaring off across the harbour to the Southside. It felt like a benediction.

Happiness filled me. I was downtown, and school—horrible school—was over for the day, and nothing called me home, for my parents wouldn't notice if I were there or not. The noise and busy-ness, horses and carts, gorgeous glittering windows of the shops left no room for sorrows. Many stores had not only signs but also objects over their front doors to advertise their business. The figures would come alive in the fog tonight long after humans were in bed, I thought as I charged down to Water Street. The ship's officer outside Parson's Watchmaker and Jeweller would stalk through the streets holding his quadrant and seeking for the sun; James Baird's lion would prowl next to John Steer's polar bear, and the giant circular saw outside Martin's Hardware would roll down the hill and slice through the Courthouse jail, setting the prisoners free. Bowring's ship would set sail into the starry night. Monstrous fish would don colossal Smallwood boots and carry Rutherford's golden fleece like a beacon up Signal Hill, and mammoth pocket watches would roll crazily through the streets, causing the saddlery's life-like horse to whinny and leap. The tall man with the feathered headdress outside Cash's tobacco store would come alive and walk across the harbour, walk on water all the way to the Southside, and he'd go to the churchyard of St. Mary's where the body of Shawnawdithit was rumoured to lie, and he'd say, *Sister, let us leave this place.*

Oh, how I wished I could leave it too.

For most of my conscious life I'd been certain that I was a suppuration, a corruption, an anxiety that the city wished to squeeze out of itself. I'd developed an idea that some day I would come into contact with something bigger than my mere self, something that would take me away. A destiny, I dared to think, elaborating on the theme.

This very day, such a thing would present itself.

THE SHIP

I darted across the busy street, earning a curse from a streetcar driver. I grinned at him and waved in imitation of the poor, dead Queen.

"Filthy urchin!"

"Ha ha!" I retorted unbrilliantly. The driver had his revenge, however; a breeze caught hold of my hat. I missed grabbing it from the air, and it skittered under the wheels. The streetcar ground inexorably by, but O miracle of miracles, the beribboned saltwater pancake emerged, skimming over granite cobblestones. I seized it, collecting a fresh curse from a cab driver and—I was almost certain—a dirty look from his horse.

A bell shivered the air.

It was Mary Kelly herself, shocking the good and pure of St. John's by shamelessly riding a bicycle.

Mary Kelly was glorious as an angel and tough as a stevedore. She was my very first memory, at my side while the city burned. She was there when my mother was first overtopped by the black moods. She'd been the Help, back when my family could afford Help. But Mary was more, far more, help than housework. She was the older sister I'd never had. She was my friend. Ever since we'd had to let her go, she'd kept up a contact with me that was, possibly, responsible for any poor ability I had to love at all.

"I'm meeting Murph at Wood's!" she shouted now, waving her arm as if commanding an army. "Come along, me duckie!"

Several passersby directed disapproving looks her way, but I noticed men's eyes bulging, zeroing in on Mary's shapely ankles. An enormous hat perched jauntily on her masses of twilight-dark hair. Any hat on Mary's head would never have the temerity to blow under the wheels of a streetcar. She had enough pins in there to dispatch a small army of ogling men.

I broke into a run, pursuing the bicycle. Wood's! It was not open yet; how could Mary be meeting Murph there? Wood's opening was awaited with great anticipation by everybody in St. John's: a candy and soda shop on the main floor, and a restaurant on the second.

I caught up to her at the entrance of the turreted brick building. She had already dismounted her iron steed, the glass door under the fanlight swinging shut behind her. Next to the door was a tantalizing ad: *Pure Fruit Soda All Flavours 5 Cents Per Glass, Ice Cream Soda 10 Cents Per Glass.*

The two-storey bay window was hung with sheets. Peering through a gap I saw scaffolding by a wall, a floor covered with vast sheets of canvas, some chairs, and several small, round tables.

I pushed open the door, and stepped over the threshold.

Plaster dust covered almost every surface inside Wood's. Mary's fiancé William Murphy was flapping a giant handkerchief over a chair so Mary could sit. Workers hammered away upstairs, and a painter reclined on some scaffolding, laying down the outline to some kind of scene, probably—if the trees and caribou were any indications—a woodland fresco. The soda fountain lay disassembled on the counter. No soda or candy in sight.

"What's happened to your face?" Mary was asking.

"Don't you like it, my darling?" Murph stroked his mustache, carefully twirling the ends. He was blond and thinning up top, but the hair on his face was brindy as a red and blasty bough, setting his twinkling blue eyes afire.

"But your beard? You worked so hard on it."

"Gone the way of the dodo, my dearest."

"Will it grow back?"

"Ha!" snorted the painter unkindly.

"You wound me, damsel." Murph now pretended to have

been shot through the heart, staggering over to the counter; however, he thought better of falling on it, due to plaster dust. "What do you think, Dor?" he appealed to me. "It's very new-century." I managed not to laugh. "Just the thing." "See, Mary Kelly?" He cast a mischievous glance at Mary. "Oh, well, then, if Dorthea likes it." Mary peeled off her gloves. "I adore it. And I adore you."

A burst of hammering from above prompted a fine mist of plaster dust to fall from the ceiling. Mary whipped a handkerchief from her sleeve and laid it delicately over her hat. "How did you get in here, Murph?" I burst out.

"My good friend Ralph, here," Murph gestured at the fresco painter, "arranged for a sneak preview, on the promise of a shout-out in the *Evening Telegram*. I'll be writing a feature for the New Year opening." He pulled a flask from his pocket and took a swig, passing it up to the fresco painter. "Ralph, fresco *artiste* for Wood's Soda Emporium and Restaurant Extraordinaire, the Michelangelo of Newfoundland... do you think that's a bit much?"

"A bit," admitted the painter. "Although I'll take it."

"Maybe I'll just say something like *a credit to all concerned, especially to the person who did the frescoing and painting*...I have a month to work on it." He began to struggle with his jacket pockets. Lead pencils, a candle stub, a box of Seadog matches, and a couple of legal pads fell onto the floor. "I have," he grunted, "a bottle of... somewhere in here... damn it... birch beer!"

"Capital!" Mary said. "Full points for Murph!"

There was a hunt for a bottle opener for the birch beer—which the fresco painter rather crankily came down off his scaffolding to procure—and Mary offered to share it with me, which I thought very generous.

She'd arrived at our house with nothing but a primary school education. Precocious, she'd listened in on lessons taught to older children in the one-room school. My father deemed it *a sin that the cleverest person I've ever met didn't finish her schooling,* and promptly took on her further education. To his delight and hers, she learned quickly, and he even taught her some Latin.

But the crash of the two main Newfoundland banks, a mere two years after the devastation of the Great Fire, meant Father lost his position. With great mutual sorrow my parents were forced to let Mary go. I'd missed her every minute since.

However, for her it turned out to be a blessing. Being Mary, she got a job at a fancier house in town, and from there, a fancier one still, until a few months ago she procured a place at Government House. Sir Cavendish Boyle, made Governor of the colony that very year, overheard her singing at her work, insisted she attempt one of his compositions, and was instantly enchanted. He determined on Mary getting lessons, and induced her to sing at parties. She soon attained fame as *the Governor's operatic housemaid.*

She also had the opportunity to observe many of the most important people in the colony, including the Governor's fellow-bachelor Premier Robert Bond (*the Great Newfoundland Bear*, she called him), and railway contractor Sir Robert Reid (*the Great Newfoundland Walrus*, on account of his tremendous wealth, balding head, and prominent, drooping mustache).

She'd met William Murphy while he was covering society parties at Government House for the *Telegram*. They'd become engaged, and so she no longer worked as a housemaid, even an operatic one. She was occupying herself making occasional appearances in local theatrics at the Casino Theatre. And I knew Mary harboured a not-so-secret ambition to move to New York, or Europe, so as to sing opera. The New York scheme worked for Murph, who wanted nothing more than to be a reporter with the *New York Times*.

If she managed to leave, I had no doubt she would become world-famous. Not only was she a tremendous singer and smart as a whip, she was the most beautiful woman in

St. John's, with the raven hair of a princess, alabaster skin, and eyes that sparkled like stars. My mother called them true Irish eyes, and she would sometimes add *put in with a sooty finger.* This wasn't a particularly lovely way to describe Mary's eyes. They were the colour of the sea on a broad day, with a dark ring around the iris like a storm coming in. But Mother had Opinions about the Irish.

"I call this meeting to order!" Murph announced.

"Hear, hear!" I shouted.

There followed an impressive silence. Murph made his mustache quiver, which caused me to snort birch beer up my nose.

"For heaven's sake, Murph, what meeting?" Mary laughed.

"The *Sardinian* has been spotted," Murph replied. "She'll be in port by the end of the week. By Friday... Marconi will be in St. John's!"

A thread of cold went running down my spine. That dream from last night peeked through Murph's words—the ship—the man with the light-filled beings glistering and yammering.

"Well, we all know that," Mary pointed out.

"Who is Marconi?" I asked.

"Ignorant child, listen and learn." Murph leaned in, mustache quivering again. "Here's the thing."

"Oh for heaven's sake, Murph, how can we take you seriously?" Mary hooted.

"Down, Rover!" He made a show of taming the beast with his fingers.

I remembered then; it had been in all the papers. Marconi was an Italian, and an experimenter with a new wireless communication system called telegraphy. My heart beat faster. "What's the thing?" I asked.

"A mustache."

"No, silly! What's the thing you said was the thing you were going to say about Marconi?"

Murph sat back and took another swig from his flask. "He claims to be visiting our fair isle to establish ship-to-shore communications. I don't believe it." He leaned forward, enjoying the theatre of the moment, but his eyes had a serious look I didn't often see there. "It's got to be something bigger. Much bigger. And he's not telling anybody what it is."

We sat in silence for a moment. Even the hammering from above momentarily ceased.

"Are you saying Marconi's here under false pretenses?" Mary asked, voice low.

Murph nodded. "I think this whole thing is a bam."

"But that would mean..." I stared at him. "He's lying to the entire Newfoundland government!"

Mary agreed. "It beggars the imagination, Murph."

"Think about it," Murph said. "He had the station in Cape Cod. It blew down. His station back in Cornwall blew down too. His investors must be lunging at him. If he doesn't do something big, and soon, all the work he's put in over the past years..."

"Will be for naught," Mary finished. "But to lie to the Dominion's entire administration..."

"Is it lying, though? It's not like he *won't* put in ship-to-shore stations, necessarily. I think he's trying to build on his past experiments. He's been going for longer and longer transmission distances. He's gotten up to—well, I can't quite remember, but something over twenty miles."

"Newfoundland is considerably farther from Cornwall than twenty miles," I pointed out.

"Clever young article. But nothing across the sea's closer to Cornwall than Newfoundland."

"He's got rivals at his heels," Mary mused. "That Tesla fellow in New York was quoted as saying he's got something big in the works too. A one-hundred-foot spark, whatever that means, at his testing facility on Long Island."

"Exactly," Murph nodded. "Marconi's got to do something spectacular. And if that thing doesn't involve his station in Cornwall, I'll shave my mustache."

"Oh, goodie," Mary responded drily.

"A public demonstration? But... you'd want to make sure it *worked*," I jabbered. "Maybe Murph is right. Just imagine if Marconi announced to everybody that he was going to get a signal between Britain and here, and then it failed!"

"He'd be a laughingstock," Murph nodded. "Hence his motivation for secrecy."

"What does your editor think?" Mary asked.

"Bah, humbug," Murph admitted. "He's got me writing up a story about that poor fella who plunged from the Courthouse scaffolding and knocked his nopper in."

"I heard about that!" I said. "He fell down three storeys onto the rocks and was still alive when they lifted him up and his *hands quivered* and he tried to speak and then he *died*."

"Barbarian," Mary said. "The poor patrick had a family to feed too."

"Yes, I was sent by my heartless editor to be there when they brought his body home." Murph looked miserable. "Some caudler was supposed to send the priest to break the news to the wife. But that never happened. So she comes out, takes one look, and starts battering at the unfortunate's corpse, shrieking like a banshee about how was she supposed to feed his brats now that he was gone. The children bivvering and bawling. They had to haul her off her man, and her still screaming that she'd bring him back alive to kill him again."

"Lord."

"How are you going to write that up, Murph?" I inquired.

"Oh, something like *the scene at the home was...* let's say *heartrending, when the wife and six children saw their bread-winner brought in a corpse*."

I whistled. "That's good."

"Don't whistle, Dor, you're not a sailor," Mary admonished.

"But about Marconi," Murph continued. "He's got the two Roberts in the palm of his hand. And the Governor has offered up whatever resources he needs."

"That's public knowledge," Mary pointed out. "It's an agreement to install telegraph stations here on the island and on the Labrador. The government's going to pay him a royalty for such-and-such number of years."

"Indeed. But here's the *thing* Dor wants to know about..." and he leaned in, mustache quivering again. "His station in Cornwall, on a point called the Lizard, he built up rather quietly. But I have it from a source in London that the place has an electrical transmitting apparatus of thirty horsepower. Thirty! There's something big on the go."

Mary sipped her birch beer, a speculative look on her face. "And, again, your editor thinks...?"

"No muckraking," Murph said sourly. "None of that new investigative journalism. No scrabbling through the dirt for him. No, no, it's all *Print what I tell you to print* and *Gentlemen's press* and all that. Even though three-quarters of our newspaper is advertisements. People will buy this story, I tell him. Even if I am wrong—and I know I'm not—the papers we would sell!"

"So what are you thinking? Because if I know you, you've got some kind of harebrained scheme."

Murph clutched his heart again. "My lady!"

"Out with it, Murph!"

"Well, he's bound to call a conference. My editor has asked me to be at the Cochrane Hotel when he arrives."

"Oh! Of course. Can I come?"

He took another swig from his flask. "Ah, the golden nectar from the family of Marconi's mother."

"What's that?" I asked.

"Jameson whiskey," Murph belched.

"Murph!"

"Please excuse me. Naturally I want you to come, my darling Mary. You can charm people into talking to me, else they will avoid me like the plague." He stared at the draped windows as if he could see through the sheets and over to the Southside Hills and beyond. "I need a spy," he muttered.

A spy? I thought.

"Whatever for?" Mary asked.

"Someone Marconi won't suspect. Someone who can spend time with him during his experiments, and report to me."

What was this energy surging through my body? A spy... Someone nobody suspected would make the best kind of spy.

"Murph!" Mary exclaimed. "Are you giving me an assignation?"

Murph looked revolted. "Never! No, Mary! As if I'd do such a thing. I was thinking more along the lines of asking the *Telegram* errand boy, but he's hopeless."

A child, a boy. Yes, I could see why Murph had had the idea.

"Hopeless how?"

Murph sighed. "He is, to be frank, a complete idiot. I've taken to delivering my own dispatches; he can't even get an address straight."

"Idiots don't make good spies."

A boy would be best. I wasn't one. But I wasn't an idiot, either. I was... What was I?

I had never felt like a girl.

And I knew with every fibre of my being that I wanted to do this thing. To meet Marconi, and be a spy for Murph. My heart began to race. "What about me?" My voice came out like a death rattle.

"What about you, Dor?"

I cleared my throat. "I can be your spy." As I said it out loud, the idea seemed bright and hard and true as metal.

"Er... you'd pretend to be the *Telegram* errand girl?"

"There's no such thing as an errand *girl*," I said scornfully. "No—I'd be a boy."

"What?"

They were both staring at me as if I was a bedlamer. "I'd pretend to be a boy."

"Now, I don't—" Mary began.

Murph was looking strangely at me. "Your voice is rather... you know. Low. For a girl's."

I seized on this. "The choir teacher at school says I sing like a crow!"

"Hmmm."

"Go home out of it, Murph," Mary rapped. "You're drunk."

"I assure you, my angel, I am sober as... well, given the state of our colony's justice system, I will not say."

"To encourage this. No, Dor, you'd never be able to keep up such an elaborate charade. See reason, my darling. And he'll be experimenting with electricity, and... well, who knows? It could be dangerous."

"No, Mary, please listen." I suddenly wanted this more than anything. "I haven't got a thing here," I puffed out my concave chest. "I'm skinny as a skinned rabbit. The girls in school all say so. So does Mother. I'm a late bloomer. That's what they all say..." Words tumbled out—I hardly knew what they were. "I could do it. I could, and I know how to swear—Jesus, Mary, and Joseph I've got more chaw than a sheep's head... I can do it!"

Mary threw Murph a troubled look. "Look what we've done. Besides, she'd miss school..."

She? The image of myself as a *Telegram* errand boy was so entirely vivid that it took me a moment to know who Mary was referring to.

Murph considered. "Today's Wednesday. The conference will be Friday evening, if he arrives when we think he will. He'll want to move fast, scoping out sites over the weekend. No school is threatened."

"See?" I pleaded.

"What about your parents?" he asked me. "Could you get out of the house without them worrying?"

"That's no problem," I said.

"No, it wouldn't be," Mary said. "I worry about you in that house, Dor. Rattling around there and nobody paying attention. But, the pair of you, see reason! You'll never pass for a boy, Dor."

"Why not?" I asked belligerently.

"Well, you're too small, for one thing, and you have the most beautiful big eyes, and... well, really. It beggars belief that you could suddenly become a boy and fool the world. And if Marconi discovered you, who knows what he would do? Call the police, quite likely." She turned her severe expression on her fiancé. "Anything to get a story, is that it, Murph?"

Murph looked ashamed. "You're right, of course, Mary, you always are." He looked to me. "Sorry, Dor. I let myself get carried away."

"But what about your story?" To my horror, my eyes filled with tears and my lips trembled.

"I'll find another way. It's grand of you to offer, Dor, but Mary is right. I can't accept."

I cast a beseeching gaze at Mary, clasping my hands. I tried to come up with some stunning logic, some persuasive reason for this plan to work, but all that came out was a whisper. "I can do it."

Outside, the short December day was drawing to its close. Electric light poles, their web of wires carving the sky, started all at once to light up. The fresco painter clambered down and began to clean his tools. Down the stairs trooped the workmen, joking and laughing. They came up short when they saw Mary, straightening up and tugging their caps at her.

We all stood. Mary clucked, attempting to brush the dust off my coat. But I didn't care about dust.

No matter what Mary said, the hard brightness of the idea shone in the air before me. I could become this boy, I could. If I had anything to do with it, my life was going to change.

ONE EYE ON THE DEVIL

Mary and Murph insisted on walking me to the Long Bridge. As we got near the north end of it, we heard the approach of wheels and horses' hooves. A pair of dark horses emerged around the curve in Water Street, drawing an ornate hearse burdened with flowers.

We stepped back and bowed our heads in respect.

It must be an important person, I thought, looking through my eyelashes at the crochet on the horses, the elaborate wreaths of crape-paper lilies.

"There's the Reverend," Murph whispered.

I gazed at the eldritch person before us. Everyone knew who he was; I'd seen his slight, bent figure all my life. If he had any occupation it was that of professional mourner. Any funeral of importance he was there, marching right behind the coffin with his unmistakable gait. He always walked bent sideways, almost doubled, so that his long black evening coat dragged on the one side.

Everyone said he lived down the Southside Road, near the Old Man's Beard, a place that stayed covered in ice far into June most summers, for it never saw the sun.

Some of the old people called him a fairy man, or changeling. Even if he was stood upright, I estimated he'd be no more than five feet tall, and with his bent-over stoop he was smaller than a child. His gait was lop-sided, for one of his legs did not bend. He planted that heel, then twisted as the other leg lurched forward. On a muddy day or in the snow he'd leave circular depressions, dimples—like a series of mots for playing marbles—in a trail behind him.

Yet we children—even Clinton Taylor, worst boy on the

Southside—never tormented him. It was said he could escape from any locked room, as if he could turn himself into mist.

And that if you crossed him, he'd turn you into a goat.

When not honouring the passing of members of St. John's high society, the Reverend often sang. You'd hear it long before you saw him, a warbling voice that lurched indiscriminately between a sweet counter-tenor and a baritone. Some said that if you heard it coming for you in the night, you'd be dead by morning.

As the Reverend pulled level with us, I saw he had a big hump on his back. He lifted his head, twisting his neck around until he fixed me with his gaze. It was all I could do not to step backwards.

He nodded at me. "Hello, young fella."

Young fella? Dressed as I was in my beribboned hat and girl's stockings and coat, I gave an awkward bow. "Hello, sir."

"Keep one eye on the Devil," he said to me, turning, "and one eye on the One Up Above."

Confused, I pulled my hat from my head, stuffing it under my arm.

"I'll see you in a while, short or long. Young ... lady?"

It was a question.

He bowed. I bowed again in return, keeping my head down. When I heard his uneven steps begin again, I straightened.

Something moved on his dark coat. I realized that what I'd taken for a hump was a crow, a crow sitting on his back. The bird, too, fixed me with its gaze. As the Reverend lurched away, the bird slowly turned on the Reverend's back to keep me in sight. It bounced up on its clawed feet and half-raised its wings. Was it my imagination, or was each pinion striped with one white feather?

"Caw! Caw! Caw!"

The sound fell dead in the fog. The funeral passed into the dying day.

WHAT A PRETTY GIRL

After bidding Mary and Murph goodnight, I trudged alone across the Long Bridge. The last rays of sun gleamed, dazzle on my back. Almost nightfall, and almost home.

As I beat up the Hundred Steps towards the Range, my crow came into sight once more. "Hello!" I cried out, waving. "Oh, hello! I didn't know you were acquainted with the Reverend!"

"Caw, caw!" the pied bird yawped. "Caw!" He flapped off down the harbour. I shaded my eyes with my hand and watched him until his black sketch of a figure disappeared into the water's reflected dazzle. Did he live with the Reverend? I wondered. Did they truly live in the Old Man's Beard? Surely it was a special day, for me to have seen him twice.

I was blinking away the flare when, to my joy and delight, Clare Taylor appeared.

She lived in the Range, one of the abutted houses containing her thousands of relatives—brothers and sisters and her ancient Nan, and her father's parents too. I could hear her mother yelling within.

"Get back here, you sons of bitches, or I'll have your guts for garters!"

I believed I was the only person on the Southside Road—or indeed the world—to truly appreciate Clare Taylor's extraordinary beauty. Her harassed mother didn't, her father appeared not even to know her name, and certainly her nasty brother Clinton had no idea that among the eleven Taylor siblings lurked a creature of such radiance that she called to mind the paintings of the Pre-Raphaelite Brotherhood. Her eyes were a strange pale green, and her hair—a dark, velvety brown— in sunlight sparked ruby fire. She had a deceptively sweet expression, but I knew well that she was wicked, was Clare. I was the one forever getting into trouble just for looking at someone the wrong way. Clare, she could have been planning someone's murder and they'd think, *what a pretty girl.*

"I ain't done nothing!" Clare shrieked, then caught my eye and grinned merrily. "Hello, Dor! Catch me if you can!" and she careened down the Hundred Steps. I turned tail and tore after her, catching her around the waist, whipping us both around and laughing.

"What did you do?"

"Put jackstones down Clinton's pants."

"Damn right you did!"

We detected Clinton flying down behind us a moment too late. He leapt past us and knocked his sister a ringing blow across the head, sending her hat flying. I sprang and caught the hat before it sailed off into the muck.

"Ow, that was a jowler!" Clare complained.

"Another where that came from."

"Lay off, Clint," I growled.

Clare and I dodged past him down the steep, uneven wooden stairs. Clinton closed in right behind us, shoving me in the small of my back and nearly sending me into a header.

"Leave her alone, Clint!" Clare shouted.

"Make me."

"I'll tell."

"Tell who? Ma?" He laughed. In truth it was an empty threat. Mrs. Taylor had enough to do without worrying about one of her sons shoving an arrogant girl from up the Hill. He chuckled Clare, grasping her throat with his hand. "You won't."

"Let her go, Clint!" I said.

"Make me."

But I was not weaponless. I had, hung on a grubby string around my neck, a pocket knife. I fumbled for it. "Let go of her!"

Clinton gave me a dirty look. "You'd never."

I opened the blade and put it to his neck. "Want to try me?"

He wasn't scared. But with a gesture of casual contempt, he let Clare fall. She grasped on to the rail of the stairs, coughing and trying to swear at her brother.

"What have you got under those skirts, a tail?" he grinned at me. "Or a bud? Because I bet my life you ain't got no slit." Then he laughed. "See you in hell, you crooked-arse bitches!" and he sprang over the next run of steps.

"Good riddance!" Clare yelled after him, rubbing her neck.

I watched Clare's brother clattering down the rest of the Hundred Steps, vaulting over the wrought iron fence into the churchyard. His lithe figure beat against the wind like the hounds of Hell pursued him, disappearing behind the rectory.

"Probably going to rob the minister," Clare spat.

What was it, I wondered, that made Clinton so obviously a boy? Even from a distance you would never mistake him for anything but that. Was it his clothes and his short hair, his roughness? Or was it also things like vaulting the fence?

Certainly there were things boys *didn't* do—like stealing clotheslines on a summer's day to go skipping, or playing jackstones on the canvas in the front hall. But other games—like Hoist Your Sails and Run, or Hiding—boys did just the same as girls did, and when Clare was taking off over the Hill shouting "First not to be After!" she covered ground with more determination and speed than her older brother, despite his long legs.

Was it simply the clothes? No, it was more. I couldn't name it, but I could feel it. I rolled my shoulders, felt it in my feet.

I'd seen the community theatrics at St. Mary's Hall, and there was always a man dressed as a woman, generating high hilarity. I'd never understood what that mincing, simpering kind of performance had to do with the real Southside women, who'd never minced or simpered in their lives. But it certainly sent the house up.

Clinton could skip school or go running through the rectory garden after supper, and he wouldn't get punished, by teacher or parent. But if Clare or I did...

"I don't mind being a girl," I said, picking my way through it. "I just wish there was more *scope.*"

Suddenly filled with energy, I put my hand on the wooden stair rail and vaulted over. I landed on the rocky path beside the stair and let myself fall, rolling down the slope, the rocky descent jarring my teeth. Coming to a flat place I leapt to my feet and finished up with what I hoped was a jaunty bow.

Clare was laughing so hard her eyes spouted tears. "You're in the fairies this evening, Miss Dor!" she called from above. She clattered down the stairs in a more girlish fashion. "You just getting home now?"

I nodded.

"I'd catch it if I got home this late for supper," she said.

Wariness gripped me. "We eat late," I lied.

"You must be half starved!"

I nodded. "Well, not long now," I said. Turning, I began the long trudge back up the Hundred Steps.

"I was hoping you were coming to see me," she said, falling in beside me.

Damn it to Hell! If only I'd lied with more skill.

"I could. They won't care," jerking my chin up toward my house.

"Don't be silly! You'd get skinned," she said, shocked that I'd even contemplate skipping supper. "But come see me tomorrow evening?" she begged. "If I don't find out what happens to that man with the Martians I will simply die, I will."

I had been sneaking Mother's old issues of *Pearson's Magazine* for weeks now. They carried serialized stories that most adults, I was sure, would have deemed *highly unsuitable* for girls. I was currently gripped by a bone-chilling story about an alien invasion in England. And I had not only been scaring myself rigid with it, but had been reading it to Clare. She could read for herself, of course. But she liked it when I read to her. *You do all the voices some good.*

And there was something about reading to Clare—her head on my shoulder as she followed along, her soft masses of thick, curling hair nestling into my neck, and her appreciative gasps at the horrible bits, both of us terrifying ourselves so I'd have to fling the magazine away while we clung to each other for a moment, shuddering in a mutual fit of the diddies—

"I promise!" I said, pulling myself from that dream.

Clare's cheeks flushed, and her eyes went green as a whiskey bottle on a windowsill. "I can't wait! Him, just wandering around with that chaplain and the aliens coming after them; I've been scared abroad ever since." She twinkled, lowering her voice. "Ma's having a card party tomorrow evening; she's wild lest the minister find out. So we can have a good natter and nobody will bother us. And, Dor. Your mother will have to come calling soon. Will you let her know?"

"Is..."

Clare nodded solemnly. "Mother's expecting again."

"Oh, Clare! I think my mother spends more time at your house than ours!"

We laughed at this much more than it deserved, leaning against each other for support.

"Go on with you, you'd better get home or you'll catch it."

I hoped she couldn't detect how hollow my laugh was. "And you, don't let that low-life Clinton oil you!"

"You can stick him with that knife of yours any day!"

Clare walked me back up the Hundred Steps, waving as she disappeared into her house. I watched her dance into the dark maw of the doorway like a bright twist of paper in the wind. When the door swung shut behind her, I felt a pain behind the crackbone of my heart, and the evening got a little bit darker.

Nightfall.

Lights had come on Over, as we called downtown across the water, trembling on the glassy surface of the harbour like stars. Over had but recently acquired electric lights. Some considered them ugly; all agreed they were useful.

I turned my back on the electric brilliance, making my way along the narrow, rickety boardwalk that led along the Hill to my house. It was known throughout the neighbourhood as the Ratline, pronounced *rattlin*. And the flat area where my house stood was called the Top, as if the Southside Hill were an enormous, square-rigged ship, and the house an anchor for the shrouds of an invisible topmast.

Seeing my home from across the harbour always engendered a shift inside me, a dislocating strangeness. It looked almost lovely from afar, with its hip roof and gracious windows, old-fashioned and quaint. It was the oldest house on the Southside, a fact of which my mother was inordinately proud. For when my great-great-grandfather had moved here, the area was no place to live, only work. Usually, I tried to avoid looking at it when I was Over. The disjuncture—the external appearance versus the lineal reality—put me into a mood, unstable even by my quixotic standards. With heavy feet I trudged up the shaky little stair. My head bowed as I walked the path alongside the dark and looming house.

The linney door hung unlatched on its hinges. We called it the back door, although it was at the side, for the house butted right up against the rock of the Hill. Living rock, it was. Often I laid my cheek against it and felt it, an energetic, dynamic thing, beating slow and cold beneath my skin. The Southside Hills had a vigour all their own.

I stepped through the linney and into the kitchen, groping for the matches kept on the windowsill. Would we ever have electric lights in our home against the rock? Something told me no, not even if we had all the money in the world.

"Hello?"

There was no answer.

Father was still out—probably, as Mother would say, on the Devil's racket. Mother would be abed. She had been for almost two weeks now.

The black mood had taken her, as it did, and when that happened Father and I would let her be. One or the other of us would bring her occasional food and drink—that was easier than when she came down to the kitchen, driven, despite her inner darkness, to feed. She'd enter the room like a wraith, faded nightdress and shawl glimmering in the dimness. She never spoke, never responded to plea nor prayer. Her long, pale hair hung down her back—she, who in the bright times was such a stickler for appearance. She was like a ghost those days.

My searching hand fell on a candlestick. The flare of the match brought the kitchen into shadowed relief, every crevice in the flagstones a ravine. The stone wall aback of it loomed like castles, the sideboard a monolith. The pump in the middle of the floor stood stark as a warning. Water ran ceaselessly beneath the house, back to front, bubbling up from a living spring gushing from the Hill. It murmured and chattered in its constant rush.

It was cold in the room, somehow colder than outside. I crept over to the coal stove and lifted a damper; the coals were dying. Buttoning my poor coat, I went back out to the linney and filled the scuttle, then tended to the stove. Once I got a good flame going—one I judged would bring the coals back up to heat for the night—I brought a basin to the pump and worked the handle.

For no reason whatsoever, the water came back into my face.

"Damn you!" I spluttered. Mother would have said it was my own clumsiness. And perhaps it was. But I couldn't help feeling that clumsiness alone failed to explain the many times incidents like this occurred to me in the house. They ranged from minor irritations—water coming back against me, a fork falling to the floor—to sudden pitches and shoves, flinging me against a wall or into a doorframe. It felt personal. And lately, it had gotten worse.

I did my best to wash my face and hands in the frigid water with a hard bit of soap, drying myself with the towel that hung on the stove handle. Then I looked about me to see how I'd fadge for supper. The breadbox had half a loaf; I seized on it with pleasure. And a trip into the cellar—across the hall, nestled back into the same rock that walled the kitchen—found me some cold chicken and an apple. Capital meal! I wolfed it down. Clare had been right; I was half-starved.

I blew out the candle, leaving it on the table for Father; he'd need it on coming home. Eschewing another wash of my hands and face, I crept up the back stairs to my bedroom, the spring chortling behind me. I slept in what would have been the Help's room. I had taken it for my own because it was the farthest from that of my parents.

Poised in my doorway, I thought I heard a movement down the hall, in the direction of Mother and Father's room.

"Hello?"

Nothing.

"Mother?"

She wouldn't answer. She never did when the dark mood had her.

A sense stole over me: the dark house was aware of me.

I flung my clothing in the general direction of the chair next to the bed, and threw my nightgown over my head. Bivvering with cold, I crawled under the blankets, pulled the covers over my head, and fell into sleep.

A GREAT ROARATION

I lay in that landwash space, lapped between sleeping and waking.

The room was pitch black. From downstairs came a din, dishes clattering and banging. Was someone flinging them around the kitchen?

Gradually I became aware that something was happening, but I could not move or prevent it: a sliding sensation, painful and pleasurable as a milk tooth coming out. And then I could see myself below in the bed. Despite the cold I lay splayed out like a split fish, long dark hair tangled across the pillow and face all afrown, eyes rolling under the thin skin of my eyelids, hands and feet twitching. My body gave a little cry, and with that my spirit cleaved from it.

I left myself behind.

My spirit flew out the window of my little room—through the panes of glass, as if I was a ghost—and hovered outside the house.

I could see my sleeping body through the wavery glass. See the house perched on its ledge on the Southside Hill, a cliff behind and a slope of scree before. See how the spring flowing beneath—from the kitchen in back all the way to the front of the house—tumbled off the Top, wetting the lips of the red rock. Icicles clung to the cliff where the iron-rich water froze blue and amber in the wintery air.

Around over to the farther side of the house my spirit was towed. Through the kitchen window I saw a crowd of tiny figures, beings of dancing light. No, not light. They were dressed all in grey, I saw then, with red caps on their heads: male or female I could not tell. I could look at them, and thought I was seeing them, but I could not describe their faces. Those kept shifting away, indescribable; my mind could not grasp what I was seeing. They danced in the corners of my eyes, flickering in the periphery, jigging and jagging across the flagstones. A figure seized a dish from the sideboard and flung it down the line, tossing it from hand to hand to the kitchen table, where it crashed down. More of Them tossed knives and forks into the air, juggling them widdershins, landing them on the table like a game of spillikins. Two worked the pump in the middle of the kitchen floor, and three more held the copper kettle beneath it. I could hear the spring gurgle as it was pulled up from deep inside the Hill.

And then my spirit was towed through the panes of glass and into the kitchen. I was pulled into the pump, shredding through all the intricate mechanism, hauled into that frigid hole beneath the house where the spring issued from the living rock. I didn't want to go but I was helpless, a twig against the tide, a great roaration in my ears. Pulled through water and rocks and frost, down below, I came to a tiny opening, too small even for a cat.

The choking passage opened up into a vast and impossible cave.

The walls sparkled with frost. Stalactites gleamed like crystal chandeliers.

A sound whispered around the cave, a threading, repetitive rasp.

There sat my mother. She wore neither coat nor sweater in that icy cavity. Her midwife's bag lay open beside her, and she smiled and laughed, easier than I had seen her for a long time. "To the health of your little one!"

There was nobody there but her.

She lifted a broken oyster shell to her lips, sipping filthy, breachy water out of it like fine wine.

The sound grew: a long, slow, repetitive wheeze. *Ooo... ah... ooo... ah...*

Mother reached out to a flat rock before her and took a living snail between her fingers. "Such lovely cakes." She popped the squirming thing into her mouth, munching and crunching and nodding her head. "I shouldn't have another, but we must celebrate."

The noise became grating, a dying person trying to breathe. The cave walls shuddered in time with the sound.

Ooo... aah... ooo... aah...

It was as if the cave were the interior of a giant lung. As if it was alive.

My mother laughed.

TOMBOY

I woke up back inside my body, unable to move. Someone was screaming, a breathless, high, frantic sound.

It was me.

"What's that caterwauling! Get *up*, Dorthea, for the love of God!"

I was covered in sweat, nightgown clinging to me, breath coming fast from the nightmare. What time was it? The room was still dark.

"Up, Dorthea!"

How I hated my full name. *Dor* I could stand, but...

"How many times... your father needs his breakfast or he'll be late to work!"

My mother's voice?

I threw the covers aside. It was like being plunged into cold water, an instant chill. I felt around in the dark for the chamber pot, forced my bare feet to the icy floor. It was a miracle my piss didn't freeze as it came out of me. From the kitchen downstairs came the clattering sounds of someone opening the dampers to get the coal embers in the stove going hot—I'd catch it now, that was supposed to be my job. Faint ruddy light glowed up the stair, dimly illuminating the hall outside my room.

We were currently "between girls." We'd been "between girls" for almost a year now, and I suspected we would remain "between girls" forever. I didn't care; after Mary left, every one of them had been horrible to me. But it was hard to go to school with my hands all grainted from housework, and the other students at school all had—not even "a girl," but—"maids." Plural.

"Dor-THEE-a!" That was Father's voice, not my mother after all; had I dreamt that? I breathed a sigh of relief.

"Coming, Father!"

Black stockings, white bloomers, woollen undershirt—I found them scattered from the night before. Lord, how that undershirt itched. Black dress, a thousand infernal buttons hard and shiny as crow's eyes up the back, and so hard to do up, especially with fingers all afrore. Comb over hair, so many knots, where was my ribbon? Pinafore—no, not that one, it had ink on it from yesterday—where was the other—there! Black boots to lace up, spitting on the toes and rubbing one after the other on the back of my stockinged legs. I grabbed my coat and was about to run out the door when I remembered—my pocket knife!

Father had given it to me for my last birthday. I suppose he had abandoned hope for a son to give it to. His father—my mysterious West Coast grandfather whom I had never met, and who had trapped with the Innu on the Labrador—had given it to him. It had a bone handle with iron bolsters and a steel blade, and measured six inches open.

For heaven's sake, what will she do with that? my mother had snapped. *Girls don't have pockets. Nor any need for a pocket knife. She's already a late bloomer; do you want to turn her into a tomboy?*

Father had laughed. *Too late.*

It had a metal ring attached to the handle, enabling me to carry it on a string around my neck. I loved the feel of it hidden down the front of my dress, cold on my skinny chest and slowly warming with the heat of my skin. I clutched it like a talisman, clattering down the stairs to face the day.

On my way down the stairs one of my feet caught, pitching me headlong. I landed on my hands and knees at the foot of the stairs.

When I looked back up behind me, there was nothing that could have tripped me. "I'm so lungy I'd trip up on a pencil mark," I muttered. I clambered to my feet, but stopped short when I came into the kitchen.

My mother crouched before the firebox, skirt ruched

up. "There you are," she snapped, poking mercilessly at the coals. "Wash your hands and make the toast."

Mother, here in the morning, meant she was in one of the energetic times, the brilliant times. It meant the dark mood had lifted. It meant she'd be scrutinizing me, finding fault with anything.

I pumped freezing water over my hands.

"Good morning." Even to my own ears, my voice was deep and ridiculously husky.

"Where you come from I do not know," Mother said. "You'd think you spent your nights with your father, smoking and drinking whiskey, with a voice like that."

She stood upright, dark skirts falling back around her feet in perfect drapery. Her white apron gleamed in the ruddy light, and the lace around her throat looked like the ruff of a queen. Her thick, fair hair, twisted and lifted into a softly swirled pompadour, shone in the half-light. She always kept spotless, somehow, despite the coal dust.

I wiped my hands on my pinafore—earning an exasperated sigh from Mother—and lunged toward the breadbox.

The kitchen table was already set, and for three. My father treated breakfast like camping out; when Mother was abed he only cooked for himself. I was old enough to serve myself, and usually I didn't. Eating in the morning made me feel like I was going to vomit. So then of course by dinnertime at school, I was faint with hunger. But still, I couldn't make myself eat first thing. I had read about geese being force-fed to render their livers a monstrous size; that's what breakfast felt like to me. Usually I'd have a little tea, with milk, if we had it, and lots of sugar, and that was it.

Mother being up and setting the table meant I'd have to eat under her eye.

Time was that would have been normal. We would have eaten breakfast all together; it had been that way when I was younger. And we would have eaten it in the dining room.

That room lay at the front of the house, overlooking the harbour and the city. It was a formal room despite its small size, with dark wood panelling, large windows, an oblong mahogany table gleaming like the surface of a still lake. But it was too cold in there; getting two fires going every morning was too much with no help. Cooking in the kitchen and then conveying everything down a hall to another room was too much with no help. It was all too much. And we couldn't afford the extra coal.

"Where's Father?"

"I sent him up with some hot water to shave. Hop to it."

By the time I had the bread sliced and stabbed through the heart with the long toasting fork, my father had appeared with a shaven chin.

"Morning, morning." His voice, deep as a foghorn and gravelly as a stevedore's, made mine sound like a piping bird. He ruffled my hair with his big hand, setting my bow even further askew. I took after him, with my single black beetle-brow, my dark hair and eyes. Mother was the odd one out in our little family, with her grey eyes and fairness. I could smell the alcohol on him from the night before; it came out his pores. I liked the smell—astringent, sharp, a little like juniper berries on a summer day.

Yawning, he poured a cup of thick black tea from the kettle always roiling on the back of the stove. He reached for a frying pan to cook his beloved eggs, but, "I'll do it," snapped my mother.

He winked at me. "Certainly, my dear." Removing a pair of glasses from his waistcoat pocket and perching them on his nose, he took up a defensive position behind his newspaper.

I scravelled over next to my mother, lifted a damper, and held the bread over the coals.

My mother cast a despairing glance at her dishevelled daughter, then confronted the wall of newsprint that was her husband. "The roof is half-off the linney again. It came loose in that wind last night."

The wall of newsprint grunted.

"It'll leak next time we get a thaw. And we still haven't fixed that door there. It bangs in the wind."

Grunt.

"Nor replaced those rotting boards in the front. We could get at it this weekend."

Father flapped the paper in half horizontally, peering over it. "If by *we* you mean *you,* meaning *I,* then certainly I could possibly *get at it this weekend* as you say. If we can get felt and tarpaper."

"Ah! *We* meaning *I* need to go Over to Templeton's and see if we still have credit."

The paper flapped upward again, an irritable angel's wing, and Mother focused on the eggs. Their sparring generally didn't go well if Father hadn't had his breakfast yet. I longed for the usual companionable silence of mornings with my father. I felt my stomach tighten. Maybe Father would simply let it go... With a start, I remembered to turn the bread.

The paper flapped down. "That'll be it, you know." Shot delivered, back up the defenses went.

"It, what *it?*" Mother poured herself some tea and flipped the eggs. "Watch the toast, Dorthea."

"I *am.*"

"And watch your tone, you saucy flinter. Lord, you're thirteen. Surely you should be acting like a young lady."

Only one right answer to that. "Sorry, Mother."

"What *it?*" Mother repeated at the wall of newsprint.

Down flapped the paper. "Last bit of original board in the place."

"Go away!"

"Once we replace that rotting clapboard in front, it'll be a new house. Nothing historical or ancestral remaining at all."

"Why, you ignorant..."

"Oldest house on the Southside my arse."

"What is it then?"

"The Ship of Theseus."

"Ship of—! It most certainly isn't. Or *is*, if one follows Aristotle. *Toast,* Dorthea!"

When my parents started brandishing their classical educations at one another, every way was likely. Mother was faded merchant aristocracy. Father, on the other hand, was the first person in his family—and the West Coast was maggoty with them, I can tell you; smeared from Cow Head to Port aux Basques, they are—to finish school. He worked as an accountant, which led some to say he was no good as farforth as a man was concerned. Unlike most of the others in his family—or most of the men on the Southside Road, for that matter—he'd never worked longshore in his life. After losing his job—along with multitudes of others—in the aftermath of the crash of the Newfoundland banks, he'd gotten a somewhat reduced position at McAuley's cooperage just down the road. But only this past September the boiler had burst, setting the cooperage afire. High winds spread the sparks, flankers flew over to Job's seal oil store, and from there the fire ate up Prowse and Sons, Baine Johnston and Company, and Newfoundland Fish Industries. Eight hundred casks of oil had to be thrown into the harbour, but even so, eight houses burned to the ground. The decks of nearby vessels were too hot to stand on, and two men—father and son—had died.

And with the closure of McAuley's, Father was once more out of a job.

It had been a grim few months for us, with only a few dollars here and there from Mother's midwifery. And not everybody whose baby she borned could afford to pay. Mother had been taught this trade by the Southside's former midwife, a Mrs. Kettle; when she passed on, my mother inherited her beat. She visited the houses of women in the family way from Long Bridge down to the end of the Southside Road, and even to Fort Amherst, after the road ran out; you needed a boat to get there.

Two pieces of toast made, I sliced and speared a third. What would Grandmother have thought of Mother's work borning babies? I was almost certain the grand old lady would have thought it beneath her. After all, her daughter's marriage to a mere accountant was enough to set her scrunching her teeth.

Well, Grandmother wasn't around to object. Nor was anybody else. I had no maternal cousins, no uncles or aunts. Each generation of my mother's family consisted of one: my mother, my grandmother, and her mother before her. One, a girl, a lone survivor.

The line ended in me. Six other children my mother bore had died, leaving me to live their lives for them.

I tried not to think of it. It was too much to bear. I didn't deserve it.

I was abominable.

That the house was never at peace was explained by some of the old ones as a consequence of it being situated on a path.

Who makes a path over a cliff? I asked.

Them, my mother said. *The Good People. Little Strangers.*

And she'd refuse to say any more.

My grandmother had been less close-mouthed, but when it was suggested a priest be called, the impossibility of bringing a priest into a Protestant home was strongly represented. A minister, then, they said. Out of the question. Grandmother did not go to church, not since the minister had had the temerity to speak to her about knitting in church. Knit she did, like a grim Fate, and she told him to his face she would never darken the doors of his church again. And she didn't, nor did her daughter my mother, and so I was raised a godless child. Three generations of churchless women; and slowly, the money ran out.

Only a week ago Father'd been taken on at the Newfoundland Railway. The fact of his employment was, naturally, a great relief to the family.

His failure to complete—while unemployed—the repairs needed by the house, was not.

Maybe that's why Mother's dark mood had lifted. Perhaps sheer irritation had brought her out of bed and down to breakfast.

"The form. Certainly the *form* of the house is the same," Father continued. "But not," and he raised a forefinger to heaven, "the *matter* of which the house is *made*. That would be entirely unrecognizable to your grandfather."

"Great-grandfather. He most certainly would recognize it. For by Aristotle's fourth formal cause, its *intended purpose* is the same."

"Is it?"

"Certainly! It is a house. We, the family, are living in it, *burning, burning!*"

I jumped; the toast was aflame. "Sorry!" I yelped, shaking the flaming bread off the fork and into the coals.

"Don't be sorry, simply *make the toast*. What a waste of good bread."

"Same? Look at us!" Father grumped. "Some grand we are, eating in the kitchen."

"*How* and *by whom* a thing is made is also a formal cause," Mother continued inexorably. "I am a scion of that line. So is Dorthea, although I have days when I doubt her origins. The tools and methods of building have changed little. Therefore, the house is the same."

"Tarpaper and felt? I don't think so."

Mother took the three plates from the table. "Great Grandfather most certainly had tarpaper and felt. Why wouldn't he?"

"Because last time I went up on the gliddering roof—risking my life in the process, I might add—I found the remains of ancient ancestral shingles, my dear. Shingles!"

"The ship is the same even though the materials are replaced." Mother cast forth eggs from the pan and slammed plates on the table, removed her apron, sat, and began to eat. "Hurry, Dorthea, don't stand there like Lot's wife!"

I scampered to the breadbox and cut more bread, spearing the slice on the toasting fork and taking my place by the stove once again. My eggs would get cold. I hated cold eggs. Eating them made me feel sick; eating anything in the morning made me feel sick. It wasn't fair, why did Mother think she could just show up some scattered morning and change everything on a whim?

And with that, the toast once again burst into flames.

"You can't even make toast, you parasite. You nasty parasite! Get out of my kitchen!"

THE CROW

A sob came up my throat. I strangled it, tossed the toast into the stove, then stalked out of the kitchen and up the stairs to my frigid room.

At least I didn't have to eat breakfast.

I heard Father leave the house, his great feet like dampers slapping out the linney door and down the path. Pictured the shapeless brown thing he called *my hat* on his head. Felt my heart hurt within me.

"Dorthea!" came my mother's voice, calling to me from the foot of the back staircase. "I am going out to arrange tarpaper for your beloved father! Get down here and present me with evidence that you will get out the door so as to arrive at school *on time.*"

I trailed down the stairs, eyes fastened on my feet. Mother was already in her coat and hat, and was pulling on her gloves, looking every inch a Gibson Girl.

"Brush your coat, it's indecent. I don't know what you get up to. Hurry now—I'm leaving—I want to get downtown for when the store opens. You're big and ugly enough to take care of yourself."

She swept out of our damp, dark kitchen. As the door slammed shut, rage burst inside me. "Devil take you!"

I froze, terrified that Mother had heard me.

Terrified too that my curse had worked, and my mother would go up in a dart of flame.

But no. Her footsteps rapped down the path by the side of the house, and continued rapping down the long line of rickety wooden stairs that led from our house to Southside Road. Ordinary as tarpaper and felt.

I shoved my arms into my shabby coat. It was too small, and made-over, turned inside-out and relined in an attempt to keep it one more season. I grubbed around for my school satchel, then remembered to forage for some food for the dinner break. Two thick slices of bread with molasses dribbled over them... Hurry, hurry, or I'd be late...

I wrapped the sticky bread in my handkerchief—licking the long sweetness off my fingers—and jammed it into my satchel, when I caught sight of the magazine.

Clare!

I had to get the next installment of the story.

I flew into the parlour. The room was furnished with a grand piano, a beautiful carpet all the way from the Ottoman Empire, a grandfather clock, two sofas of antiquated and uncomfortable design, and three shabby-genteel chairs by the fireplace. Every bit of available wall was crammed floor-to-ceiling with books. And, in the place of honour above the fireplace, hung a portrait of my great-great-grandfather.

The portrait was a copy of an ivory miniature that had been painted just before his marriage in 1817; if there had been one of his bride, it had been lost. He wore the fashion of the Regency period: dark coat molded to broad shoulders, an elaborate white neckcloth and high, starched collar points, hair arranged in careless, windswept curls, sideburns but otherwise clean-shaven.

He was handsome. But he had the cold, grey eyes of my mother. As you moved around the room, they followed you.

I looked nothing like him. I felt certain that were he to have been enabled to meet me, he would hate me. *Last survivor of my line. A girl. And this one! Better annihilation!*

Good thing you're dead, then, I mouthed back at him.

I'd see Clare tonight! That's what mattered.

I cast my eyes hurriedly over the magazine spines. 1897— there! Published when I was almost ten years old! I would never have had the courage to steal it then, but now was a different matter. Drawing it out, I ran my palm over the smooth paper, admiring the elegant lettering and the beautiful illustrated covers. Sliding the old one back onto the shelf—making sure it was level with the others so as not to excite Mother's suspicion—I slipped the new one into my satchel with slightly trembling hands.

Then I caught sight of the time on the grandfather clock.

Lunging out, I tripped over the leather doctor bag that Mother kept packed and ready by the back door, and almost fell on my face.

"Damn you to hell."

Presences quivered—my ancestors, so my mother said—whatever they were, the house was never still. *Sure, they won't hurt you. You're their last hope, you barnacle, poor spirits.*

Something—a plate?—shifted. The spring gurgled beneath the pump. The stairway let out a groan; shadows stirred.

The house rolled as though struck by a rogue wave.

Grabbing the doorframe for support, I jammed my hat on my head and ran out the door.

The linney door flapped back and forth. As Mother had pointed out to my father, it didn't latch properly. It flapped—open and shut, open and shut—sighing on creaking hinges, rendering a sound like the terrifying intaken breath-voice of a mummer.

Ooo... aah... ooo... aah...

That sighing chaw was the sound from my dream.

I was seized by an intimation that it was the house, trying to talk.

I fled down the path like a devil was after me. Mid-flight, I was flung backwards and fell on my back, wind knocked out of me. It was like running into a wall.

There was nothing there.

And then, faint laughter.

It could be gulls laughing, I told myself. *It really could be gulls...* Dread drained chill from the top of my head, sluicing through my chest, into my empty bag of a stomach.

Ooo... aah... ooo... aah...

Louder, now, the sound, full of malevolent glee.

And then the sun cracked the crown of the Hill, a dazzlement breaking over the crest. A black shape flew overhead, feathers limned with brilliance.

"Caw! Caw!"

It was the crow, lighting on the stair-rail at the end of the path.

"How are you, fella?"

He fixed me with a bright black eye. I unwrapped my hasty dinner and tossed him a bit of bread. He caught it deftly in his beak, glutching it down.

Shouts and the noise of horse-drawn carriages and hammering clattered from down below; ordinary sounds, the sounds of a city beginning a day. I grabbed my much-abused hat, scravelling to where the crow perched at the top of the Ratline. The house crouched behind me, but the dawning kissed my head. From up here I could see the streetcar barns—the new railway terminus, still under construction—the warehouses and piers.

I launched myself down the Ratline, the pied crow leaping into the air and soaring ahead.

It was working its way toward being a clear day. I took a gulp of air, a rich and complex mix of coal smoke, seal and fish oil, the tar of the railway, frost, and salt ocean. I ran headlong along the boardwalk as fast as I could, past the Range—oh, I'd see Clare tonight!—and down the Hundred Steps to the mud and muck of the Southside Road.

On the walk across the Long Bridge I noticed the wall of fog, out just past the Narrows, grey and dense, still held back—for now—by the colder air over land.

I turned and looked behind me. There, on the Hill, sat the house, black against the rocks. I felt it, windows glaring like empty eyes, all the long way across the bridge.

MY TWIN

It was my great-great-grandfather who brought the house to this place.

The story of my family began with him, as if emerging fully formed from a black hole. My grandmother told me the story, else I wouldn't know it, for my mother never spoke of it.

Your great-great-grandfather, Grandmother said, *married a young and beautiful bride.*

That's all my grandmother ever said about her, and possibly all anybody knew. She was beautiful, and considerably younger than he, and I had a distinct impression—although nobody confirmed or denied this—that she came from somewhere else, some faraway and unnamed country.

My great-great-grandfather and his young and beautiful bride emerged from their wedding to discover the city in flames. My great-great-grandfather, a vigorous man with legendary strength and endurance, carried his lovely wife to a boat. He placed her tenderly upon his overcoat and rowed her across the harbour. Every dip of the oars caused the waters to burn, like a raking of glittering embers, and the threads of her lacy veil shone rosy in the light of the burning city. As it trailed through the water her veil left a wake of phosphorescence, sparkling like the tail of a mermaid.

They spent their first night in an empty room above his merchant premises on the Southside. From there, they watched the flames lapping Over, the norther side of the harbour. It was winter, and cold, the coldest anyone could remember. Lying on silvery sealskins they watched the city burn, and heard screams and shouting, and as days went on, the looting. It was 1817, and St. John's first Great Fire.

That winter became known as the Winter of the Rals. Rowdies—gangs of rals—roamed the streets, rooting through charred remains of the town for half-burned fish to eat, assaulting and robbing everyone they met. One in three people was left homeless. Governor Pickmore put in an emergency request to England—groaning under a mad King and the debts of her extravagant Prince Regent—for provisions to feed the people of St. John's before ice closed the harbour.

But the ice clamped shut before sufficient provisions could arrive.

It was the custom at the time for governors of Newfoundland to leave the colony in winter for fairer climes. Pickmore stayed. But his residence wasn't meant for winter dwelling. Within three months the most excellent Governor was a most excellent corpse.

The harbour ice was so thick that it took three hundred and fifty men more than three weeks to chop a channel so that his body—preserved in a puncheon of rum like a pickled curiosity, a two-headed calf—could be sent to England for burial.

Grandmother told me that my great-great-grandfather determined to bring his house away from all the violence, the looting, the ruffians and rals, fish flakes and wooden piers, barns and hay and ranges of wooden houses. He would preserve the life of his lace-clad lady.

He climbed the Southside Hills, up a treacherous slope of slate scree, feet scrabbling on rocks, hands gripping like frozen claws, eyelashes frore together with frost. He made the top of the scree, and stood on a flat place. The steep Hill aback of him, he surveyed the burnt city below: brick chimneys like standing stones in an anarchic Neolithic henge; makeshift shacks thrown up against the cold; the beautiful, vast, almost land-locked harbour hard afrore; Signal Hill; the Narrows; and the open sea beyond it, the great blue drop, murmuring and surging.

His house on Prescott Street had survived the Great Fire, sitting just above its range. He determined that rather than building anew, he would tow his house to the south side of the harbour, and place it here.

With a great hammer he smote the rock.

From the place where his hammer fell, Grandmother said, *a living spring gushed forth.*

I liked to imagine that house, reinforced with wooden cribs inside and out, harnessed to a team of horses. Imagine it swaying like a ship, towed across the frozen harbour. I pictured its reflection, as if a second, twin house lay caught in the winter ice. The horses would be hard put to haul it so far, but somehow, my great-great-grandfather got them to do it. On the Southside he sank anchor points in the ground up the slope, and with the help of a crew of strong men, he hauled that house up the Hill to his chosen site. Grandmother said he pulled harder than anybody, almost bursting with the strain, but he did it. He caused several tons of large beach stones to line the excavation, channeling the run-off from the underground spring. He settled the house directly over that spring, right up against the stone cliff-face. The elaborate pump in the middle of the kitchen's flagstone floor was his invention. The back wall was living rock.

Grandfather said this house settled right in, Grandmother told me. *It just uncoiled. As if it had been waiting for him to bring it to its rightful place.*

It was a good thing he had, for the house would never have survived the next Great Fire.

My grandmother was only three when it happened, but she always said she remembered it well. It started, she said, with the ignition of a single pot of glue set to warm on the back of a cabinetmaker's stove on George Street. From there it consumed the waterfront. Oil vats exploded in an uncontrolled inferno, and the buildings on both sides of Duckworth and Water Streets were wrapped in one vast sheet of flame. And then the wind shifted to the easterly. That was the end of the city, then. The conflagration had no difficulty leaping through the closely packed town, fish flakes and shacks, wharves and wooden ships on the water.

Like the first, the second fire ate the city, only there was more city to consume by then, the year being 1846. In the end everything was destroyed, from just shy of Riverhead to the barracks up Signal Hill. The effects on my family's fortunes were confined mainly to an edict, following the devastation, that all seal and fish oil must be processed away from city, ruling out the north side of the harbour. This did my great-grandmother good, and the Southside business she had inherited from her father prospered.

Mine was the third fire. As with my grandmother's, it came when I was very young; my first memory is the city aflame. We watched it from our house on the Hill: Mother, Father, Grandmother, my brother, and I. Mary was with us too.

The summer had been one of desperate heat. Our small, hard-won garden shriveled up: drooping lilacs, gasping roses, lettuce leaves like brittle brown panes of fairy-thin glass. Brush fires burned all around the city's outskirts, and the skies were a strange, oppressive, brassy grey. Smoke hung over the city. The air smelled of burning.

One day in July a stiff breeze sprang up, blinding my eyes with dust. The usually glassy harbour stirred until the waters bared white teeth. The wind brought no relief, for it was hot and dry as a wind from the heart of the dying Ottoman Empire.

At tea-time, in a north-side barn—where Freshwater Road meets Cookstown—a driver went about his chores with the horses. He stumbled, so the story goes, and embers from his pipe fell into the straw.

At five o'clock we heard bells pealing from the fire hall at the foot of Long's Hill.

Flankers flew from barn to house, house to merchant's premises, glittering imps crawling over the wooden city. By six the flames were visible even from the Southside Road, licking pale and deadly in the long light of the summer's evening. I was scared abroad by sudden explosions from gunpowder caches, bells ringing, the groans of burning timbers. The lead panes of churches melted in the heat, and hungry flames licked inside and caught the timbers holding up vast roofs. Walls fell; black shapes tumbled and then seemed to rise, strange figures silhouetted by the infernal flames. At one point we thought it was over, for the flames appeared to subside. But then a line, glowing red, razor-thin and sharp as a needle, shot along the roofline of the newly erected Anglican Cathedral, and the slate roof went crashing in. The inferno rose again. Every merchant's building went up, and the wharfs. Even ships on the water burst into flames. The harbour reflected the burning city like a pool of blood.

As night fell and the fire ate the city, my mother played the piano. The piano had been there in the parlour from the time my great-great-grandfather had towed the house, the only grand piano on the Southside Road. I sat with little Theo, moving his arms and legs for him and singing softly under my breath; he stared at the ceiling, flickering red light reflected in his huge, clear eyes. My mother favoured Romantic composers: Chopin, Beethoven, and the like. My grandmother knit, fast enough to heat the metal needles and placing them under such tension that they bent into two arcs like crescent moons. Father smoked. Mary made a meal that nobody ate. As the tide forced its way unheeded up the throat of the river, Mother gradually morphed from the Romantics to her own music: serpentine, roiling like fire or the sea, repetitive yet ever-changing, a heavy left hand charging over arpeggios like a train. Father called her Nero, fiddling while Rome burned.

We did not sleep that night.

Morning failed to dawn, for a thick canopy of smoke hid the sun. The city was a field of charred rubble. Scorched hulls of vessels floated aimlessly across the now-still water. Brief excitement shuddered through the neighbourhood as the men, Father among them, went up the Hill in an attempt to contain brush fires spawned by sparks that had flown half a mile over the harbour.

You could hear people Over weeping from across the water.

At the height of the fire, some merchants had thrown open their doors to let the crowds take whatever they could. Now people wandered the smoking ruins clutching fine china and rich brocades: eleven thousand of them—over a third of the city—homeless. Almost nothing was left standing, from Signal Hill to Beck's Cove, LeMarchant Road to the water. The military set up tent towns in Bannerman Park and on the edge of Quidi Vidi Lake. Nearly every doctor's surgery, law office, church, and newspaper had been obliterated in the inferno.

Only four people died; incredibly, only four. Two were variously reported as an aunt and her niece, or a mistress and her maid; we never did discover the truth of it. The other two weren't counted among the dead of the fire in the annals of the town, but my family knew the fire took them. Within a week the piano lid was closed and we were waking them both in our front parlour: my grandmother, and little Theo.

Grandmother was a fine old lady who always wore black, crowned with the family jewels and an implacable belief that her daughter had married beneath her. She died in the same bed she had been born in, in the bed her mother had died in too, in the house built by her grandfather, as if two fires devastating the city in her lifetime were more than her upright, severe, black-clad body would stand.

Theo left soon after her. He died as he had lived, slipping between the worlds without a sound.

He was my twin.

I loved him; he was my little doll and I used to sing to him, play with him, and, on special occasions, dress him in the lace christening gowns that were never used and he never out-grew. We were four years old. He had never walked, never spoken, never made a sound.

I was the one who found him, pale and still in his crib.

They laid him out in a casket on top of the piano. I wanted to see if he'd move if I touched him. I took his icy hand. I shook it a little. Then again, harder. He didn't move. He was gone.

The wreaths people sent! Where people got the flowers I do not know. The stench of lilies and Jeyes Fluid lingered in the parlour for days. You could barely see Grandmother's large black coffin, and as for Theodore's small, white box, it looked like a living bower. I watched the funeral procession from the front window, standing with Mary and my mother, while Father went along behind with the other men of the neighbourhood to the graveyard. Black horses drew the hearse, with black feathers on their heads. They looked very stately and beautiful, pacing solemnly up the Southside past St. Mary's Church, turning to go across the Long Bridge, conveying the coffins and the flowers to the Anglican cemetery.

My mother turned away from me and took to her bed.

The pipe-smoker, that stumbler, whose carelessness had burned the city? People said that he was fired. And that he returned the night after he was let go, went around to every single horse in his former master's stable, and cut out their tongues.

SIGNOR MARCONI

Prescott Street was the kind of hill that reared up and smacked you in the face. It was a desperate climb to Queen's Road, and I arrived at school sweaty, crooked, and gut-foundered.

I managed to get into the classroom with little interaction beyond being called a "nanny goat," and having my hair pulled by an unknown hand—but I strongly suspected, from the sniggers elicited, a dishy-looking, whiny little creature I wouldn't have credited with the guts. I settled into my desk still breathing hard, trying to smooth the wrinkles out of my grubby pinafore, grateful that my desk sat in the very back corner. My back was to a wall.

I did not wonder why none of the girls liked me. They didn't, that was all, and it rendered my time in school a misery. I did not blame them, however. I would probably pick on me too, if I'd had friends. I was dirty, and continually cranky-looking, and smarter too. What's worse, I knew it. But somehow this intelligence was of no use to me. I lacked discernment, so my mother said. I didn't remember things properly, or rather, I paid attention to the wrong things. If only I could have cultivated charm! But my social acumen was almost nix. Knowing this did not give me the tools to address the lack.

If only I could have gone to school with Clare! But my mother considered St. Mary's on the Southside inferior—they had only two harassed teachers, and nothing but a bit of slate stood up on a chair. Clearly it was out of the question; I was to get a proper education. Girls like me—despite the long, slow draining of the family money—went to Spencer.

Our morning lesson was with Miss Addington-Acker. She had come, or been sent, from England years ago and had remained, a despairing civilizer of the colonial hordes, grim, grey, and bent. I wondered sometimes what she had done to deserve this mission—for surely being a teacher was like being a missionary, or a devout from the Catholic orders. Like an enlistee in the army, one would have little choice where to go. I tried to imagine a younger, less grey, less bent Miss Addington-Acker, standing before some kind of British Board of Colonial Education. She had a wonderful thick head of hair: dark in the back, pure white in front. No matter how hard I tried to picture her as a young woman—or a girl my own age—the white remained, recalcitrant, and the stoop in her back, and she still had glasses.

Newfoundland?! My young, improved Miss Addington-Acker gasped, hand to her heart, staggering backwards. *What have I done to deserve this exile?* Her wrist went to her forehead; would she swoon? *It is the great love between myself and Lord Lawnya Vawnya that you want to destroy, isn't it? His family vows I am beneath him. Well, we will never be parted, never!*

A great thwack echoed through the room, sending my heart into my mouth.

"Girls!" She—the real Miss Addington-Acker—had thrashed the top of her desk with a yardstick. My fantasy died in its tracks, and the other girls shut up; as one, we folded our hands atop our desks.

"Signor Marconi," she intoned, and paused, letting the name hang in the air.

My world tilted and I was once again in the plaster-dusted Wood's, sitting with Mary and Murph.

My teacher whacked the top of her desk with the yardstick again, snapping me back.

"Signor Marconi—with, it is rumoured, two helpers—is as we speak on his way to this very Dominion. Now, does anybody know why we should be interested in Marconi? Anyone?"

I wasn't about to say anything.

After a considerable silence, one student put up her hand. I watched our teacher suppress a sigh. This girl's father was one of the richest men in St. John's and sat on the School Board; in consequence, there was a tacit understanding that she was above reproach. As soon as she was deemed old enough, her parents would doubtless send her off-island for the remainder of her education. "Because he is Italian."

"Very good. He is Italian on his father's side; I believe his mother is Anglo-Irish. What does his being Italian have to do with any interest whatsoever that we may have in his imminent arrival?"

The girl giggled. "Nothing, Miss."

Miss Addington-Acker got a little shorter and her hair got a little greyer. "Anybody? What were we talking about yesterday?"

That I remembered. Yesterday Miss Addington-Acker had actually managed to capture my attention by relating the story of a scientist with a wonderful name: Jagadish Chandra Bose. He had, a few years ago, made a public demonstration of something called *microwaves*. And he had made the demonstration in a town hall in Calcutta. I had heard of Calcutta, of course. We all had. There was a prison there known as the Black Hole and something terrible had happened there in the seventeen-hundreds. We knew this because Miss Addington-Acker had *actually been born in India*, a fact that gave my teacher a striking touch of the fantastic.

I had immediately fallen in love with Mr. Bose, sight unseen. For one thing, Calcutta. And there was, too, something about gunpowder and bells. Our teacher had related how Mr. Bose had set alight some gunpowder and rung a bell using only these invisible waves... In my imagination his experiment was transported, conducted inside a tiny, perfect model of St. John's. The model was made entirely of white paper, from a flat white harbour with tiny, flawless ships at anchor—even the masts and rigging were somehow caused to be made from paper, as if a spider had spun them—to the tall ridge of Signal Hill crowned by Cabot Tower, and the Southside Hills on the other side of the harbour, and Fort Amherst. All the houses, churches, and merchants' premises were there, even my own, alone on its ledge. *Microwaves* zapped through the miniature city. A fire sprang up inside a tiny paper barn. White paper horses neighed and reared and trotted out onto tiny spit-ball cobblestones; tiny white paper men ran around, pointing useless paper hoses at the conflagration. The flames spread. The flimsy model was afire. And then, tiny charges of gunpowder had begun to go off, making a sharp report just like the fireworks set off every February by Mr. Fong Choy outside his laundry on New Gower Street, marking some festival he alone here celebrated in remembrance of his homeland: Bang! Bang! Bang! Sulphur sharpened the air. And then tiny paper bells began, miraculously, to ring.

"Microwaves!" I burst out.

Giggles spread around the classroom.

I had forgotten to put up my hand. I felt my eyebrow snap down to its usual half-mast position, and my face went hot.

Miss Addington-Acker did not bother to suppress her sigh this time. "Dorthea. Yes. Microwaves. Spencer girls do not shout out like longshoremen."

Everybody giggled some more. I slid down in my seat. "Yes, Miss, sorry, Miss."

"And please sit up straight. "

I did.

"Thank you. Don't any of you read the newspapers? Don't your fathers?"

Mine did, but I wasn't about to speak out again.

"I despair. Ignorant little beasts, Signor Marconi is known around the globe for his experiments in wireless telegraphy. Some call him a genius; others, a charlatan. Can anybody tell me what possible use wireless telegraphy could be to the world?"

Silence. Oh, they were such idiots, these girls! Didn't they care about anything?

"Don't we have an underground cable, laid at great expense across the floor of the Atlantic?" the teacher tried, a little desperate now.

The daughter of the Inspector of Lighthouses put up her hand. "Ships can't talk to one another, nor to shore, on a wire, Miss."

"Correct!" Miss Addington-Acker looked almost pleased. "You'd be ashamed of yourself not to know that. Class, wireless telegraphy—if it is possible and not simply wishful thinking—will enable ships to communicate vessel to vessel, and vessel to shore, *instantly*. The implications are immense. Any other ideas? Anyone?"

Gradually students chimed in: it was expensive to send a message over the wire. In times of war, wires could be cut. Fish could eat through a wire (this one earned a dubious look from Miss Addington-Acker, but she accepted it out of desperation). And so on.

"Mr. Marconi, if successful, will change the way international shipping is conducted. And that will have intimate consequences for this, an international port."

She looked tired, I thought. We must be a trying lot. I was under no illusions that I was a good student; too often I drifted off into reveries like the paper city; and only last week she had sorrowfully forced me to stand in the corner because, in the midst of a fantasy that I was engaged in a knife fight defending Clare from rapacious Martians, I had actually thrashed my arms so vigorously that my books had been swept off my desk and onto the floor. It hadn't been that which had inspired my punishment so much as my face afterwards.

I was aware that my normal expression was truculent and my voice naturally insolent; how could I not be, with my mother telling me so every five minutes? Awareness itself did not give me power to manage it. Other teachers—Mrs. Addington-Acker had yet to join their number, but it was only a matter of time—had given me the strap for something they called "dumb insolence." Father had explained the term originated in the British Navy, a cause for punishment if they could find nothing else. It came down, I had decided, to the thing I called my eyebrow—a black line, joined in the middle so that it was one lowering line, like bad weather on the horizon.

I suspected that if I'd been a boy, my face itself would not be cause for punishment.

"... would be what, Dorthea?"

I'd been hit on the lee side. I had no answer to a question I had failed to hear asked.

Thwack, rap! went the yardstick on her desk. "Types of *radiation.*" She began to walk down the aisle to my desk, rapping the stick on top every desk she passed. "Microwaves," *whack!* "and the waves discovered by Hertz," *wallop!* "and utilized by Signor Marconi," *ding!* "are all types," *wham!* "of radiation!" *Smack!* She stood before me, bent and grey and terrible, stick upraised. "Dorthea. I cannot tolerate this lack of attention!" *Baff!* "Arise, wretched child."

I stood, hands clasped in a desperate grip. Surely she wouldn't strap me with the yardstick?

"Go to the corner, please. You are quite familiar with it. I hope contemplation of your personal failings will lead to more tractability in the future."

My knees went weak with relief; I would not be strapped today. I untwisted my sweaty palms and walked, head up, to the corner at the front of the class.

The split second that the giggles subsided, my stomach rumbled.

It was so loud that the entire class broke into peals of laughter.

"Class!"

I sucked in my stomach, feeling my face and the back of my neck go hot. Eyes screwed shut, I wished my guts into stillness, pulling my stomach in so tight I imagined you could see my spine poking through the front. Another gurgle escaped, but only the front row heard that one.

Miss Addington-Acker continued with the lesson.

I castigated myself, for a time. I actually found the

substance of the lesson interesting—so why couldn't I pay attention? Usually we didn't learn science at all—except something called "domestic science" at which, naturally, I did not excel—unlike the boys at Bishop Feild who had a whole lab to play in. Not only that, these discoveries were extraordinary. Things had changed so very fast. I remembered when Spencer first had electric light bulbs installed. The girls still laughed about the one teacher who had climbed up on the desk at the end of the day, and started blowing at the bulb in the ceiling. Trying to blow it out. She'd never seen an electric light bulb before. None of us had.

Imagine if Marconi was right! We could talk to someone in India, in China, anywhere in the world, any time we liked...

I was lost once again. I only came back with the end of the lesson. It struck me that standing in the corner was not the most efficacious method to punish someone such as myself.

The rest of the morning passed in the usual light-headed haze.

Finally we broke for dinner. I flew outside, finding my spot beneath a bent old tree in Bannerman Park. The branches curved down almost to the ground, providing shelter from weather and prying eyes, and the ground beneath was smooth. Despite the cold, I preferred this to sitting in solitary splendor inside the school; it took some cruel weather to keep me indoors on dinner break. I examined the branches for my friend, the pied crow; would I see him twice in one day again?

But he did not appear.

I was unprepared for the desolation that gusted through me. As tough as I tried to be on the outside, my failure to find even a single friend at school was an awful, burning shame. It had to do with something wrong with me, I had long ago decided—something the other girls saw in me, something despicable—and I lived in dread for the day that Clare would see it too...

It was my daily terror, a customary self-mortification. When younger I had been certain it was that I was stupid;

nowadays, I was quite convinced that I stank. No doubt I was ugly; that went without saying. So what? No use in thinking about that. I slammed the lid down. The feelings roiled, breeding inside me. But I could ignore them. I had a lifetime's practice.

Soon I was dispatching my meal, thinking of the Great Fire, imagining the park full of tents. I invented, on the spot, an entire family of seven girls, named them all and decided on personalities and dramas between them, developed an elaborate game of make-believe they played, and as quickly discarded it as maudlin.

Fragile and rudderless, the parentless girls sailed up into the air, pastel lacey creatures bursting like soap bubbles against the sky.

Dinner done away with and fingers licked, I gobbled up the next chapter of *War of the Worlds*. It would be a rehearsal for when I read it out to Clare later. It was a petrifying episode—with equally petrifying illustrations—in which the Narrator is forced to administer a stunning blow to a ranting curate in an effort to silence him and thus escape detection from the blood-quaffing Martians. He knocks the curate unconscious, then watches in agony as his prone body is removed by a tentacled machine.

Hiding terrified in a nearby coal-cellar, he barely escapes himself.

LIKE THEY WAS MADE FOR YOU

The day crawled to its end. At last I made my flight down the hill and across the Long Bridge. Every step brought me closer to Clare. I beat up the Hundred Steps toward her house, my satchel with the precious magazine banging against my quarters.

I went in through the side door as usual; the houses of the Range, like ours, didn't have true back doors, being butted right against the Hill in back.

The hot little kitchen was numerous with neighbours, four of them gathered around the table. Mr. Taylor was not in evidence; like my father, he was often out until all hours. Mrs. Taylor always seemed happier when her husband wasn't there. Now she was in her element: dealing out cards, making fun of the crooked face Mr. Coultas pulled at his hand, telling Mrs. Horwood that they would surely win this time.

"Clare in, Mrs. Taylor?"

She gave me an irritated wave.

Her mother, old Nanny King, sat in a rocking chair by the stove. Nanny King looked at least a hundred, although I knew by math that was impossible, Mrs. Taylor being only five and thirty. Nan had snow-white hair that her scalp peeked through, and few teeth left in her head. It made it hard to understand what she was saying, at least to me; Clare had no trouble deciphering. Nan usually ignored me, but tonight her eyes fixed on me. She pointed up, and said something.

After a moment of frozen incomprehension, I realized she had said that Clare was upstairs.

I fled the kitchen, shouts of laughter following me. "I'll have the Devil after you for cheating, Bride Taylor, I will!"

"Play 'em with scrutility, now!"

The ceilings upstairs were so low that I could barely stand upright. There were four bedrooms: one for Clare's parents and the baby, one for Mr. Taylor's slightly-less-ancient parents, one for the Taylor boys, and one for the girls. Nanny King's pull-out bed was in the kitchen, as she could no longer manage the stairs. Clare slept with three of her sisters in one bed, heads and points; the youngest girl had a cot.

I felt ashamed of my solitary splendor in the house over the troubling, bubbling spring. It was a fact that not only did I have my own room, we had two empty rooms on the second floor. My great-great-grandfather had built a house to contain a family, although in the end, each generation produced only a single live girl. My mother had lost all those babies, pain enough. But it still seemed unfair that we had all that space, where Clare was jammed in like a tinned herring.

She never complained, however. The family spent almost no time upstairs, except to sleep—all life was conducted on the main floor, mostly in the kitchen at that. I had only been up here a scattered time.

"Clare?" I called at the top of the narrow, creaking staircase.

"Come along!" she yelled.

A metal trunk filled with clothes lay open in the middle of the floor, and by the light of a kerosene lamp Clare was mending something. "Sisters are out. Don't know when they'll be back," she said, "so get that story out before I dies of curiosity." She set her sewing aside and scooted over, patting the quilt next to her.

"I read ahead," I admitted. "At school today."

"You never! Well, don't tell me what happens. Just get reading, for the love of God."

The room was cold and perpetually damp; I hadn't taken my coat off, and now I was glad. Kicking off my boots, I tucked in next to Clare on the bed and opened my satchel with an air of great importance. I drew out the precious pilfered magazine, and she clapped her hands. "Hurry, hurry!" she bounced up and down on the mattress.

When I read aloud to Clare I put on a "proper" accent. The prose seemed to call for it. The education inflicted on me— teachers shipped over from England—insisted on it. But when not reading, when I was simply visiting with Clare, my accent veered. Warmth bubbled up, boisterous syllabic blurs rinsing my throat and my chest. There was no prickling sensation of discomfort, no searching for my voice. I could roll words in my throat, tender sounds, loving the shapes and sounds of them.

I did my best with the passage, and was rewarded by Clare cuddling close to me, her head on my shoulder. She shuddered appropriately at the Martian tentacles, and then, when they grab the curate, she sighed.

"Maybe this is harsh of me, but I am kind of glad they took him." She clapped her hands over her mouth, then began to laugh. "Isn't that a sin!"

I started to laugh too. "No, I was near ready to cheer when they took him too."

"He was so *annoying*," Clare agreed. "Always going on like that. He was going to call the Martians to the Narrator, I just knew he was! I'm some glad he's dead!"

As usual, we laughed until we had to wipe tears from our cheeks. Clare had the kind of eyes, the shape of them, that looked like they were always laughing anyways, but when she really got galing her eyelashes curled and her eyes tilted up, and they shone like a green glass match-striker. I laughed so hard I fell on my side and got pricked by her sewing needle.

"Don't bleed on me quilt!" she said, then, trying contritely for concern, "I mean, are you all right?" She burst out laughing again.

"Sure, sure you heartless creature. What are you at?"

"Mother's got me going over the boys' clothes and seeing what's fit and what isn't. Clint's grown out of his best and I don't know what we'll do for him now. We'll pass these on to Harvey." She held up a darling tweedy Norfolk jacket.

"That was *Clint's*?" I gasped. "Did he ever *wear* it?"

"Certainly. To church. Which means he probably wore it once the most. I doubt he'd even recognize it."

"I just can't picture it."

"Wha', Clint in church?"

That sent us off again.

"No, just... him in that," I managed. The jacket was a beautifully made thing, with leather buttons and patch pockets, and a little belt to match. "He'd be some... *sweet* in that."

"Oh, you don't know the half of it. There's breeches to match. Mother says he looked a proper little angel." Clare took those out, and a linen shirt.

"They're so precious!" I ran my hands over the garments, feeling the smooth-rough of the tweed, sniffing the sweet, musty smell.

"They'd fit you perfect," Clare said. "You're only small."

I stared at her.

"Clare..." My breath went ragged.

"Wha'?"

"Yesterday... I developed an extremely bad idea."

"*Wha*'?" Her eyes positively glowed.

"You know that fellow Marconi is coming to the city?"

"Sure! Everybody's talking about it. He's going to set up some kind of wireless contraption. Beatrice-at-school's mother says it's witchcraft, but I think—"

"Remember my friend Mary?"

"The girl from the cove? Who used to work up at your place?"

"Yes, her. You know she's engaged now?"

"To that reporter from the *Telegram*. Father says the *Telegram* is a mouthpiece for the Liberal establishment."

"Yes, that one. Well, he wants to do a story on Marconi, and he needs a spy."

"A spy!?"

"And I want to be that spy. And to do that, I have to be a boy."

Clare stared at me, a speculative gleam lighting her face.

"You'd wha'? Work for this Marconi fella?"

"Something like that."

"Sniff around for suspicious activity?"

"Yes. And then I'd tell Murph, and then he could write it up in the mouthpiece for the Liberal establishment."

Clare clasped her hands. "Sounds thrilling. Not like Martian-tentacle thrilling, but—"

"Oh, I don't want *that* kind of thrilling!" I exclaimed. "That might be too thrilling even for me."

"Well, put them on, girl," she twinkled.

My heart started hammering, my mind veered. If I could have these—they'd be my disguise. I could spring it on Murph and Mary. If I could fool them, they'd have to admit I was capable of pulling off the charade. But still I hesitated. "What if your sisters come home?"

"They're out at the Whittens, and anyways, who cares?" She put her head to one side. "Try them on."

I gulped. "You sure?"

She leaned close to me, so close I could have kissed her. "I dare you," she whispered.

I stared into her eyes. Did she know how I felt about her, how jumbled up my body and mind got around her?

I could never ask her. The very first time I'd been aware of how I felt about her, I'd known two things simultaneously. One: I was in love with my friend, and it was a love that had a lot to do with her laugh, her mind, her way of seeing the world with a twist. But there was also a great deal of carnality inside of it. I lusted for my friend's body. I'd perused that passage from the Bible, the one about Sodom and Gomorrah. I was sinful. Despite my lack of a god, maybe even because of it, the universe would see my perversion, and annihilate me. So, this led to the other thing I knew in that moment. Two: I could never, ever, tell.

Slowly, I took off my coat. I felt shy, all at once. Clare and I had changed in front of each other many times—but this felt different. I still had the body of a child, although in recent months I had been horrified to discover a new, dark fuzz on my upper lip. I was getting taller, but I simply grew up, getting no wider, as if I was being sucked through a straw... not for me the swelling hips and bust of Clare...

Just last summer we'd climbed up the Hill to go swimming in Soldier's Pond. I'd snuck a look at her beautiful breasts, her changing body. And since then, while my body hadn't altered much, hers had kept changing.

I had a feeling we wouldn't swim together again. She had the body of a young woman, now.

Untroubled by my existential woes, Clare was rummaging around in the trunk. "There's a cap in here somewhere, and suspenders. And maybe even boots... Ah!" She turned, holding out a pair of brown boy's boots. "Why aren't you out of your pinafore?" she demanded. "Turn around and I'll unbutton you."

Mutely, I stood and turned my back to her, letting my coat fall around my ankles. "This'll be hilarious," Clare said.

Slowly, in a kind of dwall, I felt my pinafore come untied and watched it sail through the air as Clare flung it on the bed. Felt her fingers deftly working loose my thousand buttons down my back. I let the dress fall to the floor, and turned to face her.

For once, I didn't know what I was going to say. It was a terrible feeling.

"Clare..."

But Clare had the shirt up in front of her, and shoved down over my head, dousing my confession like a snuffed candle. "Hurry up, or you'll catch your death. I'll get the suspenders onto the breeches, now," she was saying, and turned away while I was left to button the four buttons on the placket.

Of course, Clare had to dress her younger siblings every day. This was nothing new for her. I was like a little sister to her, I told myself bitterly. She would never burn for me the way I did for her.

"You can wear your own stockings—they're a bit nish for a boy, but hopefully nobody will be looking too closely." She held out the breeches, the suspenders buttoned on the waistband for me. I climbed into the breeches, found the fly buttons—easy!— but fumbled with the suspenders. "Like they was made for you!" The boots were a little big, stiff and heavy on my feet compared to my feminine ankle boots, but they'd do. In a fit of excitement I pulled my pocket knife from around my neck and slid it into a pocket of the breeches. It fit perfectly, like it had always wanted to live there.

"Let me braid your hair so it tucks up under that cap," Clare suggested.

There was no mirror in the little room. But the short span of December daylight had come to its end and I could see myself reflected in the darkness behind the window pane. I stared, thrilling with pleasure as Clare ran her fingers through my dark hair, pulling it up tight, twisting and braiding it into a thick knot until it might plausibly fit under the cap.

Was it my imagination, or could I see that dark fuzz on my upper lip—the fuzz that had so horrified me when it first appeared—in the glass? I liked it now; I was thrilled to have it.

Clare shoved the cap over my hair. I shrugged into the jacket and did up the buttons and belt. I looked into the dark glass.

A dark-eyed boy stared pugnaciously at me, chin lifted. My fists closed instinctively; was I going to fight myself in the glass, like a kitten seeing itself in a mirror for the first time? I grinned. The boy grinned back at me.

Were those Theo's eyes looking out at me? Did something of my brother live inside me, there in the glass?

Would Theo look like this, had he thrived?

The smile leached away, and all of a sudden grief swept through. Like the final remaining original boards of the Ship of Theseus, I was all poor Theodore had, now. Rotten.

"You look like a proper little boy," Clare said. "Don't you?"

I managed a nod, and turned to face her. "I look like a proper little pisswig is what I look like."

Clare laughed. "Ready for a scrap, are you?"

And then she kissed me, kissed me right on the mouth.

I stood there like a block of wood. My lips hadn't pushed back, I'd been that stunned. "What was that for?"

"You just looks some sweet."

I had never actually imagined kissing Clare. For all that I knew I wanted to see her, be with her, all the time—for all the vague yearnings I felt whenever she touched me, and the way I wanted to stare at her, but knew I had to conceal it, taking side-looks at her whenever I could—I had never imagined kissing her.

Some sweet? What did that mean? My mind was all in confloption.

"What's come over you, ninny?" Clare asked, dropping her smile.

I, Dorthea, the king hand at fantasy, had never imagined my lips could touch Clare Taylor's.

And now she'd come out ahead of me.

"Nothing." I tried to laugh.

My conniver looked a little uneasy. "Come on, now. You'd better get out of those and smuggle them out of the house before Mother catches us."

Wordless, I turned away and began to take off the things. I felt like I wanted to cry. Or did I feel happy?

I couldn't tell.

Clare found an old nunny bag in the bottom of the trunk, and into this she put the garments as I stripped out of them, starting with the boots. "Nobody will be looking for these right away," she said.

"I'll have them back... I wouldn't think this Marconi'll be here past Christmas," I said. "Will that be all right?" Imagining trying to impersonate a boy for weeks on end almost ended me. "Lord, I hope this is a good idea."

"Of course it's a good idea! I had it!" Clare declared. "You'll have to tell me how everything goes. Everything. You hear me?"

"Oh, I will."

Getting back into my own girl's clothes felt like putting

on a costume; one I'd been forced to wear all my life, but a costume nevertheless. I stared into the reflection in the window.

That girl there, her face... somehow she was more complete, now that I'd seen the boy.

Clare was doing up the infernal buttons on my dress when we heard the stair fill with footsteps and laughter. "Hurry!" I said breathlessly. "It's your sisters back!"

I flung on my pinafore; Clare shoved the nunny bag into my hand. "They'll never notice. Too full of themselves."

I swept up my overcoat and draped it over the hand holding the bag just as the first younger sister came prancing into the room. "Nan's reading the cards!"

Clare and I met eyes. It was a grand thing when Nanny King read the cards. Southside women were known for their abilities to tell fortunes, to see things beyond. They had psychic powers, so it was said, and Nan King was best of them all.

Clare grabbed my hand and dragged me out of the room and down the stairs, followed by her younger siblings.

The old lady was sitting at the table now, her shawl draped around her. The card players were sot back, chairs against the rail, except for Mrs. Horwood, who sat opposite Nanny King, shuffling the deck in her hands, her face inches away from it.

"Show me some money coming in, Nanny King!" she begged.

"Not up to me," Nanny mumbled. Then she said something else.

I let the bag and my coat fall behind me against the wall. "What did she say?" I whispered.

"She said, get to it and cut the darn cards," Clare replied in normal tones, raising a laugh around the room. As her nan was deaf, Clare never worried about being overheard by her. Me, I couldn't help whispering. It felt rude to let on to the old lady that I couldn't understand half of what she said.

Mrs. Horwood, obedient, stopped shuffling and put the deck face-down on the table. She reached out and bent close to the cards again, trying to cut the deck exactly in half. She lifted her fingers.

Three cards flew out as if a phantom had blown on the cut deck. They arrowed straight toward me, landing at my feet. I jumped as if I'd been burned.

"Oh!" said Mrs. Horwood. "I'll cut again."

But Nanny King raised her hand. Her fingers were swollen in every joint, the tops so bent I wondered how she managed to use her hands at all. Mrs. Horwood froze in her tracks, half-out of her chair.

Nanny King said... something.

I inclined my ear toward Clare, never taking my eyes from the old lady.

"This isn't yours," Clare said. "Someone else in this room has a fortune that needs telling."

And then Nanny King pointed at my feet and spoke. Even I could tell her meaning. I was to pick up the cards and bring them to the table.

Beneath me, right between my boots, was the Jack of Spades. Next to that was the King of Diamonds, upside down. And on the other side was the Ace of Hearts, also upside down.

Obedient, I took them to the table. Mrs. Horwood stood, indicating I should take her place.

"Oh, no, I couldn't," I said. "I have to get to supper..."

Nan King glared at me.

I sat down.

Her gnarled hands arranged the three escapees just as they had landed on the floor, and she gestured that I should shuffle the remaining deck.

I glanced at Clare. She nodded eagerly, two bright spots of colour on her cheeks. "She never reads our cards, Dor! Never!"

I gave the deck a miserable few shuffles, then caught a sharp look from Nan, leading me to shuffle with more focus and precision. I felt silly. But as I shuffled, the small, hot room receded, seeming to fall away. There was nothing but the cards and the movement of my hands. Finally I felt something click inside; a definite, sharp sensation, like the unlatching of a door.

I cut the deck, and pushed the pile toward Nanny King.

She laid them out in a cross pattern, with the Jack at the centre, the upside-down King on top, and the reversed Ace on her right. The rest of the pattern she filled with the cards from the top of the deck as I'd cut it.

There were a lot of spades on the table when she was done.

She pointed at the Jack. "You," she said. "Dark hair. You means well, but..."

But what?

Then over to the reversed King of Diamonds. "He's coming." And then she muttered some more unintelligible words. My eyes darted to Clare.

"He's lying about something," she said breathlessly.

Marconi! It had to be!

"But him? He's not the real story." The old lady's voice broke through, clear.

Not the real story? How could that be? She pointed then at the reversed Ace of Hearts. "Your mother."

I looked at the Ace, confused. "My mother?"

Nanny nodded. "It's beginning."

What was beginning?

"Your family."

I waited in agony, my eyes darting around the table. Why were the cards reversed? I knew that was a bad sign. So were spades. They tended to mean enemies, power, change, and trouble.

"*You* can change it." She pointed to the reversed King with her crooked forefinger, then over to the Jack of Spades, then described a circle around the whole table.

"The spirit is in the body," Nan said then. I nodded.

I wasn't sure why she was telling me this; everybody knew that.

She embarked upon a longer passage, lifting her arm and describing an arc through the air. I looked to Clare.

"The spirit is like a man in prison. When the body is asleep in the night, the soul leaves it to roam, free until the morning dawns. And some people—I think she means *you,* Dor!—have the ability to leave the spirit lying in bed in the night, while the body walks."

I shook my head. I wasn't capable of such a thing. I was far more interested in the King. If that denoted Marconi, I would meet him. My life would mean something.

But still Nan spoke.

"Which is why you should never awaken anybody suddenly in the night. For what if the spirit was cleaved from the body? It might not be able to get back in time," Clare finished.

Nanny glared at me, seeming to wait for a response.

"What would happen then?" I asked.

"They'd die."

And then, Nanny King swept every card off the table and into her lap.

The whole room gasped.

She seemed an ancient weird woman to me, then, the light of the lantern flickering on her face, her hands gnarled claws. She sat up straight, taller than she had been, taller than me. The light of the lantern dimmed, and shadows grew up on the ceiling. There was nobody else in the room—no Clare, no Mrs. Taylor, none of the card players. Just me and the old woman.

"It's coming for your mother, dearie. And then it'll come for you."

Then Nanny smiled. It was all gums, her smile, no teeth. The shadows shrank, the lamp grew bright, the room was warm again.

"You're a real Southsider, Dor," she mumbled. "A real Southsider. Despite your father." That I could understand just fine. It was something everybody said to me, up and down the road. *A real Southsider, despite your father.*

Everybody in the room chuckled.

It sounded like a curse.

PARASITE

I loved the passage between sleep and waking. It was a constant fight with my mother, my love of sleep. She called it laziness. But to me it felt like something essential, those precious moments riding between, drifting from dream to waking, unable to distinguish which was which, carried on waves between the worlds. Images and words would stretch out, syllables long as the passage of Time. Words signified things in the world, of course—but in that state of half-waking, they became their own ineluctable beings. Vowels would roll deep inside my body; consonants snapped and sparkled, streaking across my sleepy mind like comets, or that kind of attenuated, razor-thin, blossoming frost on the windowpane that my grandmother used to say meant the fairies had been ice-skating in the night. And then she'd say, *Don't worry, it's Monday* (or Tuesday, or whatever day it happened to be). *They can't hear us talking about Them on Mondays.*

Sometimes as I drifted, I would hear a great roaration around the house, or a throng in the kitchen. Or through the house. Hard to say. A dream? Or had the house drifted astray, like a ship on an uncharted sea? Was our house on a path, like the old ones said?

The Southside wasn't officially part of the city. We lay outside the city limits, a hinterland back of beyond. Nobody wanted us. There was even an ongoing squabble about who was responsible for maintaining various services in the district: the Newfoundland government, or the municipality. The first electric lights illuminated Over in 1885, three years before I was born, powered by a steam-driven generator in the Terra Nova Bakery on Flavin's Lane. We still didn't have electricity on the Southside. Those houses that stood right by the road had gas lighting, and cooking and heating too—for the St. John's Light Company generated its own gas at the facility just up the road at Riverhead, and merchants down on the made ground by the harbour's southern edge all used gas for lighting as well as power. The Bowrings, Jobs, Ayres, and Grieves were original shareholders in the gas light works, lending powerful merchant resistance against electricity.

Those of us up the Hill couldn't get gas lighting. But even if they could have had it, my parents eschewed the new technology, hanging onto candles and kerosene lamps and the old coal stove.

After the Fire, electric lighting took over the downtown, for it would have taken years to clear the rubble from the streets to re-lay gas mains.

And by that time, my mother had started losing babies. And the more established the new technology became, the more babies she lost. Or so it seemed.

First a miscarriage; I didn't remember that, for I'd only been one myself. Then, at four, my brother Theo had died. Next came stillborns, twins again, like poor Theo and me. Another, a boy they'd named after my father, survived six months before passing into the next world. By last year Newfoundland had its first hydro-electric generating station, built at Petty Harbour. From there the city received enough power to run the street railway and provide all the downtown's electric lighting. Bright, buzzing, perpetual light, streaming through wires, banishing shadow to the margins.

Then, another miscarriage, too young for a name or a sex, but not too young for my mother to mourn.

I was the sole survivor of seven children.

My mother, scion of a faded merchant line that somehow failed to produce large families, referred to the lights Over as *that nasty buzzing bright misery*, or even, sometimes, *that cold bright Death*. The curtains in the front of our house were always firmly drawn against them.

And last year, since the blossoming of light through the city, things had gotten much, much worse.

The house had always been imbued with a sense of menace. But on my birthday earlier this year, a rock had flown straight through my bedroom window, breaking the glass. It meant They were upset, the old ones said.

Upset with my survival?

And there were other incidents, scores of them: sounds of crashing crockery in the kitchen, dreams where I was hauled around the house, back-flying water. I tripped on nothing, fell into doorframes.

That invisible wall I'd run into yesterday morning.

There are such things that some people will see and some people won't, I remembered my grandmother telling me. It had to do with the time of day you were born. *If you're born between two lights, you're apt to see things.* Between two lights meant born in the dark of night. My brother and I, poor little Theodore, had been born at three o'clock in the morning; the clock struck the hour exactly when I took my first breath, grandmother said. Mary backed that up. Mary said Theo and I had come out within five minutes of each other—me red, him blue—and although I was small, Theo had been so tiny they doubted he'd live. He didn't even have finger- or toe-nails. They'd had to blow life into his little lungs, and he spent the first weeks of his life wrapped up in blankets on the open oven door.

Father, on being served a pair of rabbits for dinner by Mary, had leapt up theatrically and exclaimed in mock horror, *My God, the twins!!!* They'd had a good laugh about that, Mary and Father.

But poor little Theo, he never throve. Maybe it was the house never at peace, dancing ladies passing through walls, rocks falling for no reason.

Urchins, Mother called Them; or, more often, Little Strangers. I'd never seen Them while waking, except once. I'd been with Mother, then, standing in my parents' bedroom, two storeys up at the front of the house. Through that wall, from the air, came three ladies dressed in lace. All in white, white foam from head to toe. I couldn't hear them; I only saw them, laughing and holding hands, dancing in a happy line. Right through the wall and across the room they twirled, brushing past my mother and me, feet not touching the floor, and then they went through the window—through the panes of glass—leaving nothing behind but a cold shudder. It was as if they melted into the very rock of the Hill.

Did you see that, Dorthea? Mother had asked me.

I'd nodded.

We won't speak of it.

The old ones—Nanny King and the like—had their theories, but *Rocks sometimes fall,* my mother countered. *It's called gravity. Don't be foolish; this is science. There's nothing wrong with our house. If there's ghosts, they're your ancestors and you're their last hope, God help them. You threw the rock, didn't you. Now get up and—*

"...how many times do I have to call you, Dorthea? Up!"

Mother was up again this morning.

And it was cold! I burrowed further under the covers, only the tip of my nose out in the freeze.

But then I remembered. Today Marconi was coming.

"Dor-THEE-a!"

Oh, I hated that name. "Coming, Mother!"

The little actions of life are repetitive, to the point of making me want, at times, to scream. Emptying of bladder, wondering why it wasn't a frozen icicle; flinging on of underthings, hating how they felt and smelled; pulling up of sagging black stockings; doing up of black dress, a thousand tiny buttons up the back, black and shiny as crow's eyes—so difficult, especially with cold fingers. This morning I perforce left a gap in the middle of my back.

Light was beginning to leak into the sky. Grey fog pressed up against the glass of my window.

My fingers flew to my lips. There, Clare had kissed me, Clare Taylor! Right on the lips.

A glow sparked up inside my chest, a glow the memories from the rest of the evening couldn't douse.

Nan King's tangled prophecies.

My father not home for supper.

Mother and I alone at the table without him.

No answer from Mother when I tried to share my fears.

I went to bed with Mother playing the piano, angry, swirling music, until I fell into a dwall.

Late, much later it seemed, I'd heard my father come stumbling through the door. I'd heard them haranguing each other into the night.

By the time I got down, breakfast had already been served, and my parents were still arguing, now—again—about home repairs.

"Sit down, Dorthea," said my mother. "We will have untoasted bread this morning for reasons I do not need to elucidate, you lazy little article." And then, to make me frantic, she began quoting Shakespeare. "For this, be sure, to-night thou shalt have cramps, side-stitches that shall pen thy breath up; urchins shall, forth at vast of night that they may work, all exercise on thee; thou shalt be pinch'd!"

Father, perhaps taking pity on me, interrupted this recital, talking with a full mouth in a fashion guaranteed to annoy my mother. "What if *two* houses," he chewed vigorously, "two *identical* houses, had been built on this hill side-by-side at exactly the same time? Or let us return to the Ship of Theseus."

"Yes, let's," she snapped.

"The river you stand in is not the river you step in." I stared at him, working out the profundity, while Father shoveled eggs into his mouth.

"But it's still a river," Mother objected.

I wondered why he and men like Mr. Taylor stayed out drinking. Not all did. Many of the fathers up and down the road abstained from alcohol, and of course the women did. Was it some kind of weakness in the ones who drank? Clare said it was. That her father got his wages and they went down his throat, when the money could have gone to pay for better clothes for the children. On bad months, they had trouble making the rent.

We didn't have to pay rent, the house being in the family. This was, I knew, a great luxury. Food was another thing. We never needed to go hungry—the family finances were sufficient to take care of that, my father assured me. No, the times I went hungry it was because Mother had been taken by the dark moods again, and Father was too stunned to notice there was no food in the pantry.

And half the time my stomach was too roiled up to want to eat in any case.

"Picture two identical ships, built simultaneously," Father intoned.

"I'm picturing," Mother snapped.

"Sitting in the harbour, side by side." Father finished his eggs, and started on the bread. He seemed merry this morning, and I smiled at him.

My mother glared in my direction. "Like Dorthea and her brother, say? Two near-identical babes in my womb?"

My eggs, already making me queasy, turned to spongy grease in my mouth. Could not my father hear the cold anger in Mother's voice? He was bantering, but Mother—suddenly, it was always sudden—had veered into waters dark and dangerous.

"And then, let us say, one sinks the other in battle?"

Stop, stop, stop! I silently screamed at him.

"Clearly the two ships are not the same ship even before, let alone after, one sinks the other." He was enjoying himself, inexorable and light-hearted. "And yet the two have the same formal cause."

"So what?"

"Therefore, two objects having the same formal cause does *not* by itself suffice to make them the same object!" my father finished triumphantly. "And so this house is not the same house you were born in. It's another house entirely—"

"You nasty parasite! Get out of my kitchen!"

It was me she was talking to, not him. My stomach lurched.

"Helen! What in the—"

As I left the table and went back to my dark and freezing room, I was almost grateful.

I lifted the sash, stuck my head out the window, and spit the greasy eggs out of my mouth and onto the rocks below.

Now, I understood. Finally, I grasped why she had always called me *parasite*. I'd seen him myself, reflected in Clare's bedroom window.

She believed I'd killed my brother. I'd sucked the life out of him while we'd shared her womb.

One advantage of having a mother who hated you was that it made it easier to smuggle a nunny bag stuffed with boy's clothes out of the house. She didn't want to see me. And so she didn't.

I came out the door into the fog. No breeze blew, but still the door lapped and jawed.

Ooo... ahhhrs... ooo... ahhhrs.

That sound...

I remembered the time the janneys, the mummers, had come to the house. I'd been very young. It was some time just after Christmas; there was snow on the ground. Strictly speaking, mummering wasn't allowed; there'd been a ban since the 1860s. But on the Southside, people did things their own way.

There had been a great knocking at the door.

"Any mummers in tonight?" It was a strange, high-pitched, squeaky voice, spoken while drawing breath in. It made my skin crawl.

"How many of ye?" my mother sang back.

"Oh, four or five!"

And my parents had let them in, putting out rum and cakes and all manner of food for them. I remembered being pursued by a hobby horse, nails for teeth snapping at me, *Snock, snock, snock!* Remembered how the adults had laughed while I'd screamed. Remembered the mummers' awful cramp talk.

Had Theo and Grandmother been alive then? They weren't there in my memories. I did remember someone grasping me and pulling me onto their lap—a man, I believed, although the person had a lace curtain over their face, and a big pillow stuffed up under a sweater like enormous breasts, and they wore a great long skirt. They also had gargantuan rubber boots with caribou shanks tied on over, cloven hooves and all. You could see the shin-bone of the animal, poking up out of the shrinking hide.

The person had reeked, the same sweet-sharp juniper-berry odour I often scented on my father. I didn't know what it was, back then.

My father showed much delight in the cloven feet of the mummer. He kept grabbing at them, and the mummer put me down and kicked out, dancing around the kitchen so Father couldn't get at the feet. My parents went on a long process of trying to guess the identity of the invaders. The cloven feet meant it was someone who hunted; was it Mr. Whitten? Or Mr. Porter, it must be, he had a trap line and hunted too. No? What about Mr. Knight?

The mummers howled and shook their heads and growled like animals, and drank the rum put out for them and ate the cakes.

Who cleft the Devil's foot? my father shouted, and then he quoted a poem from long ago. I dearly loved it when he did this.

> *Go and catch a falling star,*
> *Get with child a mandrake root,*
> *Tell me where all past years are,*
> *Or who cleft the Devil's foot...*

Everyone roared with laughter: a list of impossible things! I repeated the words under my breath, marvelling at the power in them, the way they filled my mouth like sweet, dense cake.

Who cleft the Devil's foot?

My father continued, quietly now:

> *Teach me to hear mermaids singing,*
> *Or to keep off envy's stinging...*

My mother had joined him then, and I remember, despite my terror, noticing them meeting each other's eyes and laughing together in a way they sometimes did, when times were better.

And find
What wind
Serves to advance an honest mind.

Mother stood up and her voice grew into a song:

If thou be'st born to strange sights,
Things invisible to see...

I'd been scooped up again, then, onto another monstrous lap, the person mashing me to their swollen feathern breasts and rocking me back and forth. *There me ducky, there, me girl.*

They had spoken in that horrible, in-spired breath, all high and strangled.

I'd fought and shoved and run away, and my parents stopped their poetry and everybody laughed. I'd hidden in the root cellar, refusing to come out until the terrible, merry people with their horrible talking had gone away again.

That's what the house sounded like: high and tight, sucking air inward and never letting it out. *There, me ducky, there, me girl.*

Ooo... ahhhrs... ooo... ahhhrs...

Was it my mind playing tricks, spooked by Nanny King? Or was the house trying to tell me something?

Compared to home, school was just ordinarily horrible. Miss Addington-Acker—dinner on my own—Spencer girls.

In the afternoon, we were instructed in calisthenics.

It had come to the attention of the powers that be that treating generations of well-off white ladies like precious shattering dolls had created a class of incapable weaklings. Mild, regular exercise for the daughters of the upper classes became *de rigeur* in the educational institutions catering to their needs.

Miss Woolridge, a pretty young teacher from England, was involuntarily responsible for my single happy school memory. She taught not only calisthenics, but also led choral lessons. Most of what we sang came straight from the prayer books: warbling versions of "Abide with Me" and "We Are but Little Children Weak." However, in a fit of affection for her cold and miserable new homeland, she ventured one day to suggest that we attempt a local song or two.

A stunned silence greeted this pronouncement. Local songs were mostly about fishing, and often filthy. Surely Miss Woolridge didn't mean for us to roar like longshoremen?

But something bubbled up inside me, irrepressible, like a new spring. I knew some local songs, indeed I did, for I heard them sung over on the Southside every day on the waterfront premises, at the dry dock, in the neighbourhood kitchens.

I hummed a note. Eyes turned to me, some hostile, most merely curious. No, that would be too low for the others. I modulated up a few notes. "Mmmmmmm...."

To my surprise, a few other girls joined in.

"Mmmmmmm...."

We sounded like a medieval hurdy gurdy, a bagpiper's opening gambit.

I took a deep breath, and launched.

"We'll rant and we'll roar like true Newfoundlanders..."

The song had been written a few years before by a former representative for the Burin Peninsula in the Newfoundland House of Assembly.

"We'll rant and we'll roar, on deck and below!"

By the time I got to *I'm bound to have Polly or Biddy or Molly, As soon as I'm able to plank the cash down!* the whole choir had joined in, and the final chorus had us whipped all in a frenzy, ranting and roaring in a fashion that would have sent most of our parents mad. I felt, for once, like part of something bigger than myself. Cheeks flushed, eyes flashing, heads thrown back, we were one crew, one body, hollering the roof down.

Poor Miss Woolridge! She forbade any more forays into local musical culture forthwith. The incident didn't win me any friends, but I was left more or less alone for almost a week, which was, to my solitary frame of mind, better.

However, that had been over a month ago. I had now sunk to my former status as lowest of the low, and calisthenics classes did not improve my image. Due to the zeal of Miss Woolridge, these had morphed into more-or-less continuous rehearsals for Prize Distribution Day. This much-anticipated event, where the Bishop gave out prizes for demonstrations of an artistic nature, wasn't until June. But Miss Woolridge believed one couldn't start too early.

I was able to acquit myself passably in the dumb-bell and club exercises. My skinny arms were stronger than they looked, and I almost enjoyed the simple group movements. The terrifying and mysterious motions Miss Woolridge called *hoop and scarf evolutions*, however, were the bane of my existence. I'd been banned from the hoops ever since I'd inadvertently thwacked three girls in the face at once, giving one a bloody nose, and as for the scarves...

"No, no, no, Dorthea!" Miss Woolridge exclaimed. My scarf had entangled with those of my neighbours, grinding the whole exercise to a miserable halt. "You simply have to follow the others! Turn when they turn. I don't..." She rubbed her temples with fingers that, just perceptibly, trembled. "Again, please, class."

As the teacher turned away, someone emitted a barely perceptible bleat.

Where the idea that Southsiders should be called *billy goats* originated I had no idea, but by all I held dear I wished I could lower my head and butt whoever had made that noise into next week.

"Streel!" came another hiss. A spate of giggles rippled through the classroom.

"What is it, girls?" the teacher snapped.

"Miss Woolridge?" the wealthy girl simpered.

"Yes?"

"Dorthea's dress is unbuttoned. Perhaps that impedes her movement."

My hand flew to my back. Oh. The buttons. I might have known the buttons would come against me.

"Let me see."

Face burning, I turned around to show Miss Woolridge the gap where I had not been able to do up my own dress in the morning.

"Well, so it is. Someone help poor Dorthea with her unruly garments."

"I'd be happy to!"

The wealthy girl gripped my shoulder and spun me around. I felt her fingers grasp the neck of my dress. With a vicious tear she managed to pop every fastened button right off the dress. They scattered like buckshot across the floor. A couple of the girls let out little screams, jumping away as if the buttons were fleas.

"Oh, Miss Woolridge, look what's happened!"

Snickers spiraled through the class.

"Dorthea." Miss Woolridge visibly contained herself.

"It wasn't... I... it was her, Miss Woolridge!" I gazed desperately into my teacher's eyes.

"Dorthea!" said the teacher. "Spencer girls do *not* wear their clothes askew, and they do *not* blame others for their own infirmities! Please get the broom from the janitor's closet in the hallway *at once* and sweep up after yourself."

Hot with rage and shame, feeling the dress gaping down my back—no doubt exposing my grubby, much-mended woollen undershirt—I stalked out of the room with as much dignity as I could muster. Once in the hall I pulled the dress around me, retying my pinafore as tightly as I could. Was that stink fish-oil, seeping out of the fibres, released by heat of my shame?

I thought the day would never ooze to its end.

But at last it was time. The bell was rung. And then I was out. I was free!

The fog made a whole new city out of the old one. Buildings loomed; corners seemed sometimes farther, sometimes closer than they should. I had a secret, and it was the perfect weather to keep one in.

The *Evening Telegram* office lay just west of Prescott on Duckworth. As I hurtled towards it, nunny bag clutched in fist, I considered how I'd best be able to change into my boy's disguise. My plan was to surprise Murph, fool him the way mummers fooled you—concealing the identity of a familiar neighbour—and prove to him I was capable.

And then I heard it. *Caw! Caw!*

A crow soared over my head, so close I could feel the wind of its wings. One white feather on each pinion! He perched on the lintel of the door leading to the top floor of the *Telegram* building.

"Hello!" I said. "What are you doing here?"

He cocked his head like I was right idiotish.

I'd often seen erstwhile artists going in and out of the door of the *Telegram*, for the upper level was occupied by the St. John's School of Art. The students participated in exhibitions and competitions administered by the Royal Drawing Society. The director of the school was English, and his sketches were so life-like and detailed that newspapers often used them in lieu of photographs.

"Caw!" the crow told me. "Caw!"

A group of merry, chattering women converged upon the door. I shrank back. The women went through the entrance and up the stairs.

One last look at the crow. I swear he nodded at me.

I slipped in the door and followed the women up the stairs, the nunny bag containing Clinton Taylor's old Sunday best as heavy as if it contained lead bars.

Sliding into the artist studio, I inhaled the odour of turpentine and oil, and something else, a dusty sort of sweetness. An arrangement of fruit and flowers—somewhat the worse for time—lay on a brocade-draped table in the middle of the room; several easels were set up in an arc, catching light from the large windows. Some of the paintings were rather life-like; others looked more like a collection of croquet balls than fruit. But I had eyes only for a tall folding screen to one side of the room, panels painted with scenes of Chinese ladies in a garden. Behind there—I imagined—naked women would emerge for the life-drawing courses. If they had such a thing here. I wondered if they did. I wondered if I'd be able to get inside some day and see.

The thought filled me with thrilling, swiftly followed by dark shame.

I sidled behind the screen, quiet as smoke.

It took a bit to get into the clothes, for my hands were trembling. And I couldn't do my hair up as cleverly as Clare had—I knew bits of it were sticking out at the nape of my neck. Noise built up on the other side of the screen as students trooped up the staircase, chattering gaily and setting themselves up for the lesson.

I shoved my despised and injured girlish apparel into the bag, and peeked out.

The room had filled up. A man in a dark suit was walking about, glancing at the work and offering commentary.

I had to get past all those people to reach the staircase and the street.

Heart in mouth, I waited until the man was on the opposite side of the room with his back to me. I gulped, jammed my hat more tightly over my hair, and then, flinging the nunny bag over my shoulder with what I hoped was a devil-may-care air, I sauntered out.

A few heads turned, but not many. They were preoccupied with setting out paintbrushes and putting oil paint on their palettes. I kept up the saunter, whistling to myself, tipping my hat at one of the ladies. "Good evening, ma'am." I'd reached the door.

I tore down the stairs like the hobbyhorses were after me, bursting out the door into the fog of Duckworth Street. Around the corner, and through the great double doors of the *Telegram*.

I'd done it!

It was a dramatic entrance. I was breathing hard, as if I'd just run a long race. I sprang past three or four reporters at their massive desks, hard at work typing up copy.

The din was overwhelming. Nobody gave me a second glance.

Murph's desk was near the back. As I approached I saw a dainty pair of feet saucily perched up on the desk—Mary, not Murph. She was reading a typewritten missive, making corrections with a pen.

"Get in out of the fog before the fairies get you!" I growled.

She turned, a laugh on her face, turning to perplexity.

"Yes?" she said.

Triumph! She didn't know who I was!

"I've got a message from Murph," I said. "The plan is on."

"What plan?" She took her feet down and leaned forward, frowning a little at me. "Did Murph send... Oh, my Lord in Heaven above and all His angels! It's Dor!"

I burst out laughing. "Gotcha!"

"Are you... Oh, for..." She picked up her gloves and thrashed them around like an angry cat's tail. "Murph, you will pay for this."

"But even you didn't know! See? I can do it!"

"It's too dangerous, Dor! And, and... it's highly unsuitable!"

I thought it safest to ignore the unsuitability clause. "Dangerous how?"

"Well, you'll be messing around with electricity and, and

things! And it'll be outdoors. You could freeze to death."

"I go outdoors all the time, and I haven't frozen to death yet," I pointed out.

To my delight she was starting to laugh, now, giggling at her own objections. "Oh, Dor, you'll be the death... And what if someone discovers you!"

"Nobody will." I jutted my chin. "If you hadn't known who I was, you would never say I was a girl."

"What have you done with your hair? You've never cut it off?"

"Clare had it done up better last night."

"Turn around and let me look at you, you little rag moll."

I started to spin, then rejected that motion as too girly. What, I asked myself, would a young gaffer like Clinton do if asked to turn around? I put on a sullen look, and slowly went around in a circle, trying to look big. "Good enough for you?"

"Where did you get those clothes? They're perfect! Dor, you never stole them, tell me you didn't."

"Of course not!" My wounded innocence made Mary laugh. "Clare gave them to me. Loaned. Clinton's Sunday best that he's outgrown."

Her gaze went from me to the doorway. "Here comes Murph."

"Don't tell him," I begged. "See if he knows me." I was rewarded by a conspiratorial twinkle in Mary's eyes.

Murph came up, a harassed expression on his face. "Marconi just called a conference," he said. "Parsons is on his way here. We'd better get over to the Cochrane, darling, before... who is this?"

"Jack," I said, making my voice even deeper than it usually was.

Murph stared.

I tugged my cap at him. "I heard you could do with some help," I continued.

"Help with what? Convincing my editor that this story is

the newspaper scoop of a lifetime? Well, if you can do that, b'y, I'd like to... hear... how you'd... wait a minute."

"Wha'?" I lifted my chin.

"Dor?" His frank blue eyes opened up wide, and his jaw dropped. "I never." He looked to his fiancée. "Mary, is this your—"

"My doing? Never! It's all Dor."

"But I didn't even recognize..." He stared some more. "Really, that's grand. You're very impressive, Dor."

"Can I at least come to the conference?" I begged. "That can't do any harm, can it?"

Murph raised his hands, then dropped them again. "Mary?" he asked again.

"Oh, for... All right. We'll consider it an audition for this hare-brained scheme. I suppose we could introduce you to the great man as my little brother."

"Hurrah!" I jumped up, pumping the air with my fists. Then reality came crashing in on me in a dark blast. "Oh, but I don't look anything like you. You're beautiful where all the girls say I'm just a scrappy little..."

"Stop that, now! Don't you ever let anyone tell you if you're pretty or not. You're gorgeous, just as God made you. You've come a long way from a skinned rabbit, you have." She put her head on one side. "But we can make a convincing boy of you." Mary took the cap off, and started twisting my hair in her hands. "Not thirteen—you're too small. Say you're eleven. I have some hair pins around here somewhere... You're two children, you are, the pair of you," she muttered, but her eyes were sparkling.

"Mary Kelly, I love you. And Dor, you're a champ! This story will make me!"

"Sure, all we're doing is going to a conference." Mary tried to look severe.

"Correct. You always are, my darling." Murph winked at me. "New York, here we come!"

WIRELESS TELEGRAPHY

My excitement grew with every step toward the Cochrane Street Hotel. I would meet Marconi! A famous man who was going to change the world with his invention. I tried to call up everything I knew about Hertzian waves, and contemplate the vast global implications of wireless telegraphy... but just as much, I had to admit I was excited to meet an Italian.

I'd never seen one before. Maybe he'd be dark—almost certainly he would be! Dark hair and eyes at the very least—like me.

The steps of the hotel were blocked, for word of the famous guest had run through the town. Murph pushed through, greeting many of the onlookers by name, and Mary did the same—did they know everybody? It was always like this with them. You couldn't get out of a room for talking.

Despite the crowd, plush carpet and wood panelling soaked up sound like a sponge. Everything felt hushed, poised on a knife-edge. I'd never been inside a hotel before. I gawped at the vast brass chandelier hanging from the hallway ceiling, and admired the elaborate panelling. Murph led us down the hall to a big room, double doors flung wide.

We were just in time. The Minister of Marine and Fisheries was just introducing the man: Signor Guglielmo Marconi. I craned my neck, trying to see, but it was impossible in the crowd. Something else was said, imperceptible, but it initiated a ripple of good-natured laughter.

"Just made a hash of his name," Murph muttered, getting out his pencil and pad of paper.

"Oh, dear," Mary sighed.

Murph began a process of using his elbows and

muttering, "Press, press," to edge through the crowd, getting us closer to the front. The Minister went on enthusiastically outlining the benefits of Marconi's new system to shipping. Mary edged ahead, slipping between a gap that closed in my face, a wall of tweedy jackets.

The Minister wound down, and there was a brief stir.

Next someone introduced the Governor, the fellow who so adored Mary. I'd seen him speak before; he had presided when the Duke and Duchess of Cornwall and York had visited a few months ago to lay the cornerstone for the new courthouse. Born in the Caribbean and educated in England, he was also a knight. He had a grey mustache and a proud look to him. As some kind of back-handed reward, he'd been assigned to the governorship of Newfoundland. However, he seemed to genuinely love us; in a short time he'd become very popular.

"I admire, of course, and support scientific inquiry," I could hear him saying. "But scientists must not become so imbued in theory that they miss the point of their own discoveries. Some of these fellows even looked down upon this vulgar—as they would say, it is *certainly* not my view—practitioner. Well, we are all sure that they are now ruing the day they did not embrace Signor Marconi's experiments. This is the man to develop a practical system. Unhampered—if I may say it—by merely scientific concerns, Signor Marconi is the man who made the leap from Hertz's laboratory to practical wireless telegraphy!"

General murmuring approbation covered Sir Boyle's next sentence.

"... applications ranging from international shipping," I was able to make out, "to the touching fact of enabling our dear Queen Victoria to monitor the health of the Prince of Wales from her Isle of Wight home while the Prince—now our Monarch—lay convalescing in the royal yacht lying off Cowes."

More murmurs.

"We are honoured to have him," Sir Boyle finished, "and wish him every success in his endeavours!"

Next spoke Premier Bond, who had apartments in this very hotel. He noted that although it behooved no Newfoundlander to take pleasure in the bad weather of another country, there was no doubt that Newfoundland had benefitted greatly from a certain violent storm in Cape Cod—which raised a general laugh. "We pledge our resources and energies to support him."

The room was hot. The speeches seemed to go on forever. I wished I could take off my woollen cap. But finally, there was a bout of sustained applause.

A man began to speak. It wasn't loud, but everyone piped down at once. The voice had an easy, pleasant quality, yet somehow conveyed authority. You wanted to listen to it.

It was him. It must be him!

But the voice was disappointingly English. It was no different in accent than that of countless British officials, or my teachers. I strained on tiptoe, but an awful length of a man towered in front of me and I was packed in too tight to get past him.

The voice thanked Premier Bond and the Minister of Marine and Fisheries for inviting him to this wonderful island Dominion. It spoke of investigating the possibility of setting up wireless stations to help reduce the number of shipwrecks— something he had only moments ago been discussing with the Inspector of Lighthouses.

"My mission," the voice continued, still sounding entirely unforeign, "is to eventually establish stations along the south coast of Newfoundland, thus enabling incoming vessels to more quickly communicate with the mainland. Upon the morrow, I will investigate nearby sites and select one most suitable for my experiments." He went on to thank various people, and most especially Premier Bond and Governor Boyle for making his arrival so pleasant after what, he admitted, was a horrendous crossing.

"Welcome to Newfoundland!" someone called out, evoking laughter and a general rumbling cheer.

The volume of chatter rose precipitately. Bodies started milling about. I could now slip between groups of conversationalists, gradually sidling to the perimeter of the room. I'd get my back to a wall, and try to get my bearings.

Nobody paid any attention to the boy in the flat cap. Nobody at all. If I'd been in my girl's clothes I would have been remarked and removed from the room at once. *I look like a boy, I really do!* I exulted. If anybody asked, I'd be Jack Kelly, *Telegram* errand boy. *That beautiful lady is my sister, just ask her!*

From the sidelines I caught sight of that beautiful lady at last. Sir Cavendish Boyle was bending over her hand and kissing her fingers; the two of them laughed, and then—I scuttled along the wall to see—he led her over to another man and made what I judged were introductions. The other man was... I couldn't see through the cursed crowd, and in any case Mary's colossal hat quite blocked the man from view. Was it Marconi? It must be! Drawing a bead on said hat, I plunged into the crowd once more to dodge and squeeze toward the knot of people around the famous guest.

I made it through. There was Mary, laughing delightedly. And there, gazing at Mary, was the man named Marconi.

I knew him. Or at least, I knew that energy, that tightly drawn, cold vitality. For it was the figure I'd seen in my dream.

I looked up at a slender man, of medium height, maybe a shade under six feet. He wasn't as handsome as Murph, but he was elegant and well-proportioned.

His eyes, delivering me a crushing blow of disappointment, were grey-blue. And his hair was a dissatisfying light brown, and his skin was almost as fair as Mary's. The most remarkable thing about him was that he looked completely unremarkable.

"There you are!" Mary exclaimed. "Signor, please meet my brother. Jack, shake Mr. Marconi's hand."

Nobody had ever suggested I shake hands with anybody, never in my life. Nervously, I screwed my cap even more firmly down over my head, and held out my hand.

Marconi gazed at me vaguely. He was barely taking me in. But his grip was strong, and I made an extra effort to squeeze back, thinking this was what a boy might do. "Pleased to meet you, sir," I managed.

"I was just telling Mr. Marconi that you'd be an able errand boy for his work."

"Oh, I'd love to!" I exclaimed. Wait, was that too girly? "I mean, it'd be an honour, sir."

"Errand boy..." Marconi's eyes moved restlessly about the room. I had an impression that he wasn't really seeing the people around him. How many of these junkets had he attended during his career? Surely hundreds, maybe thousands. Wherever he went, people would be eager to meet him. They'd offer to help, want to be involved in the glory. It must be irritating.

"I wouldn't let you d-d-down, sir," I hackered. "I know every business in t-town, and I take directions, I'm bright, and, and strong, and Mary here can vouch for me."

Marconi's gaze wandered back to Mary and his vague look focused. "If Madame Mary can vouch for you, why, then, we will take you on." He bowed slightly, never taking his eyes from her face.

"Wonderful, Signor!" Mary said. "You hear that, Jack? You start tomorrow, Signor? You certainly aren't wasting any time. I do hope you have time for pleasure as well as work."

"Always. It does not do to waste time—in work or pleasure." There was something hard and brilliant about him when, like now, his diamond-sharp gaze focused on my friend.

I revised my previous opinion. He wasn't disappointing— he was fascinating. Unassuming, unsmiling, yet coolly confident, he made me feel sweaty and messy and needy and loud. A precision in his consonants, and also the scent of him—slightly spicy, soap and pomade, coffee and smoke—proclaimed him a citizen of the globe. The crystal glass of the chandelier above him tinkled, as if echoing his words. I noticed he had a red silk pocket square poking out the top of his breast pocket. King of Diamonds indeed.

He belonged to every place, or perhaps to no place at all.

Murph made his way through the knot to join us. When Mary introduced him as a reporter for the *Evening Telegram,* and her fiancé, Marconi gave Murph a look that I could only describe as evaluative, then dismissive. As for Murph, he straightened himself up and made much of the extra inch he had on the visitor.

They arranged for a meet-up the following morning. "You'll be stuck with me, Signor," Murph said with a barely suppressed trace of satisfaction. "My editor has assigned me to accompany you as you search for the appropriate site. And I'll keep an eye on Jack here, too, of course."

"We breakfast at six o'clock. At seven, we will begin the process of selecting a site." Marconi looked back to Mary, whom he evidently found a more prepossessing sight. "We had considered Cape Spear, Miss Mary, as being the easternmost point. However, popular opinion is that Signal Hill is the best..."

"The Lookout!" I interjected. "Yes, sir, it's the tallest hill around here. And a lot easier to get to than Cape Spear."

Those vague grey eyes looked down at me and sharpened. "Very well, young consultant. I will take your words under advisement." He glanced meaningfully again at Mary.

I felt my fists clenching. Marconi clearly had eyes for my friend. But I had to remind myself that I looked like an eleven-year-old boy, a child. As for poor Murph, he could only look on as Marconi flirted. It was all *Someone of your dazzling beauty* this, and *If all the ladies of the town are half as charming* that.

As for her, she sparred right back at him, slaying him in one blow by citing an article from the *Times* about telegraphy and the seemingly insoluble problem of the curvature of the Earth.

"When it comes to curvature," he interrupted her encapsulation of the science, kissing her fingers, "I bow to your superiority." I barely stifled a groan, and Murph looked like he was going to rear up and go off.

Finally we spilled out of the stuffy room into the night. The fog drifted in tendrils, and streetlights trembled into radiance, misty, uncanny globes of light floating in the thick air like phosphorescent jellyfish.

"It's gone so warm and mauzy," Mary said.

"Probably freeze the brass off you by tomorrow, weather being what it is," Murph said.

Mary sighed. "Well, mission accomplished. Charm target: check. Little brother employed by target: check."

"I'm not sure I liked your first mission."

"Ah, don't go glavauning on me. There's nothing to complain about. I have one love, and that's not him." She drew Murph's hand into the crook of her arm.

"The eyes he made at you," Murph fretted.

"He's got a fiancée, a Miss Holman. She's very pretty. I've seen pictures in the paper."

"Not as pretty as you, I'll bet."

"And she's been to university, and she knows Morse code! That probably means more to him than anything."

"Humph."

"Listen, buddy. If he gets fresh, I'll just tell him, sorry, Signor, the bank's closed. Besides, I'll probably never see him again. Cheer up for the love of God, Murph."

Impatient with this ridiculous tiff, I broke in. "So, I'll see you there at seven, Murph?"

"Sounds good, Jack Kelly."

We returned to the *Telegram* so Murph could write up the events of the evening, and I could change.

As before, they insisted on walking me to the Long Bridge. I protested, for Mary lived up on LeMarchant in a painfully respectable boarding house, and Murph had rooms in all the way back in the East End. "We aren't leaving you to walk alone in the night in this lawless place!" Mary exclaimed.

I was certain I'd be left safely to walk alone were I still in my boy's garments.

Running up the Ratline, I saw lamplight glowing softly through the parlour curtains. Piano music throbbed as if being sung by the air. My mother's stately, deeply sad, yet somehow hopeful playing beat like waves against a rock.

I floated up the rest of the stairs in time to it—a brooding music, lending everything a glamour. The door to the linney was closed for a wonder. I pushed it open, drinking in the kitchen's familiar warmth, coal stove putting out its bankered heat; and the smell, close and not quite comforting: coal dust, damp, the rock of the Hill, and the freshness of the spring bubbling beneath the flagstone floor. Because of the piano, it all felt stately, tragic, better than real life. I stood, listening, the sack of Jack Kelly heavy in my hand.

Then suddenly the heavy funeral broke into a lovely, sad sort of song, full of longing and remembrance of happy days.

The piano music ceased. "Is that you, Dor?" Mother called out from the front of the house.

"Yes, Mother."

"Come here so I may view you."

The sack! The lack of buttons on my dress!

"Yes, Mother!" I scuttled up the stairs to fling the nunny bag under my bed, shuddering in the cold—how could my room be somehow colder than the air outside? It defied science—then crept back down, taking a deep breath, and noisily making my way down the hall to the parlour.

A merry fire burned in the fireplace, light playing over the beautiful jade-coloured tiles surrounding the grate, gleaming off the dark wood of the grand piano at the room's opposite end by the window. The portrait of my great-great-grandfather presided over the room. He liked my mother, I figured; in the firelight he looked almost benevolent. And there was, too, a decided resemblance; she had inherited his grey eyes and pale skin, with rose showing through her cheeks. She wore a lovely blouse with lace all down her bosom.

Those cold, gunmetal eyes fixed on me without losing a beat.

"Look at you, coming in all hours. Barbarian."

"I was with Mary," I said.

"Mary? That's all right."

I reflected that I could probably go sailing around the world with a crew of pirates and if Mary were there, my mother would say, *Mary? That's all right.*

It occurred to me to wonder if my mother missed Mary. Most likely. We all did.

"Come tell me about your day."

Mother was in a mood to talk, then. I edged up to the fire, keeping my back to it so as to conceal from my mother the burst buttons on my dress, and drew a sealskin ottoman closer to the warmth.

"I went to school. The girls were mean. We're practicing for Distribution Day."

"Distribution Day! That's not until June."

"My sentiments exactly."

"Now, Dorthea, that's not a respectful way to speak of your teachers."

"I did well in Reading and poorly in everything else."

"As usual. Well, at the very least *pretend* to pay attention," my mother advised me.

"I try," I said, "but when I do, they think I'm being saucy."

"You have a naturally pugnacious look."

"I do. Where's Father?"

"Oh, your father." Mother began playing the funereal march from the beginning again, pounding out the left hand. "Get some more coal for the fire, Dor, there's a good girl."

I picked up the brass coal scuttle and sidled out the door, heading for the bin in the linney.

"And don't get smudges all over you! Filthy creature."

Father must be out drinking, I considered as I shovelled coal from bin to scuttle. That's why the parlour sang with repeated measures, ringing out like a funeral bell. My mother, always volatile, had to be handled carefully when Father was drinking.

"Who composed that?" I asked upon re-entering the parlour, lugging the coal scuttle. I considered this a safe question.

"Chopin. Surely you know that."

I began flinging coal onto the fire.

"He composed it while he was living with George Sand."

"Who was he?"

"*She* was a novelist, and scandalous for wearing men's clothes and smoking in public."

I almost dropped the coal shovel. "Men's clothes?!"

"Certainly. Haven't you heard of Sand? I must try and find one of her novels for you. Or perhaps not... they might not be very suitable."

I groaned.

This seemed to amuse her. Was that a smile I saw playing on my mother's lips?

"In France at the time you had to apply for a legal permit to wear men's clothes. And Sand refused. Of course, she was rich, and the rich can get away with almost anything... She said they were sturdier and easier to wear than women's clothes."

"Well, they are." Then I gave a little jump. "What's the law in Newfoundland?"

"Law about what?"

"Wearing men's clothes."

Mother's hands morphed into her own music, roiling and pounding so that the windows of the parlour shook. "Dorthea. You need to start wearing longer dresses. Put your hair up. You're on your way to becoming a young lady." She played, muttering to herself, "Although until she starts acting like a young lady I'll hesitate to call her one."

We were moving into dangerous territory. "I'm not. I haven't even started... you know."

"Mmmm. Well, when the visitor comes, you know what to do. We've had the talk."

I shuddered. The talk had been *excruciating*. That dark fuzz on my upper lip had something to do with it, for Mother had pointed it out as evidence that I needed the pile of torn rags and the safety pins that she'd handed me, and she spoke of the *visitor* in hushed tones.

The thought of this *visitor* coming—once a month, *once a month!* was that really necessary?—made me sick. This was a real thing, a malediction that happened to all females?

What if it happened while I was in school? Or—and I went cold with horror—what if it came on while I was with Marconi? While I was Jack Kelly?

"I don't want to be a young lady." I flung more coal onto the fire.

"Viz., to wit," Mother said. "Nevertheless, a young lady you are becoming, in age if not deportment."

"It's just a phrase. *Young lady.* Doesn't mean anything, really, if you look at it." Stop talking, stop talking, I told myself. Why couldn't I shut my mouth? Sometimes I wondered if I wanted to goad my mother into a fight. It was somehow preferable to waiting for the hammer to fall.

On the other hand, I sometimes felt that it was Mother who drove *me* to fight, especially lately.

She was the queen bee. Therefore I had been, most of my life, a neuter. Sexless. Not even a worker bee, as apparently I could not even turn bread into toast.

But ever since that terrible talk about the *visitor* months ago, things had gotten worse. A great and constant tension sang inside me whenever I was around her. Sometimes, after a fight, she'd say *Let's bury the hatchet.* And we would—for a time. But we'd always remember where we'd put it. She believed I'd murdered Theodore, sucked him dry inside her womb. And maybe I had. How would I know?

Of course she hated me.

Her hands banged down in a concluding, complex chord. "That's enough coal, for goodness sake, Dor, do you want to burn the house down. We are not made of money. I don't know what gets into you."

I put the shovel back into the scuttle and sat on the ottoman, hands spread to the flames. "I simply don't see why at such-and-such an age I suddenly need to start wearing a corset and put my hair up, and my ankles suddenly have the power to drive men mad. Nobody goes mad looking at my ankles *now*."

Mother gave a great shout of laughter. "Be silent, child, or I'll send you to bed."

I wanted desperately to point out the contradiction in my mother's stance—either I was a young lady, or I was a child to be ordered to bed—but managed to keep my gob shut.

"And sit like a lady! How you look like your father."

I was sitting knees apart, elbows supported on them, hands spread to the flames. I sighed and straightened up. So much less comfortable. And then I remembered. Tomorrow I would dress like a boy again! Like George Sand, writing novels and saying *no* to stupid laws. I could— no, I would *have* to—sit comfortably by default, all day long.

Mother started playing something gentle, a feeling like a ship coming into port from a storm. She seemed in an uncommonly good mood. It occurred to me that she, of all people, could tell me about the strange figure I had witnessed the other night.

"Mother? Who is the Reverend? I saw him yesterday evening behind a funeral."

"The Reverend? Well, for starters, he's not really a reverend."

"Then why do people call him that?"

"Because he wears spectacles, which gives him a learned look. Also, he is well-spoken. It doesn't take much to impress this crowd around here," Mother snorted.

"But he's... he's very strange."

"He's been in the fairies so long he's one of them. Let that be a warning for you, fine miss!"

"How do you get out of the fairies, then?"

"Shhhh!"

"What?"

"Call them the Good Ones. Or some such. Them. Little Strangers." She played some more. "In th'olde dayes of the Kyng Arthour, of which that Britons speken greet honour, all was this land fulfild of fayerye," she chanted in a sing-song.

"So is he?"

"Ah, that's just an old pishogue, as Mary might say. Of course, he's human. In fact, he bears a striking resemblance to King Edward VII." The music morphed again, to a waltz. "In 1860 they had a great ball—at the Colonial Building I believe, it was before I was born—and His Royal Highness—just the Prince of Wales at the time, of course—danced with local young ladies until almost three in the morning. One Elizabeth Warren was arrested sometime thereafter for the theft of a velvet bonnet and scarf... She was found to be in a delicate condition, and without a husband."

"What happened to her?"

"She was placed in the old jail, you know, the one on Signal Hill, to await transportation from the colony."

I shuddered. That jail—at the foot of Gibbet Hill, no less—had been by all accounts been a horrible place. It was said that ghosts still stalked the site. "To where?"

"I have no idea; they just wanted to be rid of her. But she escaped before the ship sailed. Then was recaptured a few days later..."

"Did they put her back in jail?" This seemed excessive punishment for the theft of a bonnet and scarf, even velvet ones.

"Of course. And once again she escaped from the ship before it sailed. She then exhibited symptoms of insanity, and was transferred to the asylum. Where she naturally made another, and entirely sane, escape. The government then gave up trying to deport her and the Governor issued a pardon."

The waltz transformed into a battle march.

"What happened to the baby?"

"What baby?"

"The woman's baby."

Mother played some more. "He lives down the road, child, near the Old Man's Beard. You could go and ask him yourself."

I remembered the look he'd given me. *Keep one eye on the Devil, and one eye on the One Up Above.* I shuddered. "Oh, I just couldn't!"

"What kind of Southsider are you? Honestly, Dor, sometimes I wonder where you came from. He's worthy of respect, however eccentric his aspect." She finished the march with a great banging chord, and her hands fell in her lap. She looked at me, and blinked. "Whatever happened to the buttons on your dress?"

I had forgotten to keep the back of my dress from her eyes! "As I said. Mean girls."

"Dorthea, I am ashamed of my life sometimes..." She sighed. "Give it to me. I'll fix it."

"I have the buttons," I said, guilt seeping through me. "The teacher made me sweep them up and I put them in my satchel."

"The teacher made you sweep them up?"

I nodded.

"What teacher?" Her eyes flashed cold fire. "Who does she think she is, treating you like a maid of all work?"

I shifted uncomfortably. "It doesn't matter."

"It most certainly does. I'll have a word with the principal tomorrow."

No, please, not my mother having a word. I pictured it: my mother with her precise, rhotic accent, dressing down my English principal. If there was one thing my mother did not tolerate, it was a sense of being looked down upon by the English. And then the principal would call me to the office to discuss it, and... "It will only make things wor..." I caught the look on her face, and stopped talking.

Her head cocked to one side, that rageful gleaming in her eyes. Was she contemplating boxing my ears? I hunched over a little, just in case. The room was silent except for the soft stirrings of the fire.

Then the grandfather clock struck nine. We both looked up at it. It was a family clock, of course—everything in the house belonged to my mother's ancestors—from Bristol. Its mahogany case was chequered with inlay of light and dark woods, crowned with an arched pediment and three brass finials. The hands were elaborate brass lace, and the corners of the clock face painted with fruit and flowers and real gold leaf. One of my earliest memories was watching Mother wind it, the heavy lead weights rising as she turned the key. But my favourite feature was the painted glum-faced moon. It rolled clockwise, falling behind a flattened globe of the world featuring Africa and Asia, then rising again behind the globe on the left featuring North America and the Pacific islands, alternating with a beautiful sailing frigate. Right now she was waning, the sunny frigate was on the rise, and a mere crescent—the moon's sad right eye—peeped out at us.

My mother sighed. "I'm sorry, Dorthea," she said. "Give me the dress. And then to bed with you."

And she arose from the piano bench, came up the room, and kissed me on the top of my head.

You could have knocked me down I was that astonished. Hit on the lee side, again.

I stripped out of the dress. She clucked at the state of my undershirt and pinafore, and declared me a rag moll. "Give me those; I'll wash them. They're filthy. I declare, I don't know where you come from."

First time you've noticed my dirty clothes in weeks, I thought. But then, it would behoove me to start doing the laundry myself. For my mother rose and sank like the moon. And in our house there were no sunny days, and precious little calm sailing in between.

Naked but for my bloomers and stockings, I went shivering up the grand front staircase of the house with its elaborate newel post and spiral-carven rails, and directly to bed.

THREE KNOCKS

I awoke to a bang and a thud. Then the deep rumble of my father's voice; he was, evidently, cutting the curwibbles. My mother's crisp, acerbic tones, "You drink more well than wisely."

I drifted off again, or thought I did, for when the clock downstairs struck three I found I had been almost waiting for what followed next.

A knocking at the back door. Three knocks.

Such late-night summonses were nothing new in our house. Someone—usually a man, sometimes a child—would come to our door—the back door, always the back—saying that the mother, or the wife, was "in the family way" or "her time has come." Mother would fling on her clothes, eschewing a corset, and seize that black leather doctor's bag she always kept packed. If the weather was particularly awful—and he hadn't been drinking—Father would sometimes, and grumpily, accompany her to the house of the imminent birth.

Mother would stay in the house of a woman in labour, and help born the baby. And afterwards she'd visit every day; for over a week that woman would be treated like a queen. Mother would bathe and dress the infant, wash the mother, make the breakfast, launder the diapers, tidy up the house, do the household laundry and ironing, feed the older brats if there were any—and there almost always were.

Those families got more of Mother than I did.

Lying huddled under the covers, I heard her coming down the hall past my door. She was carrying a candle, and the flame cast her night-gowned shadow across the walls and through my open door. Her soft footsteps went down the back stairs; she answered the door. I listened for the man's voice, ready to identify what local family would have the next new baby. But instead, a great draft tore through the house. My door banged sharply against the wall.

"I'll just be a moment." Mother's voice, a strange tension in her tone.

Footsteps back up the stairs. No candle; it must have blown out.

"Mother?" I called out.

"Go to sleep, Dorthea. I've been called out." She paused. "I'll be back when the baby is borned."

Well, I knew that; did she think I was a blockhead?

Sounds from my parents' room down the hall; Father mumbling, cupboard doors opening and shutting. Lamplight back down the hall; my mother's footsteps, shod now, and alone.

She hesitated by my door. "Good night, Dorthea. I'll finish sewing your buttons when I return."

That was strangely tender of her.

And down the stairs she went.

The back door banged open downstairs. When it closed, it sent a shock wave through the whole house.

Silence for a time.

And then a slow, low murmuration. It sounded like it was coming from the back cellar, deep in the roots of the house, a whispering mutter. Wind moaned, and the house began to sway and creak. The back door banged open again, resuming its wheezing flaption, lapping and jawing. *Ooor.... oouurrr... ooor... oouurrr...*

And then I could have sworn there were footsteps in the cellar, out the pantry, and through the kitchen below me, a great marching of feet. The voices rose. Many voices: murmuring, singing, a dreadful charm and racket. It grew into shouting now, a great roaration. I realized I was whimpering, huddling under the covers with the pillow over my head and my hands over my ears. What cruel crowd was having a rompse downstairs? The house was shaking. Could not my father hear it? The house would shake itself apart!

And then there was a sense of stampede, running through the house from front to back. The shaking and roaring washed over me, a tidal wave.

The door banged once more, a report like a shotgun, and was silent.

The shaking and racket had stopped.

The house had never been so quiet.

THE KING HAND

Next morning was Saturday, the seventh of December, and the day dawned clear.

I awoke without anybody having to call me. Today Signor Guglielmo Marconi would begin his work. And young Jack Kelly was going to be there to help him.

Mother would still be out on her call, and I could hear tremendous snores from Father down the hall. Other than that, the house was at peace. I felt almost happy. A burden—one I was barely conscious of at all times in the house—had lifted, like clouds going off and the sun coming out. Like that frigate of the grandfather clock, under sail on a fair day.

As I pulled out the bag sequestered under my bed and buttoned myself into Clinton Taylor's cast-offs, I wondered again where my mother had been called. Fort Amherst, perhaps? It lay right out at the Narrows, and you needed a boat to get there, for the Southside Road petered out, defeated by the steep hills at the water's edge. Or someone up the road? I wasn't aware of any pregnancies other than Clare's poor mother, and she wasn't far enough along yet to want my mother.

Dressed, I slid out of the room and down the back steps like a shadow. I washed my face at the kitchen pump and had a long drink of cold, clear water. I poked at the coals in the stove. The pot of tea at the back was stiff enough to stand a spoon up in, as my father would say. I had a cup of bare-legged tea—something he also said, meaning tea without food—and felt warmth spread through me as the astringent black stuff went down my throat, sweetened with more sugar than my mother would approve of.

Her midwifery bag was gone from its place, of course. So too was the red cardigan jacket. It always hung on a hook by the back door, for she wore it out on calls; it had pockets, and was lovely and warm. She'd knit it for my father. But, perhaps finding the scarlet too vivid for his tastes, he'd never really worn it and she'd adopted it for her own.

There was a little looking glass over the sink in the kitchen. I stood there and did my best to braid and twist my long, dark hair so that it would disappear under the cap, trying for what Clare had done. I stole a few of the newfangled spiral hairpins my mother had procured; they worked wonderfully, holding my little braids and twists into place at the back of my head. The hat went on easily over that, and the band was tight enough that I didn't fear for it blowing off my head.

One last look around the quiet room, marvelling at the peace of it. A bit of rogue winter sunlight lay in a trapezoid on the flagstones, a golden pool through the southern window.

I took a deep breath.

And Jack Kelly sauntered out the door.

No phantom hand shoved me on the way through the threshold. Nothing came up and smacked me as I went down the path, no rock flew at my head. I traversed the Ratline in peace, and all was well until I got to the Hundred Steps, and Clinton Taylor himself came strolling out his own door.

"Hey!" he said, looking at me.

"Morning." Instinctively I ramped up my accent, going for a broad Newfoundland sound. I looked hopefully behind him to see if Clare was coming out too. But the door stayed resolutely closed.

"Who are you?" The bantam lifted his chin.

Dear Heaven above, I wasn't going to have to fight Clinton Taylor, was I? I shifted from foot to foot. He'd be the clear winner. I was much smaller than he, and I'd never been in a fistfight in my life.

I thought it best to say as little as possible. Boys tended to say less than girls. And the less I elaborated, the better, right?

I jerked my head back up the Ratline. "Cousin."

His eyes ran up and down my outfit. *Please Lord don't let him recognize his own clothes.* But, "I never seen you before," is what he said.

My mind raced. I looked like Father, so... "From da West Coast."

There was a long pause. Clint stared at me some more.

"Visiting," I added with some desperation. Then I gave what I hoped was a jaunty, masculine wave of my hand. "See ya," and I rattled down the stairs past the creature.

"That Dor, she's your cousin, then?" came his voice behind me.

I stopped, frozen to the spot. I felt my cheeks and the back of my neck burning, like I was standing in the corner at school. Damn, damn, damn, had he seen through me?

"Yip."

"Ain't she the king hand!"

I gave him another look. He was grinning. Just for a moment, I saw a green light in his eye and a dimple on his cheek. He looked, in that moment, like his sister. My heart gave a jump.

"You're telling me," I said, and grinned back at him.

"See you around, then."

I jerked my head again, in that strange defiant half-nod, half-challenge thing I'd always seen boys do, and rattled on down the stairs.

When I got to the bottom, I dared to look back.

Clinton was nowhere to be seen.

I'd done it! I'd walked past Clinton Taylor in his own clothes and he'd not known me!

That Dor, she certainly was the king hand, oh, yes indeed.

I ran up to Cochrane House just as Murph was arriving.

"Good morning, Jack Kelly!"

By this time my opinion of myself had swollen to monstrous proportions, for I had not only negotiated my toughest critic on home territory, but run past the dry dock, streetcar barns, and through most of downtown's West End without a single strange look from man, woman, or child.

"Morning!"

"Turns out it'll be quite the delegation today. We'll have yourself, and Signor Marconi of course. His two assistants Kemp and Paget, as well as Minister of Marine and Fisheries T. J. Murphy. Also Inspector of Boilers James McLoughlan, Inspector of Lighthouses Richard White, and myself!"

I went speechless. That was a lot of important personage for one small 'boy.'

"Don't worry, just look lively."

I gulped, and nodded.

"And be helpful if you can," Murph winked. "You'll be alright. Shall we go in?"

I shook my head. "You go on."

Murph looked at me curiously. "Don't you want to warm up?"

"I'd have to take off my cap... I didn't last night but it'd be noticed now..."

"Ah!" He squinted up into the sky. "Correct. We shall await them out here, then, Jack Kelly."

The two of us waited on the steps, stamping feet and blowing on fingers. It wasn't a bad day, but the cold got you if you weren't moving. Finally, just a little past seven o'clock, six men came trooping out of the hotel.

I recognized the Minister and the two Inspectors. White towered over the others, all long legs and big beard. Next came a short, broad man with a red face and blunt features; Murph identified him as Kemp, Marconi's right-hand man. Kemp was ramrod straight with a military bearing; he wore neither hat nor gloves. A man Murph told me was called Paget came out next. He had a fur cap with the earflaps tied down, and the tip of his nose was red; as he emerged onto the steps, he gave a shudder.

Marconi emerged last. He wore a dashing fedora, a long, woollen coat, a paisley silk scarf, and the most beautiful leather gloves I had ever seen.

He nodded to Murph. His pale eyes passed right over me.

Taller than the Minister and Kemp, Marconi was nevertheless slight, the smallest man in the group if you had to guess by weight. But there was something that drew your attention to him. It was that confidence, I decided, twinned with an unassuming, modest air. He didn't say much, but everybody listened when he did. A sort of energy vibrated off him.

No wonder I had dreamed of him covered with vibrating light.

"Signal Hill is just the place," Inspector White was saying.

Kemp nodded. "Much closer to supplies. It only remains to determine exactly where."

Ah! So it had been decided that Marconi would set up on Signal Hill.

Murph leaned into me. "The significance of the name of the hill can't be lost on him."

I nodded. Signal Hill! If he succeeded, it would be perfect.

Two cabs came rattling up to the hotel, horses tossing their heads, breath smoking in the chill air. Marconi, Kemp, and Paget got into the first one with the Minister, while Murph and I climbed into the second with the two Inspectors. I was glad to get out of the cold. The little jacket wasn't meant to keep one warm in the winter! But there was nothing to be done—I had no boy's overcoat, and that was that. I made a note to myself: Jack Kelly would double up on long underwear on the morrow.

It was my first time in a cab. I felt very grand! Crammed between Murph and Inspector White, I craned my neck, watching the streets go by. Heads turned as we passed. Even at this early hour, everybody was interested in Signor Marconi.

Over to the east end of Duckworth we flew. Then the horses had to throw themselves into the harnesses, hauling our carcasses up the steep hill. The road switchbacked, the cabs jolted side to side. I wriggled my feet with nerves, my eyes continually drawn to the Inspectors. Were they on to me? But they ignored the small boy entirely, absorbed in their own discussion.

It seemed the Government was happy to provide Marconi with whatever he wished; over breakfast, the revelation had been just how quickly he intended to begin his experiments. He'd need local men to assist in the work. All his equipment would have to be transported up to the site. He would be fed and housed, as would Paget and Kemp. And perhaps most startling, the entire ground of the testing site would have to be covered in zinc plates.

"It'll be on T. J. mostly," Murph pointed out, meaning the Minister of Marine and Fisheries. The Inspectors nodded, and some jokes were thrown about at the Minister's expense.

And finally, there could be no iron at the testing site, lest it interfere with the equipment.

They don't like iron either. The thought came unbidden. It's something my grandmother had told me: iron was said to repel, contain, or harm the Wee Folk. I folded my arms over my chest against a shudder.

The cab toiled on, past the site of the old jail and Gibbet Hill. Had the Reverend's mother really been incarcerated in that place? It was all ruins, now—nothing but crumbling, poetic foundations.

Further and further up. Wind began to buffet the cab, booming and whistling. Nobody lived here; red rock shrugged through thin grasses and patches of snow, and the wind always blew.

"It's worth it." Inspector White's expression became resolute as we drew to the top of the hill. "If we can prevent more shipwrecks, it's worth whatever we can give."

I wondered if everybody would be as accommodating if they knew the King of Diamonds was telling a lie. I believed what Murph suspected; Marconi wasn't here merely to establish ship-to-shore communications, as the Government and most people believed. He was here to try for a signal the likes of which the world had never seen—a signal that would go from Signal Hill across the whole North Atlantic Ocean. Using us for his own glory and gain.

One way or another, I supposed, I was going to find out.

IT CAN'T BE DONE

It was windy up here, much colder than in the city. The men had been walking around for what seemed like hours, discussing the site in minute detail. In desperation I took shelter from the wind with my back to the rough rock of Cabot Tower, looking over the city. Looking for home, despite myself.

Signal Hill and the Southside Hills formed two arms that protected the Narrows. I'd always thought of Signal Hill as a great domed skull, some prehistoric giant glaring across the harbour. It soared up five hundred and fifty feet, and descended precipitately down into the deep blue drop.

The Southside Hills evoked a colossal, long-wrecked ship, foundered as she tried to ram her way inland. The stern was Fort Amherst, tiny from this distance and height, with a lighthouse attached to the fort's barracks building. The long keel of the phantom ship lay all along the south side of the city, with the slowly crumbling bowsprit pointing out into the country.

Time was, I'd been told, the Southside Hills were covered in spruce woods. All that had been cut down long ago, and the Hill was bald as pictures I'd seen of the Scottish Highlands.

Turning toward Riverhead, scanning the houses and busy merchants' premises straggling along the Southside, I found that aloof dark thing, our house. A thin white line—the waterfall issuing from the spring beneath our kitchen—juddered down in front of the house, disappearing into a steep, grey, sloping fall of scree. The scree came to rest by the side of the road like the drape of a lady's train.

Why had my great-great-grandfather chosen that top-lofty site? When he'd hauled the house across the harbour, there hadn't been another dwelling on the Southside; he could have placed it anywhere he chose. Our house had an old-fashioned hip roof, like a pyramid pointing up to the top of the Hill. It must have been sheer hell dragging it up that slope, I thought. Not to mention the grand piano. But he'd done it anyway. He must have been a stubborn man, convinced of the rightness of his own decisions. Like Mother. Like me.

I screwed my cap more tightly onto my head and scowled at the house.

Had Mother come home yet?

My stomach rumbled, so loudly I thought anybody would be able to hear it even over the beating of the wind. I sucked it in hard. Maybe we'd have a break soon; maybe there'd be food. I had no idea.

On our arrival at the crest of Signal Hill, Paget had unintentionally caused general offense by referring to the newly opened Cabot Tower as *the blockhouse*. One of the Ministers had stiffly informed him that the structure commemorated poor dear Queen Victoria's Diamond Jubilee.

After making some perfunctory compliments on the building, Marconi had begun striding energetically around the site, with Kemp, Paget, and the others trailing behind. He eventually settled on a flat area around the old fever hospital, just below the tower. It was slightly sheltered from the wind in a small depression, and the rooms would provide a good base for the delicate receiving equipment and the men, he said.

I wondered if there were old germs still in the walls of the abandoned hospital. How long did germs live, anyway?

Also, people had been hanged up here. Gibbet Hill lay just a short distance below us. There'd been a scaffold so that everyone in the city could see the hanged bodies of criminals, left swinging until the flesh clung like rags over pale bones, slowly pecked by birds, rotting away. The pond below us was called Deadman's Pond. It somehow went below even the ocean they said, like the root of a giant tooth. Bottomless.

Clare had frightened me rigid by telling me that for

particularly horrible crimes, you'd be put in a barrel full of nails and rolled down Signal Hill. Then taken out. *Then* covered in tar. *Then* hung.

I pictured this: being forced into a barrel. Nails tearing at my skin; my last glimpse of sunlight; the lid hammered on. Air cut off, the stink of fish soaked into the staves. And then rough hands, lifting it. Feeling nails driving into me. They'd toss it!—more nails thrusting through my flesh. The horrible jolting rolling. Face punctured, eyes gouged out! But you wouldn't die, no, that was the terrible part of it. You'd still be alive when they took you out and splashed you with hot tar—oh, how it would burn!—and then, they'd hang your tattered body on the gibbet...

"... iceberg as we came in. And whales," Marconi was saying.

I castigated myself for a fool and sidled closer to the men. It wouldn't do for me to be inattentive; I needed to be poised for action.

"We heard it was a rough crossing for you," Murph answered.

"The ladies were quite overcome," Marconi said.

With a jolt I remembered the crying voices in my dream. Passengers in distress, the ship rising and falling on the high seas. But not him, not that faceless man, with his taut, focused, relentless energy... The shimmering small beings battered at him, yammering, but he remained oblivious...

"Ladies!" Kemp snorted. "So was Paget! Sick as a dog. You'd get used to one kind of sea, and another would roll up and take you sideways."

I shook the vague horror of the dream away from me. "Were *you* sick, sir?" I dared.

Marconi gazed vaguely over my head.

"Him?" Kemp shook his head. "He likes that kind of thing. Spent the whole trip flirting with the ladies. The ones who weren't laid out praying for death as preferable to sea-sickness, that is."

I instinctively liked Kemp. He seemed like a loyal and practical friend.

Marconi was eyeing the old fever hospital. "That's the place. We will begin unloading," he said.

"Mr. Murphy, do you have men lined up to help?" Kemp immediately changed his teasing air, getting to business with the Minister.

Leaving Kemp to sort the details, Marconi walked away toward the far edge of the little plateau, overlooking a steep drop. Beyond that, the ocean.

I followed him.

He stood, leaning into the wind a little, gazing out across the ocean toward Cornwall. The water was blue today. You could see the long groundswell, roughened on top.

I cast around for something remarkable and masculine to say. "Real screecher might be coming our way, sir," I tried.

He looked down at me. "Screecher?"

"A storm."

"Why do you say that?" Again, I had the feeling that his eyes weren't really seeing me, that his mind was elsewhere.

"Because of that short sea on top of the longer swells, see? It's all loppy." I wasn't really sure if I was right, townie that I was. Maybe a lop meant a storm had already happened. But Marconi wasn't to know it, I reasoned. And in any case, in my country you weren't likely to be far wrong if you forecast a future wind.

"Then we'd better get to work." But still he stood, hands in coat pockets, staring out to sea.

"I used to think you could see England from here," I said.

He looked down at me again. Was I being too chatty?

"Someday it won't matter if we can see it. Someday, it will be as close as this." He held up his gloved hand, forefinger and thumb making a ring. "As close as you and I are now."

"That's amazing, sir!" I burst out.

"Not amazing." He stared back out to sea. "I have worked very hard for a long time to make it happen. Only those who don't understand the work are amazed. They say it can't be done."

"Because of the curvature of the earth," I dared, suddenly grateful to Miss Addington-Acker for having described it to us in school.

"Very good. The curvature of the earth." He made a grand sweeping gesture with his arm. "From here to England stands a wall of water a hundred miles high."

"Cor!" I'd never said *cor* before in my life, but schoolboys were always saying it in magazine serial stories from Britain.

"But I have sent signals well beyond the line of sight. I will..." He stopped. "Someday," he went on, more quietly, "you will be able to stand here and speak with England, boy. That's a promise."

"I believe you, sir." And I did.

Kemp hollered from behind us. "Marconi! They'll hire some fellows at a dollar a day, sir!"

"Very good!" Marconi called back. But he didn't stir from my side. I realized I was holding my breath with excitement.

"So, boy... what is your name?"

"Jack Kelly."

"Jack, your sister Mary... she is engaged to that journalist."

I nodded. "William Murphy, yessir."

"For how long have they been engaged?"

"Not long," I allowed.

"And Mary, is she happy?"

"Oh, yes, sir, very!"

"Hm." He stared at the water. "She's very beautiful. Her eyes."

"Yes," I said cautiously. Then thought I should elaborate. "Lots of people really admire her hair too."

"Certainly her hair is beyond compare."

I mustered some local masculinity. "And she can sing some good, b'y!" Was that a bit much?

"Can she?"

"Like an angel. She wants to sing opera, and she'll do it, too, someday."

Marconi placed one hand over his chest. "My mother too was a singer."

"Was she?"

"Oh, yes. She still sings, but only to me." His mouth quirked. "She came to Italy from Ireland to study bel canto; it is how my parents met. This Mary Kelly becomes ever more interesting. Mary Kelly. What an unworthy name for such a creature."

My fists twitched. Did Marconi, like my mother, have Opinions about the Irish? His own mother was of Anglo-Irish stock, I remembered; they were particularly prone to such Opinions. But his next question was a bit of a stunner. "You are sure she is... happy with this reporter?"

I stared. "They're in love."

He looked away, clicking his tongue.

"Don't you like beautiful women to be happy?" I asked, very daring.

"Oh, I do." He met my gaze directly, and there was a glint in his blue-grey eyes. "That is why I am asking, of course."

With that he turned on his heel and walked away toward the group.

I'd been dismissed.

The penny finally dropped. He had just been feeling me out to see if I, the putative brother of Mary, could arrange a liaison.

Was this how boys and men talked when there were no girls or women around?

I'd never do anything to break up Murph and Mary. I loved them dearly and looked up to them as ... well, not parents, exactly; more like mentors. Maybe somewhere at the back of my mind I thought that if I absolutely *had* to get married, a guy like Murph might be tolerable.

Although now that I thought of it, I really imagined myself not *marrying* someone like Murph, but *being* someone like Murph. A writer. Shaping the world through words.

I stared out at the ocean. From what Marconi had just

let drop, Murph was right. He had far greater ambitions than ship-to-shore communications. What he had in mind would change the world.

I ran toward the group of important men, ready to take messages down to town should they need it.

I loved being Jack Kelly, I really did.

LET SOMETHING SLIP

I knew from my father's former job at McAuley's that coopers were seasonally employed; knew too that most of the merchants had their own cooperages, but that recently there'd been attempts to consolidate the trade. Coopers were some of the best-organized and most vocal workers in the city. I gained some errand-boy points by suggesting to the Minister that such men would be strong and reliable workers for what Signor had in mind, and he sent me down to the waterfront to inquire whether any would be available. If so, they were to meet Kemp shortly at Shea's Wharf, where the *Sardinian* was docked. I was also to request that Marconi's gear be unloaded and transported up the hill.

Running down the Signal Hill road got the blood moving in me again. Clint's heavy boots on my feet felt strange; on the other hand, they handled the rough surface better than the girls' boots I was used to wearing. By the time I got down Hill O' Chips to the waterfront I was almost sweating.

I ducked onto Shea's wharf, looking for someone who could help me with my mission. The place was noisy and numerous with men, for a ship had come in laden with Christmas goods and its cargo was being unloaded: crates of Valencia oranges, Malaga lemons, grapes, tins of pineapple chunks, syrup, fancy biscuits, tea, plugs of tobacco, tweeds from Scotland, Christmas cards, calendars, corsets—the world. I got in the way and earned a curse, gleefully dodging the hand of a man aiming to hit me across the ear.

I knew I shouldn't love being sworn at and struck. But it signalled that my cover was secure.

Scravelling around the wharf, I spied a doorway into

the offices and slipped inside. There was a man at a desk, in shirtsleeves but with a fur hat upon his head, scribbling away madly in a ledger.

"Good day, sir!"

He didn't deign to glance up. "What do you want?"

"I've been sent down by the Minister of Fisheries. He's up on the Hill with that Signor Marconi." He looked at me then, I can tell you. "They're looking for men to help unload their gear from the *Sardinian*, sir."

"Signor Marconi! Really."

"And they need help with the experiments up there over the next few days. I thought there might be some coopers looking for a job, sir. They're paying a dollar a day."

He put down his pen. "Marconi, you say! How about that!"

The clerk got to work at once, commandeering wagons and horses. Kemp arrived soon after, and a mate aboard the *Sardinian* opened the hold. Soon Shea's longshoremen were dragging out a seemingly endless variety of equipment and materials, all labelled as belonging to Marconi's Wireless Telegraph Company. Crates of receiving equipment, aerial wire, twenty-five cylinders of hydrogen gas, two immense hydrogen balloon skins, and—to my delight—six enormous kites were loaded onto the wagons. One had to be over nine feet tall; the others were as tall as the tallest longshoreman, over six feet. I had flown my own kites up on the Hill many times, but these made my toys look like gnats.

"I'd love to try to fly one of those, sir!" I said to Kemp, adding for good measure, "Cor!"

"They'd take you out to sea, boy!" Kemp told me. "They were developed by Baden Powell during the Boer War."

The kites were sailed with sturdy cotton cloth, with linen tape around the outside edges and gleaming brass grommets; the frames were made of bamboo. A gust of wind came up as the big one was being carried out, and two longshoremen were almost lifted from the ground, struggling as if under sail until they managed to turn the kite edge-on to the breeze.

"What are they for?"

"We'll attach the aerial wires to them, in lieu of a pole. We have to get as high into the air as we can, to catch the signals."

I put on my most innocent expression. "Signals?"

Something in Kemp's face changed. "From the ships, boy," he snapped. And then he turned away, castigating one of the fellows for manhandling a hydrogen cylinder.

I should have kept my mouth shut, I thought. He'd forgotten himself, talking to me. I could have sworn he'd almost let something slip.

SUCH AMBITION

I was allowed to ride on top of the cargo in one of the wagons, and ascended Signal Hill like a triumphal Queen Boudicca.

No, I reminded Jack Kelly. Like Caesar.

At the summit, the men went to work unloading the gear into the old hospital, Marconi examining everything for damage. He was very particular about where things were put, keeping track of every detail. This was why he was famous, I thought. He never got distracted, never went into a reverie. When he was thinking, it was about one thing: wireless telegraphy.

I'd never be famous. I was distractible as a gull.

My stomach gave another great rumble; in the excitement, my hunger had gone into the background but I now felt I was going to faint dead away. I climbed down off the wagon and trailed to Murph's side.

"What are you at, b'y?" he said, eyes twinkling.

"I'm awfully hungry," I admitted.

"Here." He reached into his ever-bulging pockets. "This'll keep your strength up." To my delight he handed me three barley sugar candies. I shoved them into my gob, not even bothering to pick the lint off.

"Murph, you're best kind," I murbled, sucking on the candies. "So, I think Kemp almost let something slip today. So did Marconi."

"Really! What?"

I told Murph about Kemp and the kites, mentioning *signals* and then shutting himself up. And Marconi, before that, going on about how someday we'd be able to talk with England.

Remembering Murph's jealous turn after the Cochrane

Hotel conference, I omitted Marconi's searching queries about Mary.

"Thank you, Jack Kelly! That's good intelligence. Wish they'd actually let the thing slip. But to talk openly like that about such an ambition..." He chewed on his pencil.

"Maybe I'll get something better tomorrow."

He shook his head. "Looks like they won't reconvene up here until day after tomorrow."

"Not until Monday!" My heart sank. "Why?"

"The Minister's men will be all over the site tomorrow, laying down those zinc plates. In the meantime, Marconi will be busy visiting with the cream of our society."

"But I'll have to go to school on Monday," I said, dismayed.

"No worries. You've done a grand job. Here." He rummaged through his pockets again and came up with fifty cents.

"No, I want to..." I stopped, feeling my throat choke. "I want to be here when they start the experiments."

"Mary will have my hide if you miss school! No, Dor, you've done enough. Take your money, now. Pretty good pay for a bucky feller such as yourself."

As I turned away, mumbling my thanks, I caught sight of Marconi, dashing in and out of the old hospital building, gesturing at the sky.

I wondered if I would ever see him again.

STRONGER THAN SENSE

By the time I made it to the bottom of Signal Hill I was truly gut-foundered. I felt the world coming too close to me, invading me—sounds, lights, people—then receding away mirage-like, heat shimmers over a summertime rock. The walk past the waterfront was worse than a crawl; I thought it would never end.

But that fifty cents in my pocket was a king's ransom. I made a slight detour up Church Hill, stopping at the Henry Street factory where Wood—the fellow about to open the fancy restaurant and soda shop on Water Street—manufactured candies, syrups, jellies, and marmalades. If you were lucky and asked nicely, they'd sometimes sell direct. I procured enough candy to make my pockets bulge: barley sugar, pear drops, humbugs, liquorice allsorts, and more... I shoved a stick of rock into my gob and drowned my tongue with sweetness.

It was now about one o'clock, and Jack Kelly had to figure out how to get home without alerting either of Dorthea's parents, or anybody else in the neighbourhood. As emboldened as I'd been fooling Clinton, I didn't care to press my luck.

The Long Bridge felt like it more than lived up to its name, hungry as I was.

Coming off the south end of it, I saw several neighbour ladies clustered together having a natter. I pulled my cap low, and forced myself to break into a run.

They didn't give me a second glance.

Next I had to toil up the Hundred Steps and make it past the Range. Just my luck; the steps were maggoty with Taylors. The entire extended clan seemed to be out for the day: women bashing mats, children playing Hiding and Away, men soaking in a little of the weak, winter sunlight and smoking their pipes.

Nothing draws attention like a stranger. Eyes were upon me. I kept my head down.

"Who're you?" a little girl asked. She looked enough like Clare that even a stranger would have spotted her for a sister.

"Clare in?" I grunted, thinking it best not to answer the question directly. Men—and boys—often didn't, I'd noticed. It was a maddening tendency when one was a girl. As a counterfeit boy, I was finding the tactic extremely useful.

"She's up at the house." I caught the bold barnacle staring beady-eyed at the stick of rock I had out the side of my mouth like a cigarette. I fished around in my pocket and held out a handful of pear drops. She stared at me with delight, took them in her cupped hands, opened her mouth wide, and began running round and round in circles making a noise like a whistling tea kettle. She then pitched over onto her back, still making that same breathless scream, raised her hands into the air like a chute, and unclenched her fists so that the candies cascaded into her mouth. Her eyes, green like Clare's, stared into the sky, then her eyelids closed in ecstasy as she mumbled and sucked at the sweets.

A child after my own heart, I thought as I made my way up the side of the house and into the back door.

And, *What are you doing?* as I risked exposure with every step closer to Clare.

I wanted to see her. That was all. The compulsion was stronger than sense.

In the kitchen Mrs. Taylor stirred some boiled dinner on the stove, and Nan sat in her rocker. And Clare, she was there too.

She gave me one look, and the same tea-kettle noise as her sister had made came out of her mouth. She clapped her hand over the leak.

"Who're you?" her mother said, glancing at me, then turning back to her business on the stove.

"Cousin of Dorthea's up the hill," I mumbled, tugging at my cap.

Clare tore her hands from her mouth. Her eyes were so sharp I thought they would cut holes in the walls. "He's visiting from the West Coast. Clint told me." Then the hands went over her mouth again and she rocked back and forth. If I hadn't known she was laughing I'd have thought her in the throes of deepest grief.

Nan King's black eyes peered at me. She mashed her gums together and mumbled something that sounded like, and probably was, *saucy flinter*. But she merely folded her arms together and accelerated her rocking.

"Get the pease out the pot, Clare," Mrs. Taylor said. Clare, stuffing her knuckles in her mouth, seized a large fork with the other hand and fished a well-used canvas pudding bag from the giant boiler of cabbage, carrots, turnip, potatoes, and salt beef galloping on the stove. She upended it over a large platter, opening the bag with much snatching of burnt fingers, using the fork to mash the peas up. "Can Dorthea's cousin stay to supper, Mother?" she asked, eyes down.

Right on cue, my stomach gave out a great rumble. It sounded like a storm was coming it was that loud.

Mrs. Taylor threw me a glance full of sympathy. "Sure, now," she said. "He's half-starved, poor little thing; turn sideways and he'd go invisible. Set the table for me, Clare."

I helped Clare lay out the battered collection of knives and forks and plates. She kept bumping her body against me whenever she could, but I dared not meet her eyes. At one point she smacked my arse. That got a look. She mouthed something at me but I couldn't tell what it was. I reached into my pocket and retrieved a candy, sliding it into her hand. Her eyes widened, and she popped it into her cheek, then blew me a kiss.

Being Jack was getting better all the time.

And all the time, Nan sat and rocked.

Nobody mentioned I should take off my cap, a request for which I was, I realized, totally unprepared. But in fact two of the little boys kept theirs on the whole time, evidently so as to speed the instant when they finished shovelling food into their gobs and could go back outside to play.

There was one sticky moment when Mrs. Taylor remarked that Clinton used to have a Norfolk jacket exactly like that one, why she'd sewn it herself. But then Clare deftly knocked over the salt and got a scolding, averting the crisis. "Three pinches over your left shoulder, quick!" her mother shrieked. "Hit Satan in the eye!"

Clinton wasn't at the meal, which seemed to cause no consternation whatsoever. "Probably out murdering somebody," said his fond mother, setting aside a generous serving for him.

"Down at Fort Amherst kissing Jane Cooper!" shouted the little pear-drop girl.

Clare began to croon. "And her golden hair was hanging down her baaaack!"

"But oh, Jane, doesn't look the same! When she left the village she was shy!" The children belted the chorus, even the little ones, the whole table joining in the popular song.

"Stop that, now," said Mrs. Taylor, but it was inevitable.

"But alas! And alack! She's gone back, with a naughty little twinkle in her eye!"

"I said pipe down!"

Clare quavered theatrically, "'Now, gentle folks, I warn you all to shun the simple maid, When her golden hair is hanging down her back!'"

"Alas! Alack!" shrieked the pear-drop girl, earning a cuff from her mother.

I laughed so hard I almost choked on my food, and had to rein myself in. Was my giggling too unmanly? In their merriment, nobody seemed to notice.

The only person who seemed to be on to me was Nanny King. She stared at me the whole time while ingesting tiny bites from her plate; Mrs. Taylor had cut up the dinner for her in such little small pieces that the meal was practically a mash. But she didn't say a word.

I mentioned too many times how good the food was—and truly, it tasted like the best meal I'd ever had. And afterwards I made another error, starting to help Clare clear the table, earning a strange look from Mrs. Taylor. "Get on with you. You'll smash everything."

Boys didn't clear tables.

"Come up to the house," I whispered to Clare, then turned to her mother. "Thanks, Mrs. Taylor, that was some good."

"So you said, me love. You'd think you'd never had some poor boiled dinner before."

"But it was!"

"Get on with you."

I gave what I hoped was a jaunty masculine wave, winked at Clare, and went out the door.

I flew along the Ratline, then skidded to a halt. Before entering the house I had to ascertain the whereabouts of my parents.

It seemed likely that my mother would still be out attending the birth that had called her away. No matter what the outcome—whether it was a live baby, or stillborn, or worse—my mother would be the maid of all work at the woman's home for at least a week. But she'd still come home for supplies, and to sleep.

My father wouldn't be at work, not today. But usually, when my mother was called away, he spent time at the tavern. I knew this, and although Mother must have suspected, I'd not tell.

I crept to the front of the house and peered through the

parlour window. Great-great-grandfather glared at me through the panes of glass.

My dress, the one with the burst buttons, lay folded on the sealskin ottoman, and my mother's sewing basket lay next to it.

Why did that sight give me such a terrible pain in my heart?

I sidled around the path to the linney at the back. No sign of Father in the kitchen.

Which meant—almost certainly—that he was out.

I pushed the door open—for it was closed, not flapping back and forth as was its wont. It made a terrible creaking, and I froze.

Nothing.

I tiptoed across the linney floor and into the kitchen.

The house was quiet.

A quick check upstairs proved me right. The house was empty.

Within moments I heard a light, quick step on the Ratline. Clare!

"I saw you!" she burst in. "I saw you this morning, talking to Clint. Walking along so proud. I almost called out. But I didn't want to blow your cover. Oh, Dor, you're a live boy!"

Laughing, she hugged me. I hugged her back. Then I flexed my arms and legs, picked her up and, with increasing confidence, swung her around.

She shrieked. One foot caught a kitchen chair and knocked it over, but I didn't care. I put her down and we both laughed like banshees, like we always did when together.

No, not like always. This felt different.

She took the hat off my head, running her hands over my hair. "You did a good job," she said. Her face was inches from mine.

"I found these pins," I said, suddenly shy. Reaching up I pulled one of Mother's spiral hairpins from my hair; a braid fell down. Clare exclaimed over the cleverness of the pins, pronouncing them very 'cute.' Her fingers went into my hair, finding other pins, taking it all down, arranging the heavy dark coils over my shoulders.

The desire to kiss her was a thrill down my body, coursing through my torso and sluicing through my thighs. It was a craving that left my knees weak. She must have felt something too, for the smile left her face, replaced by another look. Her eyes went almost blank, and her lips curved, but it wasn't a smile.

Her cheeks were flushed. She took hold of a strand of my hair, and wound the long hank around and around her wrist.

Was it... did she feel that way too?

There was only one way to find out.

A STARRY WAR

A heavy step came up the Ratline.

"It's Father!" I hissed. "Upstairs, quick!"

I dragged Clare unresisting to my bedroom. "I have to change before he sees..."

The door below banged open. "Hello!"

Clare and I froze on the threshold to my room, still holding hands. "I'm up here!"

I heard Father's heavy footsteps scuff across the kitchen floor.

"Come here," I whispered, and pulled Clare to me.

"Ooh," she breathed. "Aren't you a bold article." Slowly, she started undoing the buttons of the jacket.

Father yelled again from below. "Your mother home?"

"No!" I hollered.

Clare stifled a laugh. Leaving the bottom button still done up, she put her hands inside the jacket and pushed it off my shoulders, trapping my arms. We stood, eye to eye and thigh to thigh.

I thought my heart would burst.

And then her eyes got a ferocious glint, and she put her fingers on my ribs and tickled me. I made a strangled sound and writhed, which only made her laugh more, pressing her body against mine.

"What's going on up there?"

"Clare Taylor... Clare Taylor's here!" I gasped.

"Hello, sir!" she managed. She had the jacket off me now and was snapping at my suspenders, while I danced and dodged.

"Sounds like a witches' sabbath up there!"

We could hear him knocking off his boots, then falling onto the settle in the kitchen with a groan.

Staving off Clare between gusts of giggling, I got out of the rest of Clint's clothes myself, and found my second-best dress to put on. It was too small for me now, but at least it buttoned up the front.

As soon as I did the last button, I felt like some magic had leached out of the room. Clare was still there, and still prettier than a queen, but she no longer wanted to kiss me. I'd not pick her up and swing her around now.

Was all that in the clothes?

The sound of Father's snoring coming up the back stairs seemed to take more of the sparkle out of the day with every wheeze.

"I'd better go," Clare whispered. I could only nod.

"Here." I rummaged through the jacket pockets. "Take this! If I eat it all I'll be sick."

Her eyes widened. She refused to take all I offered, but made a twist in her skirt to take a good handful of the humbugs— her favourite—with their shiny, tiny, black and white stripes.

I led her down the front stairs so she wouldn't wake Father in the kitchen. "It's bad luck not to go out the door you came in," she objected.

"Don't want to wake him when he's been..." And I mimed a glass to my lips. "He gets all cranky."

At the door, she objected again. "I didn't even find out what happened. Did you meet him? Marconi?"

"Yes."

"What's he like?"

"He's... different." I searched for words. "He knows exactly what he wants."

"Oh," she said uncertainly. I didn't blame her. I felt uncertain myself.

"He's up on Signal Hill, now, and that's where the experiments are going to be," I said. "And I've been dismissed. Oh. Right." I forced myself to ask, "Do you want the clothes back?"

"Later," she said. "When I can sneak them back into the trunk. Why were you *dismissed*?"

"He doesn't need an errand boy tomorrow. And," I blinked back tears, "... Murph says I can't pip off school."

Clare made a face. "Meanie."

"I'll say."

I unbolted the scarcely used front door, and she made her way to the top of the Ratline. "Thanks, Clare," I sang out softly.

"You're welcome, Jack." And with a merry grin, the most beautiful girl in the world vanished down the staircase.

I could hear her reciting the kissing game as she skipped along the rickety boardwalk. "King William was King George's son, and all the royal racy run, and on his breast a starry war, compointing to the governor's door."

Her voice was very faint, now. "Come choose to the east, come choose to the west..."

I could no longer hear her.

I whispered, my voice disappearing on the wind. "Choose the very one that you love best."

INSIDE THE SILENCE

That evening, Father went out again.

Before he left, I pulled together a poor cold meal for us both: bread and butter and some hard cheese, with the last of the cold chicken—a bit on the dubious side, now—from the back cellar.

"Any word from Mother?" I asked, as we ate, sprawled out with our elbows on the kitchen table.

He shook his head.

"Should have heard by now," I spoke through a mouthful of bread and cheese.

"Naw, b'y, she'll just be getting started," he asserted.

I knew he was right. She'd only been out slightly more than twelve hours. But underneath that assertion, something gnawed at me.

Still chewing, Father arose, put his plate in the sink, jammed the shapeless brown thing he called a hat on his head, and headed off into the evening.

The short December day was drawing to its close. I lit the kerosene lamp in the kitchen. Then, on an impulse, I went into the parlour and lit the kerosene lamp in the window. If Mother was coming home this evening, it'd be a beacon to light her way.

There again I noticed my dress and the sewing basket. Mother had gotten about half the buttons sewn on, I realized, before—what? Father came home? Or she'd tired of waiting for him and gone to bed? I had never pictured my mother like this: alone, waiting for her husband to come home, sewing buttons on her daughter's dress. It made me immensely sad.

It had been nice of her to sew on the buttons, I thought. I was an ungrateful wretch, and a trial to her. I'd thank her for putting up with me when she got home...

The mood of the house was disquieting. It was not peace. Rather, the house had been rendered speechless. I felt myself rattling around inside the silence, like a dry pea in a blown pod.

Reflected in the window glass, I saw a grim girl with a lowering brow, Great-great-grandfather's portrait shimmering behind, a faint apparition. The clock, I realized, had stopped. The moon's right eye gleamed dolefully from behind Africa.

The hands were pointing at three o'clock, the time when Mother had been called out.

I fell asleep there in the frigid parlour on the cold, hard, horsehair couch, dreaming of Marconi, of grasping the tail of a big white kite and sailing up into the air, higher and higher. The clouds admitted me, soft and drenched and yielding as damp strands of gossamer. Stars glittered all around, thousands of bright blue fires. Below, the earth spread out like the flattened worlds of the clock. To my startlement I realized I had flown all the way to Africa; there it was below me, striped gloriously with latitude and longitude, black and white as a humbug candy. I turned, veering northwest.

I would leave this vast imprisoning island, where everybody knew who I was and who I was one of. I'd ride the kite, soaring on celestial winds, all the way to New York City.

Something awoke me. I started up. What time was it? No way to know, for the clock still pointed at three. What had awoken me?

I heard it again: a long, low scraping. Something moved outside, along the side of the house, like something heavy being dragged.

The hair on the back of my neck stood up.

Grasping the lamp in the parlour window, I made my way down the hall, shadows jumping on the walls. "Father?" My voice quavered.

I'd left the lamp unattended in the kitchen; I could have burned the house down. "Father?"

"Goddamn fairies!"

It *was* my father! Relief swept through me. There was more of that scraping sound—ordinary, now, as paint. I ventured out through the linney, cold biting into me. I had not only dreamt a clear night. The sky was full of stars, and the air burned with frost.

He lay on the path, feet fretting at the ground, trying, unsuccessfully, to get up. "They struck me down!"

He was far gone indeed. I wished my mother was here to deal with him; then thought how angry she would be. I'd have to get him in myself. "You're only drunk."

"I tell you it was the goddamn—"

"Shhh!" Remembering Mother's reluctance to name Them, I hushed him. "Come inside."

"I can't." He struggled another time, then lay back down.

I'd seen him drunk before, but never this translated. My heart began to flutter with panic. "Well, you can't stay out here."

I put the lamp down on the linney floor, and stepped out into the glittering night. "It's freezing."

"Certainly I can stay here. I *am* staying here, aren't I."

I grasped his hand and tried to haul him to his feet. He was a dead weight.

"Where's your mother?"

"She went out on a call. Remember? Last night."

"When?"

"Last night," I repeated. "Three o'clock."

"You're lying. I don't remember that."

His great big feet scrabbled for purchase on the stones, legs going widdershins. It was exasperating, hilarious, and frightening all at once. "Because you were drunk. Like now."

"Don't be saucy with me."

"Then come inside." I gripped his arm and hauled with all my strength. There was a brief moment of triumph when he seemed to be on his feet; then his state overtopped him and he went down again, folding graceful as a swan's neck to the ground.

"Leave me here, leave me here, save yourself."

"Don't be silly, you'll freeze to death. Come inside."

He stared up at the stars. "We can't. We're too far out to sea."

I lay on the path next to him, the cold of the stones burning through my thin dress.

"Where's your mother?"

I snuggled into his open overcoat. "Where are we going?"

"Where?"

"At sea. You said we were at sea."

He didn't answer.

"Can we go to New York?"

"Why would you want to go there?"

"To..." I struggled. Why indeed? Some inchoate notion struggled inside me, a lodestone pointing to magnetic north. New York was a place where I could find... something. My future self? True love? A pot of gold at the end of a rainbow?

"You don't want to go there. Anywhere in the world, and the girl picks the Sodom and Gomorrah of the modern world."

I flinched inside. He didn't know what I was, and I would never be able to tell him. "England, then."

He snorted. "Why?"

"To visit Marconi."

"Shag that. Too cold. Like here."

"Bermuda?"

Suddenly eloquent, he began quoting an old poet. "Lightning was all our light, and it rained more, than if the Sunne had drunke the sea before. Some coffin'd in their cabins lie, equally griev'd that they are not dead, and yet must die. ... Compar'd to these stormes," he shouted, "death is but a qualme, Hell somewhat lightsome, and the Bermuda calme!" His deep voice echoed against the rocks of the Hill, coming back at us in an echo.

"Sunne had drunke!" I hollered. What sounds! "Nnnnnnn! Kuh!"

The echoes flung a jubilation of consonants back around my head.

"Seasick," my father muttered.

"Father, we're not at sea."

"Where are we, then?"

"We're on the back path."

"Then what's that light?"

"What light?"

He pointed up at the sky.

"It's only the moon."

"But it whirls around."

"Yes, Father, you're drunk. Nnnnnnnn—kuh!"

"Drunk, you say? Why, so I am."

"So come inside."

He thrashed around. "Something's holding me down."

"That's me." I suppressed giggles. "I'm on your coat."

"Well, gerrof."

It took much doing, and once on his feet he cut the curwibbles, veering so suddenly that he almost overtopped me. I wondered what that was like—being so drunken that a simple walk through your own back door was beset with dangers. I was scared abroad and laughing at the same time when I got him inside at last, depositing him on the kitchen settle with his coat for a cover.

That night, in my small iron bedstead, I dreamt the house was a ship, and Father and I adrift. We were looking for my mother, but she was far beneath the water, where all is dark. I realized in the dream—mermaids may indeed sing. But none can hear them, and live.

THE CLOCK STRUCK THREE

My spirit was pulled again, down into the spring beneath the house. Pulled through water and rocks and frost, suffocating in the dark, ribbed passage, until it opened up into the glittering cave. As before, a sound whispered, that threading, monotonous wheeze.

There was mother, no coat on her, with her midwife's bag next to her. She drank filthy water from the oyster shell, laughing as if she hadn't a care.

The sound grew, the long, slow, repetitive wheeze. *Ooor... aaahrs... ooor... aaahrs...*

My mother was not alone.

On a bundle of rushes and withered ferns lay a tiny old woman. Her hair shone white beneath a red cap, her face was white, and her eyes shone out from sunken sockets like two hard blue stars. And beside my mother sat a tiny man all in grey, also with a red cap upon his head. And he too was old, older than old. A beard seeped down his front; it snaked, twitching, across the floor of the cave.

And there was a third, for the tiny old woman held to her withered breast a baby bigger than herself, with a great lolling head. Its eyes were open; it could see me, and it bared teeth sharp and orange as a rat's.

It was no dream. I could smell the rank and filthy air of the cave, feel frost creeping sharp into my nose. I tried to call out, tell Mother it was all a fab, a trick, but my throat was as dry as if I'd drunk sand. I began to bivver and shake, but no tears would come in that terrible, arid place.

I woke making the high-pitched, threading sound of panic.

She was with Them!

Shaking, I pulled the covers back over myself. I'd thrashed them off in the nightmare and I was freezing. *Just a nightmare*, I told myself. *It was only a dream.*

Then I sat bolt upright. Mother was elsewhere, and she had no idea of the danger.

I got up and flung on my clothes, then clattered over the back stair to the kitchen. Father was curled on the settle, one arm over his eyes.

"What's the racket?" he mumbled.

"Where's Mother? We should have heard by now."

He cracked a lid. "What's that you say?"

"She's never stayed away this long without letting us know where she is. We don't know who came for her."

He rolled over and pulled his coat over his head.

"Something's wrong."

"Quiet, Dorthea!"

Desperate, I grabbed at his arm. "We've got to find her!"

"Hell's fiery flames!" He sat up in one swift, angry movement. "Get out! Evaporate!"

I was a king hand at transforming painful, humiliated anguish to rage in a split-hair second. "With pleasure!" I yelled in his face. I stomped out the door, banging it shut behind me and earning another curse.

The clarity of the night before had been overcome by stealth. It was a pea-soup day, grey and wet. It had been foggy too the night my mother had left, I remembered. She had walked out into a murk. Led away by some stranger.

Why hadn't I paid more attention? I was the only witness to my mother's last night with us, for Father was useless.

Fog-loom made a distortion of everything. The house seemed an immense dark beast; the rails of the Ratline ran out into the air, thin as threads. My feet clattering down the stairs fell dull and thudding, and smells carried close: damp fog, salt ocean, tar from the waterfront, coal dust. A smell of something frying. There'd be breakfast getting made in some of those houses. There'd be shouts, and laughter.

Clare. Clare would help me.

Mrs. Taylor was tipping a bucket of night soil into a gully as I came along the boardwalk; the foul smell hung in the fog. "Good morning, Dorthea. How's that cousin of yours?"

My mind whirled. I nearly said, *What cousin?* "Gone Over." To the north side; we all knew what that meant. "Mrs. Taylor, I'm..." I stopped, uncertain what to say.

"What's the matter, girl? You're white as a sheet." She looked tired as always, did Clare's mother, but there was a softness to her face that I hadn't noticed before. She'd always seemed, somehow, older than my mother, but looking at her now, I remembered that in fact she wasn't all that old at all.

"It's Mother," I burst out.

"She's never ill?"

"No. I don't know where she is, and I'm worried."

"She get called out?" Mrs. Taylor turned and began to walk back into the house, leaving the soil bucket by the side door.

"Yes, two nights ago. But she's never been back, nor sent word where she is."

"Who called her out then?"

"That's just it." I stepped over the threshold, feet tripping on the torn-up canvas in the hall. "We don't know, neither Father nor I. And..." I'd heard a voice? No, not even that. "I heard the clock strike three. Three in the morning."

The kitchen was numerous with Taylors. "Sit down, sit down now."

"And nobody we know was at her time."

She really gave me a look then. "You're right about that."

I bit my lip and tried not to let my eyes tear. "I just know something's wrong."

"Maybe we could ask up and down the road, see if anybody knows who was expecting," Clare appeared, pulling me into a one-armed hug. "What do you say, Mother?"

"No harm doing that. I can send Clint or Father in a rowboat to Fort Amherst."

"I'll go!" Clinton shouted, and shoved a sweater over his head so fast he trapped his head in a sleeve.

I was surprised at his helpfulness, until Clare warbled, "And her golden hair was hanging down her baaaack!"

"Shut up." He struggled out of the sweater and aimed a blow at her head, which she let go of me to dodge.

"Clinton's got a sweetheart!" one of the little girls sang, and soon the entire choir of younger Taylors were singing out, *Clinton's got a sweetheart, Clinton's got a sweetheart!*

"Shut up I say, or I'll have yer guts for garters!" Clinton turned red and struck out around himself at his siblings until his mother picked up a broom and threatened to thrash them all if they didn't settle down.

On his way out he gave me a funny look. "Don't worry," he said, awkward. He opened his mouth, closed it again, then rubbed his head. "We'll find her." To my astonishment he patted my shoulder, and then went out the door, cap in hand.

Clare stared after him. "That was almost *sweet.*"

Mrs. Taylor sent out the more reliable younger children, asking all of Southside below the bridge if anyone knew who my mother might have been called out to attend. I sat, Clare by my side, and Mrs. Taylor fed me—unbeknownst to her—for the second time in two days.

"Maybe I'm just being silly," I confessed to Clare.

"Why would you say that? It's never happened before, her going out like this and you have no idea."

"Where's your father?" Mrs. Taylor asked.

"Up at the house," I muttered, head down.

I sensed rather than saw Clare and her mother meeting eyes. "I see," said Mrs. Taylor.

"I had a dream," I said, still staring at my lap. "I just know...something's wrong."

"A dream?" Mrs. Taylor said.

But then her mother gave a sharp cough. We all looked at the old lady. She stared at me, and then nodded, slow, like she'd seen something she expected.

My heart sank into the ground.

TOWED ASTRAY

King William was King George's son,
And all the royal racy run,
And on his breast a starry war,
Compointing to the governor's door.
Come choose to the east, come choose to the west,
Choose the very one that you love best,
And if he's not there for to take your part,
Come choose another one with all your heart.
Down on this carpet you may kneel
As the grass grows in the field,
And kiss your partner as your sweet,
Then you may rise upon your feet.

All the long hours the search was going on, I gabbled the rhyme through my head.

Clinton came back from Fort Amherst, and the little Taylors came back from up and down the road, and Mr. Taylor asked the men, and finally my father came down from the house, eyes bleared but willing.

But nobody could find a trace of my mother. No woman was close to her time that anybody knew of. Nobody could say who had called my mother out.

I overheard Mrs. Taylor and Mrs. Horwood whispering about the man who had shot himself in the bushes up on the Hill in the fall. The chaplain of the *Charybdis* he'd been. One of the neighbourhood children, a dishy-looking girl with terrible freckles all over, had found him, the brains of him blown out amidst the alders, and she'd attained a sort of celebrity status for a time, although I thought that'd be a very hard way to become popular.

Why are they talking about him? I wondered. They caught me looking, and hushed.

Surely they didn't imagine my mother would destroy herself?

Would she?

The men mounted a search up the Hill, Father in the lead, now, for he seemed to have come alive. "I blame myself," he muttered. "I blame myself."

Clare never left my side.

It was Mr. Coultas, he who jokingly accused Clare's mother of cheating at card-dealing, who found the sweater up on the Hill, just behind my house.

It was my mother's red cardigan jacket. And it was inside out.

Mr. Coultas held it out to me, as if wanting me to take it. I stared at it. Why would my mother leave her sweater behind, on a cold and foggy winter night? Why was it inside out?

My mother was like a schooner slipped anchor in the dark.

She'd never abandon the sweater, and certainly not in that weather, in December. *This is science,* I heard her voice in my head. *Rocks sometimes fall.* It was absurd. And what had she been doing up on the Hill behind our house? Nobody lived up there.

Had someone pulled it off her?

I saw my hand reaching out; watched, as if it were someone else's hand, as it took hold of the sweater. I let it fall into my lap, bold redness spilling off my legs onto the floor.

"She's been towed astray."

Old Nanny King rocked, staring at me with her black eyes.

"Towed astray, I says. And you knows it too."

"Mother. Don't frighten the girl," Mrs. Taylor scolded. "She's out there, lost, or... We'll find her, Dor, don't you fret."

My father came into the Taylors' kitchen, took one

look at the sweater in my lap, and tried to say something. But the sound that came out was something that might have left the throat of an animal in a trap.

"She's gone," he managed.

"No!" I sprang to my feet, letting the sweater fall.

"It was a foggy night." His face was hard, his voice low and rough.

"She's not dead, I know it!"

Clare's hand clutched at me, but I tore away. I ran out of the kitchen, leaving them all behind.

My mother wasn't dead. I'd seen her. She was elsewhere, but she wasn't dead.

"She fell off a cliff in the fog!" I heard Father's voice behind me, deep and broken. "She fell and the sea took her!"

I couldn't go home. But I couldn't stay in that kitchen either. I ran up the road, away from the sea.

THE REVEREND

The morning fog had been swept away by a great, cold wind, and a heavy scad of snow came on top of that. I dashed up the Southside, hardly knowing where I was going. The wind whipped into my eyes, stinging my cheeks. Every surface was white, and I was very cold.

Up past the bridge, on the part of the Southside I rarely went to, I saw people going into a house, all heads down and well dressed. All the blinds were drawn. Someone had died.

Among the visitors come to pay their respects I glimpsed an extraordinary, bent figure: the Reverend.

As in a dream, I followed the people inside. There was a press in the hall, everyone shaking snow off their coats. Nobody minded a neighbourhood girl come to pay her respects.

Where was the Reverend? I couldn't see him.

The coffin would be laid out in the parlour at the front of the house. I slipped into the room. The blinds were drawn, and the air stank of Jeyes' Fluid, just like when my grandmother and Theo had been waked. There was a face in the coffin, deathly pale, with a band of fabric tied under the chin to keep the jaw closed. The eyes mustn't have wanted to close, either, for there were two bright copper pennies on the lids. *So mean he'd steal the coppers from your eyes!*

Was the Reverend here?

Suddenly my stomach gave a rumble. I hadn't eaten that day, and hunger gusted through my frame like a wind. It left me swaying, all thoughts of my mother, of everything that had happened, wiped from my mind. In a haze I let myself be carried along in the wake of some genuine mourners, following the scent of food down the hall to the kitchen.

I sidled around the table, palming little diamond-cut sandwiches and sliding them into my gullet, feasting mechanically on lemon rings and date cake, washed down by tea from a pink-rose tea set.

Sated, I wandered back down the hall to the parlour, and quietly took a seat on a chair against the wall, head bowed. Nobody paid any attention to me. People came and went, murmuring condolences. *Sorry for your troubles. Sorry for your troubles.*

If my mother had fallen over a cliff, there would be no body. We'd never have a wake like this. Nobody would be able to tell us they were sorry for our troubles.

Somebody came and sat next to me. They smelled like lilacs.

She would just be... gone astray. For ever.

I didn't lift my head.

I felt the person lean close to me. I leaned away. They leaned into me further. I closed my eyes.

"We are dust, and to dust we shall return," a sweet voice said in my ear.

It was the Reverend.

A top hat crowned his mess of white hair. He wore black trousers, with a lacy shirt like a romantic poet, several strings of ladies' pearls around his neck, and gold earrings gleaming in his ears. Over that rig-out went a black tailcoat, as when I'd seen him before at the head of the procession.

His eyes had a peculiar luster. In the dark of the room I couldn't determine the colour—they could have been onyx, could have been amber, or amethyst, jade, or the deceptive grey of labradorite, deep blue with tawny striped through.

He seemed to expect some kind of answer.

"All of us go down to the dust," I ventured.

He smiled. "Yet even at the grave we make our song. Come and visit me, Dorthea."

With that he stood. Or, rather, slid from the chair and stood bent double, his body in the same relation to itself—bent at a right angle—as it had been while sitting on the chair.

"Oberon is very keen to have a proper conversation," he twinkled. He then processed out of the room, whirling one wrist over and over as if bowing royally to those assembled.

Everyone made way. "Sure, it's no funeral if the Reverend don't come," a woman murmured.

Visit him? My mother had told me he lived near the Old Man's Beard.

I didn't know who Oberon was—surely the Reverend wasn't cohabitating with a fairy king from the woods of Athens. And if there was a house near the Old Man's Beard, I'd never seen it.

But I would visit the Reverend, if I could find him.

If anybody could help me find my mother, perhaps he could.

Time felt to me now like a great ocean. Our old house, that creaky, swaying Ship of Theseus, sailed upon it, sure as the frigate sailed over the face of the grandfather clock. But could there be different currents running through time?

If one thing could be changed—if I hadn't let that girl burst the buttons from my dress, say, or if my father hadn't been logy with drink—would a new current come into being, a new wave, carrying time and our house off in another direction? Would my mother still be at home?

Could these other, possible currents of time spread out like waves? How many? Thousands? Millions? Where was this current, the one I was living in, on that great sea? Was there another tide where my mother would walk up the steps right now, having only lost her old red sweater?

Previously, my little stream of time had been a thread. One thing happened and then another, all in a line like the string of pearls around the Reverend's neck.

Now, the necklace was broken, the pearls scattered and lost in the depths. I could not find them.

It was Monday, I realized with dull shock. I should be going to school. The sun was coming up behind the Hill. Our house and the Southside were still cast in the shadow of that great tor, but on the north side, the city was lit seashell pink, gold, blue, and glittering silver. Rose-coloured gulls flew out to sea. The Hill loomed, bleeding darkness, an expanding density like a tidal wave making landfall. There was a sense of breath held, of the world coming to a stop.

And then the sun cracked over the summit, a line of pale sparkling fire, and everything was limned in brilliance.

We'd had a silver thaw. Snow had come down heavy in the night, and then, sometime before dawn, changed to freezing rain. Everything was covered, now, in ice.

I should be on my way to school, not sitting huddled at the top of the Ratline, looking across the riverhead at the ice-glistered city.

I would not be going.

Father was in the house, asleep or awake I did not know. He was inconsolable. Mother had fallen off a cliff, in the fog and the dark, and the sea had taken her. That was his implacable belief.

He blamed himself.

But then who had come and called her out? I had thought and thought about it, all through the night.

No, I wouldn't believe Father was right. Not yet. Nor did I believe those whispers from the neighbours comparing my mother to the chaplain who'd destroyed himself. She'd been called out, and she'd gone, and now we didn't know where she was. But she wasn't dead. Not yet.

The Old Man's Beard was the name for a particular patch of snow on the Southside Hill. It was in a deep ravine; the sun never shone in it. Long after the rest of the world was covered in green leaves and grass and flowers, ice and snow remained in that long, dark, frozen cleft.

Old Man, or the Old Fellow, was also what some people called the Devil. I didn't believe in the Devil; Heaven and Hell were stories that other people told. But still, to live in a place named after Satan, a place that never saw the sun?

You'd be crazy to live there.

I decided to climb up the Hill rather than walk down the road. The thought of encountering the inevitable neighbours, having to endure sorry looks and whispers, overtopped me. No, I'd climb the steep slope behind the house and make my way along the Hill, and come on the Old Man's Beard from above.

I plaited my hair in two rough braids to keep it out of the way, tying them together at the crown of my head. Then I buttoned my poor coat, and set off.

I remembered my father saying, *Don't go off without bread in your pocket.* It was to do with Them; having bread staved them off. Or maybe it was just to have something in case one got hungry. But my pockets were empty.

I couldn't turn back now.

It was a cruel scramble up the first bit of cliff, especially with the ice. But I knew every foot- and hand-hold, for in summertime my parents and I would tote a billy can for a boil-up, seeking blueberries and partridgeberries, crow berries and brambles. I spent many hours up on the Hill alone too: picking berries, making wreaths of daisies and laburnum blossoms and tangles of wild roses, glaring arrogantly over the city as I crowned myself king. Sometimes, pockets bulging with bread and apples, I'd go all the way over into Freshwater Bay, alone or—better—with Clare, and occasionally some other Southside children. We'd run rampant on the large, crescent-shaped beach of boulders, collecting sea glass and skipping stones, getting in the way of the small collection of people who lived and worked there. I was insatiable for the empty green shells of sea urchins— *tests*, they were called. I loved setting them afloat, tiny viridescent coracles running races on the tide. I'd bring them back home in pocket-loads, piling them on windowsills. *Whore's eggs,* my father called them. *Sea trash,* my mother replied, sweeping them into her apron and out the window. But I'd always bring home more. I was fascinated by the shells' cupola-like structure, pale and perfect green, covered in delicate braille. Sometimes they'd still carry vestiges of prickles, like oceanic hedgehogs. I'd never seen one alive, although I knew, logically, that they went about their business in tidal pools and on the ocean floor.

You couldn't tell, looking at them, if they were male or female. Perhaps, I considered, sea urchins didn't have boys and girls. Or if they did, perhaps they didn't care.

Irritated adults often called me an urchin. Girls rarely were, but me...

A long, smooth, blindingly white slope stretched up before me, a thick layer of glittering ice crusting treacherously over soft snow. I went forward on my hands, my feet chopping steps. The sound of my boots crunching through ice—how I wished I'd thought to wear Jack's boots!—the smell of cold snow, the panting of my own breath, the calls of gulls all served to ground me. My mittened fingers couldn't break through the ice—it was too thick—but each foothold, once I'd pounded it out with the toe of my boot, felt secure. Crystalline rainbows glittered in the ice. My fingers and toes were cold, but the rest of me got very warm.

I hadn't slept or eaten, but I felt no hunger. The climb seemed endless, but I was not tired.

I sang under my breath.

King William was King George's son,
And all the royal racy run,
And on his breast a starry war,
Compointing to the governor's door...

The words themselves, the ineluctable shapes and sounds of them, gave me mechanical comfort. I thrust an English accent into them, then switched to a broad Southside. The way Clare said it.

Why did that feel so warm, rolling around on my tongue? The words themselves meant something darker and richer said this way—thick, dripping, and gleeful.

Clare.

Was it my imagination or were voices singing, whispering, murmuring around?

I looked about. Nothing.

It must have been the wind, I thought, although there wasn't a breath. The day was still.

I'd come up higher than I'd thought. The Southside was out of sight beneath the Hill; it was open country before me, all the way to Freshwater Bay. The ice was very thick over the snow here, and slippery, and I pictured myself losing my footing and falling away. Who knows where I'd land? There would be nothing to stop my slide until I went off a cliff. I bent over again, walking like an animal.

> Come choose to the east, come choose to the west,
> Choose the very one that you love best.

I *was* hearing something, a dull murmur. "Hello?" I straightened up again.

There was nobody there.

I began to pick my way laterally across the slope, heading east toward the Narrows. How would I know when I got to the Old Man's Beard? All landmarks were obscured by this dump of snow and ice. Well, it was a big gully. I felt fairly sure I'd be able to mark it.

> Down on this carpet you may kneel
> As the grass grows in the field,
> And kiss your partner as your sweet,
> Then you may rise upon your feet.

As if it were my sweetheart's face, I touched my lips to the ice. It did not push back.

The murmuring grew louder. If there had been grass, I would have thought it was the wind rushing through. As it was...

Licking my cold lips, I stood, arms out for balance.

I was in a place I'd never seen before.

The snow and ice were gone. I stood on green grass, pouring down the slope in smooth emerald tussocks, like water on a high river. Strange, tall trees stood around me in a circle. They were unlike any I'd ever seen before, towering above with naked trunks and clusters of odd, flat leaves high over my head, obscuring the sky. They flipped this way and that, the leaves, showing one colour and then another; unnatural, unnameable colours. The smooth bark was pale green, with knots all the way up on every trunk.

The murmuring whispers swelled, filling my ears.

The knots on the tree trunks were eerily uniform, swirling ovals. My eyes were playing tricks on me, for the knots were shifting, moving—the mouths were moving. They looked like the faces of old people. And that talking, murmuring, all around...

I felt the hair on the back of my neck rise.

It was coming from the trees.

The ground seethed beneath my feet, like I was standing on a carpet and some vast hand was trying to shake me off. The tussocks shifted, like bodies stirred below the grass...

Was that my name? Had someone said my name?

I turned, trying to see if anybody was behind me. And in that moment I lost my footing.

I was sliding, down and down, headfirst on the icy crust. No trees above. The blue sky shook and whirled. I flailed my arms and hands, kicked with my feet, trying to break through the ice and slow my descent. One heel managed to catch and I wrenched around sideways, momentarily halted; then my foot slid off the edge of the ice and I was off again. Terror seized me. I'd fall onto someone's roof, or worse—I couldn't stop—I pounded with my fists, kicked with my heels, I yelled.

Then there was a tree, not one of the strange ones, but something old and bent and leafless, coming up fast. I was headed toward it. I would hit it.

I screwed my eyes tight shut and flung up my arms.

There was a sound like a train and a bright light.

And nothing.

DARKNESS

"Now you've done it."

I lay in snow. I was so cold.

One eye didn't want to open.

With the other, I saw a crow. It stood on the ice not an arm's-length away, moving its head about as it gazed at me.

It ruffled its feathers, and half-raised its wings. It had one white feather on each pinion.

"You've done it indeed."

Darkness took me again.

OBERON AND THE DOCTOR

Next thing I knew I was hearing opera.

A soprano voice and orchestra warbled and crackled. It wasn't in the room. It was a phonograph. I'd heard one before, in the school, for a teacher had brought this marvellous new invention into class and played a cylinder for us.

Another voice joined in. This one *was* in the room, lurching indiscriminately between a high falsetto and a baritone.

I lifted my head, or tried to. Everything hurt. Everything blurry, whirling. I closed my eyes again. Why did my head throb so?

I reached up and felt it. And wished I hadn't.

At the crown of my head was something sticky and hard, with sharp little bits, stuck to my hair. And my head itself...

My fingers went into a cleft, soft and painful and warm, and came away wet and bloody.

I remembered then. I'd fallen on the icy slope, skidded down fast as a sled, and struck a tree headfirst.

"She's awake!" A harsh, metallic voice, the same voice I'd heard out on the icy slope when I'd thought a crow was talking.

"Ooooo-ahhhhhhh!" The songster warbled a grand finale along with the recording on the phonograph. Then singing and orchestra fell silent, leaving only a soft, mechanical, repetitive sound. Footsteps. The soft sound ceased.

The steps came close to where I lay. I forced myself to crack a lid again. The room still whirled, but I could make out a person in white, with a nimbus of white hair. They had gold earrings, I thought, and pearls around their neck; they were dressed all in white...

"Reverend?" I managed.

He bowed. "The same." He leaned over and I heard trickling water. Then a warm cloth was laid on my brow; it felt heavenly. "You struck the apple tree. She is quite upset about it. Says you dinged her trunk."

"It wasn't on purpose..." I managed.

"She says her apples this summer will be all dented in on one side, like your head. This may hurt a little." Another warm cloth went to the crown of my head, pressing and dabbing gently. "How is that?"

It didn't hurt, and I said so.

"Good thing you had that thick beautiful hair of yours at the crown of your head, else you might have broken your skull. You'll be needing some stitches, though. One or two or ten. *That, now, that* will hurt. We'll have to call the Doctor."

I forced my eyes open again. The Reverend had stepped away from me and was dancing, bent like a hoop, hands delicate like two birds.

"Doctor!" came the harsh, cawing voice. "Doctor!" The crow flew to the Reverend's shoulder and perched, looking at me. "Doctor!"

It was my friend, it had to be, with those white-striped wings. "He can talk!" I gasped.

"Certainly I can talk," the crow said.

"Dor, meet Oberon. Oberon, Dor."

"I know who that one is. I found Dor, remember?"

The Reverend danced about some more, and began again to sing in his high-low voice.

"Doctor!" the crow—Oberon—cawed. "Doctor!"

"Oh, yes, I am so distractible. He is around here somewhere..." The Reverend passed out of my sight.

"Is there a Doctor here to be found?" cawed the crow, sounding impatient now.

"Yes! There's a Doctor here at hand!" Whose was that high, breathy, strained voice? The Reverend came back into my line of vision, now with his top hat on his head. "I can cure your

Brother Champion of his deadly wound and make him stand. Now," and his voice went back to normal. "We'll need to shave your hair a little around the split, I'm afraid, so we can stitch it up good and clean. Where is it... ah!"

He brandished a straight razor in his hand.

I fainted dead away.

When I came to, it was with a muttering in my ears. "Itch, stitch, the pox, the palsy, and the gout. And if the Devil is in him, I can root him out."

I remembered this. The mummers. It had been part of their play, the ancient text they'd raucously enacted that time they'd visited the house those years ago.

Something tugged at my scalp. I opened my eyes.

The Reverend leaned over me. He was still wearing his top hat. "Ah! You're awake." His hand came into view, wielding a sewing needle. "Almost done here. Edges coming together neat as two pins. You won't have much of a scar, and your hair will hide that."

He was sewing.

He was sewing my scalp.

I wanted to scream. But I was too afraid to move.

"She's frightened to death," came the crow's voice. "And who wouldn't be, you daft creature?"

"Don't be frightened, Dor, there's a good child."

"The Reverend's not mad, nor bad. Mostly not, mostly not," Oberon yawped.

"I'm almost done. You can't feel any pain now, can you?" the Reverend queried anxiously.

I thought for a moment. "No," I admitted.

"Good! That's because I have a little bottle." His voice changed, and he spoke like a mummer again, high and tight, words on the inhale. "Called ice, some tice; some gold for lice; some, the wig of a weasel; the wool of a frog and eighteen inches last September's fog. There." He gave the thread another tug through the skin of my strangely numb scalp. His voice became his own again. "I'll knot it now."

"Who are you?" I whispered.

"There are several possible answers to that question, as for any person. Many people call me the Reverend. I am, as you know, at present, the Doctor. I am also a gifted singer—"

"That's debatable," squawked the crow.

"*And* possessor of the first phonograph on the Southside Road," the Reverend talked over him, "although I have heard that others a little further up have recently acquired one."

Something was dancing round the edges of my vision: sparkling crenellated sequins, every colour. I blinked. They scattered, then coalesced again, like moths around a light.

"Oberon and I are also," he said, deftly snipping the thread at my scalp, "wanting to help you find your mother."

"Do you know where she is?" I began to sit up, but the room whirled again. I fell back with a whimper.

"Now, that's another question with several possible answers."

I felt something on my legs, sharp and light.

"You're irritating, irritating." The crow was hopping up the bed along my body. With a convulsive leap he sprang up to my shoulder, gripping with his scaly feet. Hardly daring to breathe, I laid a fingertip on his breastbone, feeling skin hot under feathers, his alien heartbeat, flickering and pulsing with life. His feathers were on my cheek, and his voice reverberated in my ear. "*Do* you," he said to the Reverend, "or do you *not* know where the woman is?"

"Let's have something to eat. I shall return."

The Reverend doffed his top hat, and twisted his way out of the room.

I eyed the crow. "Is your name really Oberon?"

"'Course!"

"Have you always been able to talk?"

The bird made a noise that, in a human, would have been a contemptuous snort, and didn't deign to answer.

As long as I didn't move my head suddenly I could focus without the world going widdershins. I was lying propped up in a soft bed with gorgeous satin hangings, all spangled and embroidered with gold. Good feather pillows cradled my head, satin covers decorated with crewel embroidery. The room didn't seem to have any windows, but lamps and candles burned everywhere, golden light gleaming on the draperies and tapestries hanging on every wall. There must have been hundreds of yards of satin, velvet, and silk of every colour imaginable, sewn into quilts edged in sequins and embroidered over in the most fantastical fashion; even the ceiling was covered in rich fabric. There were vines, flowers, lyres and harps, cherubs, centaurs, and mermaids, stars and moons and suns; but also an embroidered printing press, a phonograph, a carriage but with no horses attached, a bicycle, and a strange box with wavy lines coming out of it and an antenna on the top.

A real phonograph—the one I had heard when I first awoke—sat on a table draped with crimson velvet, cylinders in their boxes lined up behind it.

"I just wonder if I'm dreaming all this..." I gestured around.

Oberon gave my shoulder a quick peck.

"Ow!"

"You're not dreaming," he yawped.

Above my head the bed curtains depicted, I saw now, a beautiful old apple tree. Her trunk was all in silver threads, and her branches bent over to the ground, just like the tree I had struck. On this curtain, she was covered with gorgeous apple blossoms all made of silk, each one with tiny gold-thread stamens and pistils; the delicate petals shaded from snowy white to deep pink in the throat of each and every flower.

"Did he embroider all this?"

"He is an expert-expert in embroidery, and textile crafts of all kinds."

"It's like Queen Titania's bower."

"Exactly right," Oberon said, and then he threw back his head and jerked his body, laughing, the scant weight of him firking on my shoulder.

"What is so funny?" The Reverend re-entered the room, pushing a tea cart with a squeaky wheel. It was laden with food—cakes, and dainty little sandwiches, and meats and cheese; a teapot covered in pink roses steamed gently.

I was starving. "Did you make all that?"

"I'll put a girdle round the earth in forty minutes!"

Oberon's feet pushed off as he left my shoulder to perch again on the Reverend's. I sat up with care, not wanting to make the room go around.

"I hope you like ham?"

My mouth watered. I couldn't remember the last time I'd eaten ham.

A large black cat jumped on the bed, licking its lips. "That's Snug, naughty creature. And Peter Quince is around here somewhere... Ah." He pointed to a graceful black-and-white tom with a tattered ear, sitting on a mat and washing a worried-looking face. "Nick Bottom, terrible tabby girl, small but mighty, is out killing mice; Francis Flute is that shaggy, demented old tabby on top of the bureau, and Tom Snout is most likely hiding under the bed. Robin Starveling will be in directly, as soon as she senses the service of bodily sustenance and libations. I must beg you not to encourage her."

"You are very fond of *A Midsummer Night's Dream*," I ventured.

"Ridiculous play. Can't abide it. Teeny gossamer fairies and all that. Christmas cake I made myself; be careful, it's rather boozy."

He pulled the cart up to the side of the bed, handed me a plate, and perching on a chair, began to fill one of his own, balanced on his knee. He was wearing, I saw now, satin breeches of a very pale blue and an ivory satin waistcoat embroidered all over with tiny, life-like lilies-of-the-valley. His stockings were white, and his gleaming black shoes had large, old-fashioned brass buckles.

The largest cat I'd ever seen in my life sashayed into the room, white belly swaying from side to side. "Robin Starveling makes her entrance; what did I tell you? Oh, and here's Tom Snout." A sweet-faced one-eyed grey emerged cautiously from under the bed.

"Do they talk too?" The cats, thus arrayed, looked at me with unblinking eyes. "Meow?" I tried cautiously. They stared some more, with barely concealed contempt.

"Yes," Oberon said, "You're very clever. You've learned to speak Crow, but that doesn't mean you can suddenly speak Cat as well."

"We'll have to save that for another visit," the Reverend said.

We ate, saying little beyond me exclaiming over how delicious everything was. It was real food, substantial and nourishing. I felt my dizziness receding, and the sparkles at the edges of my vision dispersed.

"Now," said the Reverend, "some facts." He dabbed his mouth with a lace-edged napkin and put his plate back on the cart. Reluctantly I made as if to put my own plate away, but he waved his hand. "Keep eating, keep eating. I'll be doing all the talking for quite some time."

Grateful, I took three more tiny sandwiches and an iced cake, and helped myself to more of the perfect amber tea. Oberon flew up to the Reverend's shoulder and sat. The cats settled down in various attitudes of comfortable indolence.

"They already hate electricity," the Reverend said. "And ever since the scientists began those experiments in Europe, They've been in a frenzy."

"They?" I said through a mouthful of food.

"Why, yes, child." His strange eyes met mine. They were amber, I decided. Definitely a rich, glowing yellow, like those of a fox. "They. Them. The Little People, the Strangers, the Good Folk. Whatever it is you want to call Them. Don't worry, it's... it's... what day is it?" He wrinkled his brow. "Well, whatever day of the week it is," he waved his hand, "They can't hear us."

"They've been doing experiments?"

"No, you daft punk," cackled Oberon. "The scientists, scientists. Bose and Hertz and Righi and Lodge and all."

"Yes. There's been a terrible disturbance in the world of the Wee Folk since 1888."

"That's the year I was born!"

Both Oberon and the Reverend gave me withering looks, and the crow cackled. "It has nothing to do with you being born," said the Reverend. "Or if it does, that's too subtle by half. No, round about the time of your illustrious birth, this fellow Hertz discovered how to generate and detect these waves in his lab. He observed that the oscillatory discharge of a Leyden jar through a wire loop caused sparks to jump a gap in a similar loop a short distance away. You follow me?"

"Not really," I admitted, stuffing some more of the boozy cake into my gob.

"It doesn't matter. What matters is that Hertz was the first not only to detect such waves, but also to start *producing* them. Which caused terrible problems for our Friends. But that was nothing compared to what came later."

He paused, evidently waiting for something.

"What came later?" I asked thickly as I chawed.

"Well, that's the issue of deep concern to you today."

He rubbed his hands together. His fingers were very long and thin, I noticed, and his nails were perfectly filed and clean.

"In the October 1893 issue of the magazine *L'Elettricità*— I am an avid subscriber—there was an unsigned article in which one reads that—if I remember aright—*the slow vibrations of the ether would allow the marvellous concept of wireless telegraphy without underwater cables, without any of the expensive installations of our time.* Now. What do you think of that?"

Wireless telegraphy? "If my friend Murph's hunch is right, it sounds like Marconi's work."

"Ah! No doubt the young Marconi read that very article; it caused quite a stir when it came out. But nothing suggested a connection between Hertz's work and the communication of intelligible signals. No, that has been Marconi's innovation."

"And that bothers the... Them?"

"Correct. You see, that's how They travel—those slow ethereal vibrations. That's Their realm. Shakespeare knew: *I'll put a girdle round the earth in forty minutes.* And now we've invaded it. The generation of artificial waves and the attempts to signal have sent Them into a frenzy. Every time it happens—every single time—it traps Them. Freezes Them, if you will. And for beings of such perpetual motion and shift, this is tantamount to torture and death."

I thought about this. Marconi's experiments, according to the Reverend, were painful to the Little Strangers? Trapped them? "How do you know?"

"One can't *not* know." He threw his hands in the air. "What a din. We haven't had a moment's peace around here since Marconi started his Cornwallian shenanigans."

I remembered what my mother had said about the Reverend. *He's a wise person and worthy of respect, however eccentric his aspect.* "Reverend, do you know my mother?"

"Know her? Of course I know her. We grew up together; we're both Southsiders, aren't we? We are practically the same age, although my hair has grown unaccountably white..." He stroked his snowy mane. Then he turned his eyes on me again. They weren't amber, I realized. They were purple, like amethysts. "They have her, Dor, you know."

A FAIRY PATH

My mouth went dry. "They have her?"

But I knew the Reverend was right.

"Who called her out that night?" he asked.

"I don't know. There wasn't a voice, only... The house shook."

He leaned forward, intent. "Yes?"

"And Mother... she was sort of tender with me."

His eyes stared into mine, unblinking.

How had it been? I remembered the tension, her hesitation. "Like she wasn't sure she shold be leaving. but felt, somehow, compelled."

He sat back in his chair so forcefully that it rocked on its legs, and Oberon raised his striped wings.

"They don't have babies, only once in an awfully long, long time. Centuries. And they've had one now."

"I saw!" The nightmare came back to me. "At least, I had a dream..."

"Didn't feel like a dream, did it?"

"No," I said. "No! I could smell, I could feel it. She was below ground, and there was a horrible baby, and an old man and a woman."

He nodded. "They have her in their power. They called her to be midwife to them, and that never ends well for the midwife unless..."

"Unless what?" I wanted to scream, to cry.

"Your house is on one of Their paths. You know that, right?"

I knew it. I'd known it all my life. "What do They want?"

He shook his head. "Who knows? It is as if They mimic human kind. Rituals of coming and going, birth and death, eating and making merry. But They aren't of us. They are Themselves."

"A fairy path." I pushed my plate away, suddenly sick. "What can I do? I can't move the house!"

"You can't make bargains and deals with Them; They don't see the world as we do. You have to trick Them. You have to be very brave, and very clever."

Despair choked my throat. "I am neither of those things," I whispered.

"Don't be ridiculous. You're one of the bravest, cleverest people we know. Back me up, Oberon!" he appealed to the crow.

"Certainly, certainly!" yawped Oberon. "Wouldn't waste my time with you otherwise!" He spread his wings and alighted on my shoulder once more. His claws digging gently through my clothes, his scant weight of feather and muscle, his trust in me, all left me gobsmacked. He nibbled at my ear, crooning gently.

"Remember what I told you. When Marconi sets up to receive the signals, They'll be trapped. Frozen. Yammering and miserable and tortured. That's your chance.

"You'll have to be there. Capture Them, and bargain with Them. Set Them free in exchange for your mother.

"You'll have to sabotage Marconi's experiments as a bargaining chip with Them. You'll have to do it, to set your mother free."

"Reverend," I said, my eyes filling with tears and my heart with wonder, "who are you?"

"My dear, I am the Illegitimate Queen of Albion." And he gave a smile of great sweetness and simplicity, warm as the sun.

I LOOK LIKE MYSELF

Always this fight with Mother about getting out of bed. *You wretched angishore, get up!*

My eyes were so heavy, and my head hurt so much.

Lazy barnacle! Parasite!

"I'm trying," I whispered. "I'm trying!"

And then I remembered. She was gone.

"I don't know who did this, but I couldn't have done a better job myself." A man's voice. Definitely not the Reverend. The man smelled like chemicals, wet wool, and a bit of booziness.

"Will she be all right?"

I forced my eyes to open.

Leaning over me, face filled with anxiety, was my father. Next to him was a man. He looked familiar... small white beard and spectacles... my eyes went in and out of focus. He had visited our house last year, when Mother lost that baby...

"She's awake!" Father said.

I was in my old room. Dark and dismal it seemed, after the Reverend's splendid bower. Why did my head hurt so? I reached up and felt, at the top of my skull, a bald patch, and bumps, tiny... stitches.

"What happened?"

"Your father found you up on the slope behind your house. You've hit your head, young lady. May I?" This last to my father.

"Dor, this is the doctor. He's here to examine you."

The doctor shouldered my father gently aside, and put a thumb over one of my eyelids, then the other, looking into my eyes. "Pupils same size, that's good," he muttered. He put a stethoscope to my chest. "Heart's regular, nice and slow and strong. How do you feel? Are you seeing things normally? No double vision or anything like that?"

I shook my head. "But my head hurts."

"No wonder. You came smashing up against a rock."

"No, it was a tree. The apple tree. She's upset about it. Her apples are going to be dented..."

The doctor and my father exchanged a look.

"What do you remember, Dorthea? Who stitched you up?"

I remembered the Reverend, Oberon, everything in a rush. And Mother.

They had her, Them, down below. I had to get back to Marconi.

I was about to tell Father when suddenly I thought the better of it.

Would he believe me? Even if he did, it would only complicate things; adults tended to fixate on the wrong things. Would the Reverend get into some kind of trouble? And if I told them—about the talking crow, the feast, the satin bower, the apple tree—I'd sound touched in the head. Would the doctor lock me up as a bedlamer? Prevent me from getting up Signal Hill?

That would be disastrous. I had to be there when Marconi began his secret transatlantic transmissions. I had to insinuate myself with him, and then sabotage his work.

It was the only way to save Mother.

"Where were you, Dor?"

"I was looking for Mother." That much was true.

"Dor! You can't, she's gone—" Father turned away.

The doctor looked grave. "And what did you find?"

"I can't remember." This seemed the safest response.

The doctor started feeling at my throat, clucking a bit. "Does your throat hurt?"

"No."

"Not at all? Stick out your tongue and say ahhhhh."

"Ahhhhh." I was obedient.

"Looks normal... but clearly there must be some kind of... you can put your tongue back in now, young lady."

"My throat is fine, it's the rest of me."

"But you must have some kind of sore throat... or infection... your voice is so roughened."

"That's just my normal voice."

"It is?" The doctor looked at my father, bewildered.

"Tis her usual voice," Father confirmed.

"Well, well," the doctor said. "Surely a remarkably deep voice for a young lady." He looked embarrassed, or rather, as if he thought my father and I should be embarrassed, and cleared his throat. "But in any case, call me at once if anything changes." He caressed the top of my head. I could feel his fingers gently skittering over the strange numbness of the wound. "Really remarkable job on those stitches. Wish I could meet the person who did that."

My father walked the doctor down the stairs and out the front door, the two of them speaking in low tones. *Keep her quiet... no stimulation... send for me at any time.*

I touched the top of my head again. Yes, tiny stitches, tiny, for the Reverend was a master embroiderer... I moved my fingers, counting. Seven, seven stitches.

I hoped that was lucky.

The shaven spot felt strange and cold. I must look a fright, I thought. Braids still hung on either side of my face. I undid them, and hanks of hair fell into my hands from where the Reverend had shaven the crown of my head.

I heard the front door open and shut, my father's footsteps back up to my room. He hesitated on the threshold.

"Are you hungry?"

I was still full from the feast the Reverend had given me. I shook my head.

He stared at me. And then he burst out, "And you don't look a thing like her, child!"

"Who?"

"Who do you think? You're just the spit of me. I don't see her in you at all!"

"What's wrong with that?" I cried.

"Not a sign!"

I jumped out of the bed in a rage, all weakness leaving me. "I don't care! I don't look like anybody! I look like myself! And if you two would just leave me alone—"

Alone? Mother was gone. Gone, and she'd be gone forever if I couldn't get her back. I clapped my hands over my mouth and sat back down on the bed as if I were a puppet with the strings cut.

"There she is now, looking out of your eyes. God forgive me, I'll be after wanting to make you angry for the rest of my life, just to see her." Father's voice shook, and he stumbled from the room.

I listened as he went down to the kitchen—rustling around, coughing—trying to cover his own tears.

My poor, poor father.

But she wasn't dead. I knew it. And I was going to get her back.

I slipped quiet as a shadow down the hall to the front stair, and descended noiselessly into the parlour. Mother's sewing basket was still there. I took out her sewing scissors, and went back up to my room. There, standing before the cracked little mirror, I cut off my hair.

It fell around my feet like long, soft, black feathers. I left it a bit longer on the top. If I parted my hair on the side I could cover up the shaven spot and the stitches.

The face that looked back at me when I was done was harder than my own, leaner. The eyebrow glowered, the chin lifted. I liked how I looked. My hair had a slight wave to it, unencumbered by the weight of length. My eyes beamed out.

Jack Kelly would ingratiate himself with Marconi, and Jack would bind the Little Strangers to his will. For Jack was going to get Mother back, if it was the last thing he did.

MUCH TO BE DONE

It sounded like someone knocking on my windowpane with a finger-bone.

The house was rocking like a ship, like a cradle; so peaceful. I was so tired. All I wanted to do was sleep.

It kept on. Three raps—then silence. Another three. Three more.

Would I never be left at peace?

Sheer irritation finally prompted me to crack a lid. There was someone else in my room. My father, asleep, had propped himself up in a chair against the wall.

Why was he here? Was I in trouble?

My iron bedstead lay along the wall, the window at the foot of it; I'd have to sit up to identify the beastie making that infernal, irritating noise.

I wasn't prepared for the agony sitting up entailed. Pain shot through my head, and the room whirled. My body felt like someone had worked over me with a birch billet. All around the edges of my vision sparkles danced, like crenellations in a childish drawing of a king's castle.

My neck and ears felt abominably cold.

Then I remembered. The fall. The Reverend. My shorn head.

Rap-rap-rap!

Suppressing a groan, I forced my aching, bruised body to shimmy down the bed. There, on the windowsill, perched a large, black crow with white-striped wings. Oberon.

When he caught sight of me, he glared and ducked his head up and down, unmistakably telling me to open the window sash. Carefully, so as not to wake Father, I pressed the heels of my hands on the sash and pushed upwards. It opened with a groan.

"Finally. Don't make me come down the chimney," Oberon scolded.

"Shhh!" I said, jerking my head back at my father.

He ruffled his feathers and glared some more, then hopped onto the foot of my bed. Chuckling, wings half-raised, he yawped, "Let's make a dart, make a dart over to Signal Hill!"

"Shhhhh!" But my father's breath didn't even hitch. He looked very tired and troubled. My heart hurt to look at him.

Quickly and quietly as I could, I pulled the nunny bag out from under my bed. The wind was rattling around the house quite smartly today; remembering the chill of Jack's first day on Signal Hill, I hauled on a double layer of long underwear, and donned my boy's garments over those. Every joint ached, my neck was stiff and sore. But gradually the glistering at the periphery of my vision faded away, and as I moved I started to limber up.

Casting one more glance at poor Father, I shoved my nightgown under my pillow and placed Clint's hat upon my head. On the instant, Oberon flew up to my shoulder. He nibbled gently on my earlobe, and made a soft noise in his throat like he was rolling marbles.

As I slipped past Father out the door of my room he gave a mighty snore. I froze. Oberon froze too, talons digging into my coat. Father murmured. "She's been towed astray, she's astray..."

He was dreaming of my mother.

But he settled down, murmuring things I could not understand, and the snores began again.

As I crept down the stairs I heard something moving around in the kitchen. Could it be Mother? But then I felt Oberon dig his claws through the shoulder of my coat. I went cold. Dishes clinked, feet tramped.

Was it the wind, that whispering and laughter?

I went down the last few steps quiet as a mouse, then jumped through the door.

I had a brief impression of a crowd of people dancing through the air, smears of light.

Then nothing.

The table was set for three. And the doors—from kitchen to linney, and the one to the outside—both hung open. The outer door creaked open and closed, hanging on its hinges.

Oooour... ouuuuur... oooour... ouuuur...

It was as if the house, having slept, was awakening again, like a person emerging from the somnolence that follows a very large meal.

Oberon cleared his throat. "There is much to be done."

It was a glorious day, sunny and clear, the wind a fine, cutting breeze, but the house was still in shadow. Looking down the Ratline, I saw I was up before the neighbourhood. With Oberon balancing on my shoulder I ran down the steps and along the walkway, stiffness and aches working themselves out with every step. Oberon crouched on my shoulder, talons a pleasant sharpness through the coat—and then he took flight, leaving me marvelling at the strange, intense sensation of his launch. He flew ahead of me, cawing joyously at the dawn.

All the way across the Long Bridge he led the way, wings rowing the air; all the way through downtown.

I remembered that I still had candy in my pocket. I took out a barley sugar and sucked the sweetness with my tongue. I made it up Signal Hill's cruel slope at a run.

Early as I was, Marconi, Paget, and Kemp were at the hospital before me. "Good morning, sir!" I said, breathing hard.

They looked over at me, a little surprised.

"Hello, boy," Kemp said. "Here to offer your services?"

"Oh, yes, sir, please, it'd be an honour."

"Isn't there some school you should be attending?"

"Er..." I froze like a rabbit. I thought quickly. "My teachers let me off." I stood up taller and tugged at my cap. "Said it was a good opportunity to study telegraphy, sir."

"Ah." His eyes twinkled. "Well, in any case, boy, there's some kites to fly today. You could help with that."

Relief coursed through me. "Anything I can do to be useful."

"Paget, Kemp." And with that terse utterance Marconi disappeared into the hospital building.

A miserable-looking, cough-rattling Paget trailed after Marconi.

Kemp held back, eyeing me. "Gusty gale today."

Gusty gale? What was he on about? It was a lovely mild day with a nice breeze. "Pretty normal for here, sir."

"Is it? Well. Hmph." He didn't look happy. "Normal, you say?"

"Pretty much."

"That'll make it hard to keep the aerial at a stable height... Hmmm..."

He followed Marconi and Paget inside, leaving me alone.

They'd been busy over the weekend. The ground was covered in metal plates; zinc, I remembered, as they'd said they needed. There were crates—some open and empty, some still sealed—neatly stacked in the lee of the old hospital building.

A black thing whizzed past me, making me jump. Oberon laughed openly at my startlement, circling around and coming to light on the roof over a window of the hospital. He cawed. Obedient, I approached the window.

There was a wire coming out of a hole drilled through the frame. Standing on tiptoe, I could see into the room. Paint was peeling off the walls; the cupboards were battered. A potbellied stove stood in one corner. On a table sat an array of unfamiliar equipment, and the wire led to all this: wooden stands, brass fittings, knobs, wires, black cylinders and other strange shapes, their purpose arcane. One in particular caught my eye: a thing shaped like a butterstamp, made of brass and black metal on a wooden base.

I could hear the men's conversation, slightly muffled.

"... damned good time," Marconi was saying.

"Exceedingly nice," Paget rattled.

"Have you ever seen so many good-looking women?" Kemp exclaimed. "Every one we meet..."

"An unusually high proportion. The jammiest bits of jam, no doubt," Marconi nodded.

"We've been invited to a reception at the Governor's

tonight," Kemp rubbed his hands. "He has told me he is going to ask some *charming* ladies."

They all chuckled. Was this how men spoke to each other about women?

"... now know practically everyone here and they all do their best to entertain me." Marconi gave a theatrical sigh, caressing the butterstamp. "But I have to carry out my experiments on the highest hill on this side of Newfoundland, and am working all day long."

He raised the receiver to his ear, striking a pose. He was grinning, and the others burst out laughing. I realized it was the first time I had seen him smile. Was this jocularity between men something I needed to learn?

Marconi put the device back down on its cradle and stood up, levity falling away. "We'll start with a kite, then."

"Tough to keep it grounded in these gusts."

"The men will be up shortly. And if it gets too windy, we can tie the boy to the tail."

They laughed again. *Very funny,* I thought, *laugh it up.*

Marconi began to talk through the merriment, and I couldn't make out the first part, but, "... tomorrow signals starting at dusk in..." and then he said something that sounded like *pole dew.* What possible meaning could be attached to *pole dew?*

And *signals...*

Could it be the Lizard? Murph had told me that Marconi's station at the Lizard was in Cornwall. Sure, they had all kinds of strange place names in Cornwall. Pole Dew could be a place. And Marconi had said *tomorrow.* Of that I was certain. Tomorrow. Pole Dew. Signals.

It was the signals I was interested in. For according to the Reverend, the signals were, for Them, a trap, a life-ending net of invisible threads.

And it wasn't only the Reverend's word I had to go on. I was marked—my whole life was marked—by Their antipathy toward electrical devices and currents. My family was scarred irreparably by it. Six babies sapped, drawn down to the dust.

Why had I, the abomination of my mother's seven children—why had I been left to live?

Perhaps I would never know. And maybe it didn't matter. This being, my body and spirit, was the only hope. Marconi's station was going to transmit signals. And the transmissions would trap Them. And while They were trapped by the transmissions, I could bargain.

I peered again through the window at the incomprehensible, fascinating array of wires and devices. Brass knobs gleamed in the half-light; rich mahogany bled red on the battered table. Their sheer complexity and mysteriousness demanded belief in their efficacy. A childish part of me wished for something much larger, a truly gargantuan machine, to achieve the unbelievable feat of receiving signals from across the vast Atlantic. At the same time, the very neatness and precision of the arcane devices commanded my respect. I was strongly attracted to the strange instruments. Excitement ran hot.

Oh, how I loved what he was doing! It was extraordinary, fascinating!

But then regret rinsed chill through my chest, twisting my guts.

For I had to wreck it, wreck the whole thing. It was up to me to find a way to sabotage this marvellous experiment.

Offer Them freedom, for the freedom of my mother.

I was swiftly revising my estimation of the day. It was, I decided, windy enough indeed.

Paget stood on the leeward side, holding the great kite to the ground, while myself and three hired men held a longer line. Marconi would bark out an order, Paget would release the kite, and then, we'd pull.

The idea was that a six-hundred-foot-long wire attached to one end of the kite was supposed to stay grounded, touching the zinc plates. Another wire—attached to the kite—connected with the wire leading through the hole in the window of the old fever hospital. And the kite itself, with all that aerial wire attached, was supposed to sail up to a height, and stay there, acting as a receiver. All this in the tumultuous winds of Signal Hill.

We hadn't achieved it for more than a split minute, not even once. And we'd been at it for two hours. Our arms ached; Paget was looking increasingly miserable hunched in his coat, nose red and dripping. My hands, even through the gloves Kemp had given out, hurt from all the grasping at the recalcitrant cord. As for Marconi, he was practically incandescent with irritation.

"What kind of fool would come to Newfoundland in December to fly a giant kite?" one of the men grunted.

I had to agree. Reducing shipwrecks was a laudable goal, but why now? Marconi could have come in the summer to test ship-to-shore. He could have kept experimenting back in Britain. No, to have decided to come here, now... Surely Murph was right. It had to be a grasp for something bigger.

All the time I was aware of Oberon, alternately perching on top of Cabot Tower, or circling around us in the air.

The scattered glitter darted around the edges of my vision. I couldn't look straight at Them—They danced on the extremities, flickering like sunlight on leaves.

A memory of my dream—so long ago it seemed now—when I saw the man on the storm-tossed ship came to me. Those flickering beings of light!—it *had* been Marconi I'd seen in that dream, it must have been! They hadn't wanted him to come! And in the dream, They'd sensed me too. Recognized me. Fastened onto me. The thought struck me with a bolt of fear like I was a lightning rod. They needed me. But were They friendly? Uncaring? Or did They want to destroy me?

It seemed to me, now, that Marconi was surrounded by a crowd of Them: darting, jabbering, enraged. Tiny sparkling figures crystallized on the kite, thick on the cord, swarming the aerial wire. Only with my peripheral vision could I see Them, however. Look straight on, and They weren't there. *What do you want?* I bent my thoughts at Them. *Why do you have my mother?*

Suddenly the heavy cord went taut. The kite pitched wildly from side to side. Our feet scrabbled on loose scree, and the man at the front of the line lost his footing and went down. Without thinking, I leapt forward and took his place. The wind checked for an instant, giving the kite a bit of slack, and I wrapped the cord around my wrist several times for an anchor. *Is this wise?* came the thought, echoed by a volley of warning caws from Oberon.

And with that, the wind surged. I was borne into the air, into the singing wind, clinging to the cord with all my might.

Who was playing piano up here on Signal Hill?

It was my mother's favourite piece, by the man whose lover, she'd told me, had been unafraid to dress in men's clothing. A funeral march.

Why was my mother so enamoured of death?

A great flashing brightness flared around the edges of my vision. It expanded, becoming an enormous semicircle stretching from ground to sky, with jagged, flaring edges, bright as the sun. It was as if flames of every colour had stabbed down from heaven and into my eyes.

Inside the shining They danced and yammered.

The sparkling crenellations shook and shimmered like a shower of falling stars. They fell into blackness, a great nothing straight ahead of me, a black, blank tunnel.

Floating in the abyss, I began to make out a lighter shape, a pale blue shadow.

I could not see her face, but I knew her. It was my mother. She sat in the abyss, rocking her body back and forth.

They laughed.

"What have you done with her?" My arms ached. The cord around my wrist tightened until I thought my hand would be pinched off. I could not tell how high off the ground I was— I could not see, nor could I hear, for there was a great roaring in my ears. I could be over the sea, or mere inches from the ground. I could not tell.

A thin and threading sound, as of a baby crying, turned the marrow of my bones to ice.

Then a great shrieking crowd cried out, falling from the kite, jagged stars into the chasm.

Through the glitter and mayhem tore a big black feathered figure. "Caw! Caw! Caw!"

The sparkling at the periphery of my vision gave one last flare like fireworks, dispersing outward. The black chasm sucked away, like water going down a drain, and with it, the pale blue ghostly image of my mother.

"No!" I cried.

The laughter faded into mere wind.

I came back to myself. I was suspended up in the air, arm in agony. Above me the kite wrenched and yawed. I was a rag doll in the jaws of a black dog, helplessly jerking up and down.

The kite, with me tangled in its cord, was being pulled toward the cliff-edge by the inexorable winds.

Below me the men shouted and heaved, trying to get the kite back to earth. "Dig in yer scrapers!" the tall man cried. But it was futile. We were all, as one, being pulled toward the edge.

They were hanging onto the kite to save me.

I let go of the cord. I was terrified at the fall, but it would be better than being hauled off the cliff. But my one wrist was hopelessly entangled, and the rope held on to me although I did not hold on to it. My arm would be hauled out of its socket, my hand would be severed. Terror surged through me. I had to let go, lest everyone die for my sake, but I was trapped. I yelled into the wind. "Let me go!"

The men below hung on still, getting dragged inexorably toward the cliff.

"Caw! Cut it! Cut the cord!" Oberon circled my head.

Swinging from my arm, the world whirling, I shut my eyes tight, feeling in my pocket. There it was! The pocket knife my father had given me.

I managed to get it out, and then... despair. How would I open it? I clenched my front teeth over the exposed spine. Could I do it without dropping it or slicing off my lips?

The blade popped open, wrenching my teeth.

My mouth tasted of metal and blood. Risking one last glance downward, I saw that the cliff edge was close, so close now.

I cut the cord.

With a spring, the fibres unravelled under my blade, and spun away.

I fell like a stone.

"Good thing the cord broke," Kemp was saying. "We could have lost our whole crew!"

My wrist burned where the cord had sawed it. Blood trickled from a cut at one corner of my mouth.

But I was on solid land, and I was alive.

As we walked back to the hospital, one of the men slapped me on the back. "Next time, let her go, b'y. Not worth our lives nor yours!"

I looked up at him, a tall, thin man with a nice face. He was a cooper, and I wondered if he'd worked at McAuley's where my father had been clerk, before it burned. I was about to ask him when I realized I didn't want to get into awkward questions.

I merely nodded. "Good boy," he said, and gave me another pound on the shoulders.

But no. I wasn't a boy, and I wasn't good. I'd sabotaged the kite string with an iron blade.

Incredibly, nobody on the ground had perceived the knife, or realized what I had done. I looked into the sky, but Oberon was nowhere to be seen.

That had been my own test. I knew, now. If They insisted on it, I could sabotage Marconi's experiments.

My mother's life depended on it.

It was a long, cold trudge home.

"I overheard them," Oberon chuckled as we crossed the Long Bridge. "The King of Diamonds and his friend. They'll start sending the signals tomorrow."

"From the Lizard?" I asked, feeling stupid. All at once I was so tired I thought I would drop where I stood.

Oberon cackled. "From across the sea. From Pole Dew!

Pole Dew! Pole Dew!" He took to the wing, making a great sweeping circle in the air as if he loved the sound of the words.

I don't know if it was some magic Oberon wrought, but no neighbours were out to see the mysterious cousin of Dor toiling up the Hundred Steps. No awkward questions to answer, no encounters where I was required to explain myself. Which was a good thing, for I was so gut-foundered and bewildered that I'd have made a poor account of myself. The sparkles at the edges of my vision receded, replaced by a throbbing, blinding pain.

By the time I got into the kitchen I was light-headed with hunger. Failing utterly to consider what I'd do if Father saw me in this rig out, I crept through the door with one intention— to find food, then get my weary body back into my bed.

To my delight, there was food on the table: a baked fish, and a figgy duff! I fell upon it, not even getting a plate. Pity food from a neighbour, I collected, brought to Father and me in our tribulations. Whoever had brought it, I was beyond grateful, and shared bits with Oberon; he glutched down fragments of fish with alacrity.

"Where's my father?" I mumbled through a gob full of delicious duff.

"By your bedside, of course. He'll not leave you."

Still chewing, I trudged up the staircase.

I stopped in shock on the threshold to my room. The window yawned open, and the room was fresh with frigid air. Oberon jumped off my shoulder and landed on the foot of the iron bedstead.

As for Father, Oberon had been right. He still slept, propped up in the chair.

And in the bed was a girl.

Me.

My shorn head on the pillow looked pathetic; dark shadows were stamped under my eyes. I was in the nightgown I remembered taking off and stashing under the pillow that very morning.

I gasped.

But when I looked again, the girl-me was gone.

Father moved in the chair, arms wrapped around himself and shuddering.

The room started going round, and sparkling crept over the periphery of my vision once more. I flung my cap from my head, got out of my boots. Darkness bloomed, zig-zag colours flashing around its edges. Shutting my eyes tight, I felt my way out of my clothes, shoved them under the bed, and crawled under the covers. I risked one last look. Oberon leaned over me, his feathers ablaze with jagged fire.

"Sleep, now, now." He soared out of the window, an inky blot. The edges of my vision closed in, and all was dark.

SOUL ROAMING

There were children down there in the gloom.

Some of them wore white christening gowns and bonnets; some were naked, blue and throbbing as a vein under the skin of a pale wrist. Six of them, six lost children. One, a little older, I knew so well; I could not bear to look at him for long. But in this place, he walked—he toddled—and he smiled and did not look unhappy.

The old man and woman hopped among the babies, which made the little boy laugh. His laughter caused the shining that rippled around the edges of the dank place to tremble.

My mother was nowhere to be seen. What had They done with her? I tried to speak, but I was a ghost in this place.

The babies mewed and wailed. Theo, my silent little brother, dead now these nine years, looked at me with his big, shining eyes but I did not know what he wanted. He opened his mouth to speak—

Caw! Caw!

Why was I so cold?

Caw! "Wake up already!"

Had I left the window open?

I opened my eyes. Something was pricking at my foot.

I sat up.

Oberon perched on my toe. "How are you today today?" he shrieked.

Where was Father?

He still sat, poor man, in that uncomfortable chair. Why didn't he go to his own bed?

"He's too worried about you to leave your side, idiot," Oberon cackled.

"So how did I get past him yest–"

I stopped, remembering. The figure in the bed that I'd seen on coming home yesterday... Nanny King's words echoed in my head. *The spirit is like a man in prison. When the body is asleep in the night, the soul leaves it to roam, free until the morning dawns.*

Perhaps my spirit was travelling? Or my body?—for all the sensations of the day before were vivid, and my wrist—yes, it bore burn marks from the kite cord.

"Today Marconi gets signals from the Lizard!"

I scrambled to my feet, all confusion forgotten.

"How are you feeling?" Oberon chuckled.

"Wonderful!" My body felt fine—not even an ache in my battered nopper. I threw my head back and laughed.

Swiftly I drew on my Jack disguise. Before I left the room, I cast a last glance at my poor father. He stirred as if he felt my eyes on him. Carefully I drew the window closed, and tiptoed down the stairs.

Oberon flew ahead of me, straight as an arrow, and I followed in his wake. We made it through the city and up onto the crest of Signal Hill before any of the others arrived.

He flew to my shoulder, and nibbled my ear. "They're coming coming, up the road. Good luck, Dor!" He spread his wings and soared off to perch on Cabot Tower.

I gazed out to sea. It was a foggy day and I could see little enough. I looked behind me, to where the house croochied on its Southside ledge.

They had my mother. And today, if I had any power in me at all, I'd find out how to get her back.

Soon I heard rolling wheels and clopping hooves, and a cab hove into view. The horse snorted, mist coming out of its nostrils as the driver brought it to a halt. Marconi emerged first, leaping to the ground with his customary precision. Paget trailed out next, fur cap with ear-flaps so tightly tied beneath his chin that I could barely see his face. Kemp wasn't far behind, red face breaking into a grin when he saw me. "Ah! Our most enthusiastic worker."

Coming up the road behind were the three hired men, on foot. They hadn't been offered a ride.

Marconi vanished into the hospital building, followed by Paget. Soon smoke from the little stove was coming out the chimney, twining into the fog.

Kemp, meanwhile, told us all what we'd be doing that day. "Mr. Marconi wants to try a balloon. It'll be steadier than a kite, and keeping her steady is the issue we need to address. The aerial wires need to be suspended at the maximum possible height, and stay steady. The kite didn't seem to be a plausible solution, in that gusty gale."

"Sure we're bet to a snot, trying to keep that one up yesterday," complained one of the men, rubbing his arms.

"Exactly," Kemp nodded. "So first order of business is to inflate one of the balloon skins."

"How big is it?" I asked.

"Fourteen feet in diameter, all told," Kemp told us. "It'll hold a thousand cubic feet of hydrogen gas."

I whistled, then wished I hadn't. My whistle was feeble, not at all the proud shrieking blast someone like Clint could have managed. But no one seemed to have noticed my unmasculine skirl. The men were all looking up into the air.

"A balloon that size... if a wind comes up..." the tall, thin fellow trailed off, questioning.

"It's perfectly calm," Kemp asserted.

Another fellow shrugged. "It's your money."

Kemp laughed. "Oh, no, it's the investors' money. Our job is to give them something to show for it."

It took some time to inflate the balloon. The men were kept busy bringing hydrogen canisters to it; my job was rolling the empty ones back to the lee of the hospital building. It was fascinating watching the vast thing inflate. The white mass was ribbed and textured with a sheen on it, like a partridge's crop.

Marconi emerged from the building to supervise the attaching of four copper wires to the vast bloated thing. I watched him giving precise orders in his quiet voice. His coat, his hat, his gloves and boots—everything fit perfectly, and the fabrics were fine, giving a sense of elegance without being flash. What was he thinking right now, I wondered? What was he feeling? To look at him you'd not imagine anything momentous was occurring. You'd never think he was trying to receive signals sent across an ocean, do something that leading scientists of the day categorically proclaimed could not be done. He must, I thought, have a will of iron. Failure would have never occurred to him.

I wondered what that was like.

The final canister of hydrogen was emptied into the balloon.

I drifted close to Marconi. He glanced down at me, eyes vague but with a faint twinkle. I smiled at him. "Are those wires aerials, sir?" I asked. I knew damn well what they were. I felt we both knew I was getting him talking, and we both knew he wanted to talk.

"Indeed."

"You're hoping to receive signals." I bounced on my toes.

"Correct."

"Signals from... Pole Dew?"

"Kemp, replace that wire, it's damaged..." Marconi strode over to the balloon, now a huge writhing globe.

He'd not denied it, not said that the signals were *not* coming from across the ocean. If Oberon were right, today they were hoping to communicate two thousand miles across the sea, Hertzian waves curving impossibly around the Earth, from Cornwall to Newfoundland.

Imagine, imagine being able to speak with anyone, anywhere in the world! I could talk with that scientist in Calcutta! Or better—better than that—a strange girl in that strange city. A girl with long, straight black hair and an eyebrow like mine.

Someone who was in love with her best friend and wanted to kiss her.

I tried to picture her, this Indian girl. Somewhere across the globe there was surely someone who wanted more than her city could hold. Someone who would understand the inchoate yearnings inside me, because she felt them herself.

Someone who knew that a whole vast battered island wasn't enough to hold her as she truly was.

But I couldn't want that.

I couldn't, because it was up to me to make sure wireless telegraphy never happened. Not until They let my mother go.

The balloon glimmered above us in the fog, a glimpse of a whale's belly to the drowned. We knew how high it was because Kemp had made sure the cord was marked with little pieces of coloured ribbon, one for every five feet. It currently stood at fifteen feet, holding steady, which made Marconi happy. He'd ensconced himself inside the hospital, calling Kemp in at intervals. Kemp would then emerge to tell us to let the balloon out higher, or lower, then higher again.

I had been banned from hanging onto the rope after the events of yesterday. Gradually I edged my way over to the old hospital building. The door hung open.

"... a more sensitive reception system when we get back to England," Marconi was saying. He seemed fretted.

"And get the Lizard back up to full power too," Kemp said.

Paget, huddled by the stove, sneezed. Nobody blessed him.

"Goes without saying," Marconi snapped. "I can't get anything on the coherer."

"Maybe you'd better do it, then. Use that rigged Bell telephone receiver."

"But then we won't be able to use the Morse inker."

"That'd be disastrous. There'll be no evidence," Paget muttered.

Marconi's narrow face looked dangerous. He thrust the butterstamp thing at Kemp. "Can you hear anything?"

Kemp placed the thing to his ear, listening intently.

Paget sneezed.

"Please be quiet, Mr. Paget," Marconi said between clenched teeth.

"Sorry, sir," the miserable man sniffed.

Kemp listened some more, and shook his head. "Just atmospheric noise. But you know me. Deaf as a haddock."

Marconi looked at his pocket watch. "They'll be transmitting now. They know to do it." Then he paced up and down a bit, excitement radiating off him. He reached for the butterstamp thing. "Let me listen again."

Kemp passed the butterstamp over and began to turn toward the door. I slid around the corner, back to the wall, and gasped. I'd been holding my breath the whole time and not even knowing it.

It was true! They were listening for signals not from passing ships, but from the Lizard itself! From Cornwall, across the sea!

I had to tell Murph. If he was the one to break the news about Marconi's real reason for being here–

But at that moment, above us, the fog shredded and whirled. A wind sprang up. The cord attached to the balloon aloft began to thrash in the men's hands. Soon they were digging in their heels, and pulling with all their strength.

"Getting blustery," one man sang out.

"God's having a rompse," grunted another.

"Well, I wish He'd lay off," said the tall fellow.

Cabot Tower, shrouded in fog a moment before, emerged sharp and clear. A black silhouette glimpsed on top of the wall told me Oberon was still there.

A soft pulse, a whisper, emerged from the red rocks beneath my feet, slow as a heartbeat. A chorded sound, and a vibration.

Oberon took to the wing. "Caw! Caw! Caw!"

A pulse began behind my eyes. Light darted in from the edges of my vision, flaring in time to the pulse. Suddenly sparkling crenellations burst into the air, soaring from ground to sky in one long arc.

There were figures in the arc, and they were screaming.

Through the glister I saw Kemp emerge from the building. Small figures darted in his wake and flooded inside, where Marconi was listening for signals from the ether. Others flashed around Kemp's head.

"Keep that balloon steady, now! Steady!"

The balloon was smothered in small, glittering figures. It weaved and thrashed in the burgeoning wind.

And I too was surrounded. My ears filled with yammering and crying.

Let us go! Let us go!

They were trapped, transfixed.

The pulse in the rock strengthened and resolved. Signal Hill was a vast, ruddy stone heart and it beat in time, an immeasurable, geologic piano playing my mother's favourite music, slow and deathly.

The glittering apparitions clashed and chimed against the music. *Let us go let us go let us go let us go!*

"The signals!" Oberon called to me. "Signals!"

It was the signals trapping them, as the Reverend had said!

I reached out, grasping at the shimmering, shrieking figures. "Only if you'll do for me!"

Screams and moaning; no words.

"You have my mother. Why?"

Ahhhhhh!

"Why? Tell me, or I'll let you fry!"

She birthed us a baby.

My heart went cold.

They began to chant in time with the slow beat of the music. *She's... ours... she's... ours...*

I shook my head, trying to rid my vision of the angry glister.

"Let her go and I'll let you go!"

Darkness bloomed in the middle of my eyes. I could see, now, only in a small space between the void in the middle of my sight, and the violent saw-toothed shimmer at the edges.

And another part of me sensed Dor, lying in bed, limbs twitching, eyes jerking microscopically beneath thin, blue eyelids. I was unravelling like an old rope.

Gasping, I made my way to the men holding the cord. As before, I launched myself at the cord ahead of the men, in guise of helping stabilize the balloon.

The music beat at my ears. The creatures yammered and cried, that slow chant. My nightgowned spirit-self thrashed. *She's... ours... she's... ours...*

My weight on the rope was enough to stabilize the balloon. "Good!" cried Kemp. "Keep her there!" He hurried back into the hospital.

"If the wind will let us," muttered one of the men.

I forced myself to focus on the here, the now, thrusting other awarenesses to the margins. Carefully, making sure my body blocked my actions from view, I got my bone-handled knife from my pocket. Carefully, I clenched my teeth on the spine and opened the blade. I tried to focus on the rope in my hand, but I could not see... I shifted my eyes. There! Using the small space of clarity between my glittering peripheral vision and the void in the centre, I got the rope in my sites.

A great gust of wind roared overhead, and one of the men cried out. They all threw themselves into the rope, hauling hard.

And with one swift movement, I slashed the fibres with my little knife.

Bless that sharp little blade my father had given me. The rope parted with never a sound, and the balloon was aloft.

"Kemp! Mr. Kemp, sir!" the men called out.

Both Kemp and Marconi came out of the building.

"God's eyes!" Kemp swore.

It was almost impossible to see between the void and the glittering zig-zags bisecting the world. But I saw—and sensed— the screaming multitudes riding the balloon as it tore off across Signal Hill.

I went after it.

Of course I didn't imagine I had the strength to haul that balloon down by myself. I wanted only to keep those filthy yammering creatures within my sight. The shimmering balloon sailed gaily up toward Ladies Lookout, and I went after it.

It seemed to me that fog shrouded the hillock, like a gauzy dress slipping off a lady's shoulder. Where was the balloon? Surely I hadn't lost it. I shut my eyes. Arcing pulses of shattered light burst behind my eyelids.

Yes, I could hear Them. Over there, just where the fog grew thicker, a great yammering crowd of Them. I followed.

Over here... over here...

My feet stumbled over rocks; the land was climbing. That pulse came through the rocks again, the funeral march.

"I freed you! Now you do for me! Let my mother go."

Their utterance became non-verbal, a creaking door. I'd heard it all my life. *Oooour... ouuuuur... oooour... ouuuur...*

The funeral march grew louder, more insistent.

A sound: carriage wheels and horses' hooves on cobblestones. Yet there was only snow and rock, no road here.

It was a funeral procession, hearse driven by the Reverend! Resplendent in a gauzy white gown of the style popular when my grandmother was a girl—tight at the waist, long, full skirt—his neck and shoulders were smooth and bare. And he shone with a wonderful mess of jewellery: strings of pearls encircling his throat, rings on every finger and his thumbs. His feet were shod with crimson ladies' slippers embroidered in crystals and gold thread, his mustache was elaborately curled, and he wore a top hat. He looked marvellously beautiful.

The coffin was open on top of the hearse, as if the body inside were being waked at home in a parlour, not drawn to a burial. The contraption came to a halt. I approached, standing up on my tiptoes to look inside.

The coffin contained no body. Instead, it held my mother's red sweater, inside out.

Oooour... ouuuuur... oooour... ouuuur...

I understood, now.

My mother was held prisoner in the gut of the house. And I knew, now, what the door, the mouth of the house, had been telling me, all these many years. *Oooour... ouuuuur... oooour... ouuuur...*

You're ours. You're ours. You're ours.

THE GIRL IN THE BED

When I was small, my parents took me on a trip across the island to visit Father's family. On the way we detoured to Cape St. Mary's. It seemed an endless journey, and after being jolted half to death on the road I wondered why on earth they thought we should go there. We had tea and fruitcake at some lady's house in a nearby community; I got the impression she was a distant relative of my mother's. And then we'd had to walk for a long, long time, across barrens and bog, until something in the air had begun to throb. I felt it before I heard it; the air beat against my cheek in constant vibration. Only slowly did you become aware of it as a sound.

And then, a smell, rank and sharp.

Gradually, as we got close to the sea, the sound sharpened, became a vast, yammering cry. The smell grew to an unbearable stink. We began to follow a sheep's path along the tops of the cliffs.

"Pay attention, here," my mother had said to me. "Don't stray from the path. If you fall, there's nothing either of us will be able do about it. You'll just die. You'll be dead, and that's all."

Thus warned, I had edged along the path with such caution that my parents—striding ahead—soon left me behind.

The tops of the cliffs were green, and the ocean was blue, and the sky was dark as sapphire. Across the cove I could see sheep, white against the dark cliffs, leaping fearlessly from ledge to ledge.

What was that great throbbing yammer? And what was that smell? It stank like a dead bird I had once found, and buried, only to dig up days later out of morbid curiosity. Maggots had swarmed out of the thing, and the smell... it was like that now, or the closest thing I could compare to it, only much, much vaster, a stench so strong you expected it to bend the air.

The distant figures of my parents had come to a halt, looking at something in the sea.

I came up, gasping from the stench. But all my complaints died on the sight: a great white knuckle of rock, rising sheer from the ocean far below. All over it were birds, birds, birds. Gannets they were, big white birds with black-tipped wings and gorgeous creamy yellow heads, and a perfect black line around their blue, blue eyes. Their beaks were pale blue-grey, looking as though they'd been dipped in tempera and outlined in black, like a stained glass window.

The stink was their droppings, staining the grey rocks white. The sound filled the air and my head and everything else; they all spoke together in one continuous yammer.

That was the closest thing I had now to describe the yammer of the Things that surrounded me. I was trapped, taken prisoner by it, and I'd never get out.

"Caw! Caw!" Across the fog and glitter shot a black, feathered bullet. Oberon! And back he came again. Every time he passed, his trail cut a swathe of clarity through the black fog and glittering light that pulsed through my brain. Every flight was a swipe against the glamour, a blow in a campaign for clarity.

At last the yammering and the shimmer were all wiped away.

I stood, teetering on the brink of a cliff on top of Ladies Lookout. The sea pounded hungrily, nearly six hundred feet below me. The fog was gone.

Is this what had happened to my mother? Was my father right, and in the fog she'd fallen off a cliff to her death, swept out to sea? We'd never find the body. The currents here were something awful...

"Caw!"

I saw myself as if in a dream, from above. The girl lay in the bed, with her shorn head. She was thrashing in her sleep.

And then I fell off the cliff. I'd fall into the water, or be dashed on the rocks below...

I landed, in my body.

I was back in my bedroom, dressed in my nightgown, spread out on my bed.

MAD FOR TRICKS

Night fell, and day dawned again before I was able to move. Vague impressions came and went: my father rising, laying his hand on my forehead, and weeping; stars wheeling outside my window; the sky paling, stars winking out. And all the time, the wind rose. It howled around the house. The house shook, the timbers swayed. The wind was a live thing, an unchained beast with the house in its jaws. The noise was tremendous, so loud I almost didn't hear the sound of a crow on the windowsill.

He rapped at the window with his beak, insistent, penetrating, until I finally sat up.

Why was my neck so cold?

My hand went up, felt the shorn hair there.

Memories came charging back. My mother in the night. The Reverend. Hitting my head. Poor father, his vigil in his chair. Marconi. The kite, the balloon.

Them.

And if I believed my vision, Mother. Trapped by Them, below the house.

Below me now.

Rap rap rap! Oberon glared through the window.

I opened the sash. The cold, hungry wind sent its teeth into the room, ripping the covers from my bed and sending my nightgown flapping.

"Caw! It's a regular screecher!" He hopped inside. I shut the window, panes rattling angrily.

"You better get dressed. It's a big day, big day." He laughed inordinately, as if this was the funniest thing he'd ever heard.

"Shhh!" But my father did not wake. His face worked and worried as he slept, propped up in the chair by my bedside.

Oberon crooned. "He has been at your bedside all this time."

Was it some magic Oberon wrought, to keep my father sleeping? My heart gave a pang.

But, obedient to Oberon's impatience, I got into my clothes. As for my hair, all it took was a bit of water from the washstand rubbed through it. Lowering my head, I examined my wound. The stitches were beginning to itch, and the top of my head felt tight; but there was no redness. It was healing. One rake of my fingers through my hair to cover the shaven patch, and on the cap went. I was dressed.

I stared at myself in the mirror. Yes, I liked this short-hair version of Dor.

"I never want to wear a dress with a thousand tiny buttons ever again so long as I live—and as for corsets, I'd like to see someone try to get me into one of those..."

A creeping feeling crawled over my skin, then. What of the girl I'd seen in the bed?

There wasn't anybody in the room but myself and my sleeping father.

"How did I get home yesterday?" I asked Oberon.

"We got you home, the Reverend and I. Very touch and go. But you landed, you landed."

The wind outside moaned and skirled, shaking the house, rattling the washstand.

"But... who was the girl in the bed?"

"Girl?" Oberon put his head to one side, looking at me like I was a bedlamer. "You, of course."

"How can I be two places at once?"

But before he answered, I realized I already knew. Nan King's card reading, Clare's voice whispering in my ear. *Leave the spirit lying in bed, while the body walks...*

If only Clare were with me now. I could stand anything if she was by my side.

Oberon hopped up onto my shoulder, nibbling my ear.

I would be all right, I told myself. It's not just anybody that wins the trust of a talking crow.

And my mother was counting on me, for I was her only hope. Poor Mother, what a poor hope that was.

With one last look at Father, I crept down the stairs.

On my way through the kitchen I saw another offering left by a pitying neighbour—boiled dinner, and more thick slabs of figgy duff. My stomach rumbled so loudly it almost drowned out the wind. I hadn't had a thing the day before, I realized. I seized a bowl and spoon from the sideboard and stuffed myself, thinking I had never tasted anything so delicious; Oberon too looked contented after glutching down a chunk of meat and some carrot. I forced myself to leave some dinner and one of the slabs of duff for my father for when he woke.

"Hurry, now," Oberon said. "The Reverend is waiting at the bridge."

"Is he coming with us?" Hope sprang up in my heart.

"He has technical details he wishes to convey." Oberon opened his beak and jerked his body, laughing his crow laughter.

When I opened the door it almost tore out of my hand. The wind pressed my breath back into my body; I had to turn away to gulp air into my lungs. Oberon leapt up and got caught by a gust; twisting, he fought the air.

As we descended, I saw that a small, bent, beautiful being awaited us at the foot of the Long Bridge. He seemed to float rather than stand, dressed in the outfit I'd seen the day before. *Seen, or dreamed?* I wondered. The long, white, voluminous dress, the top hat. His concession to the bitter gale was a gauzy wrap thrown around his tilted shoulders.

"Aren't you freezing?" I ran up to him, breathless in the wind.

"Silk. Marvellously warm," he said, wafting the wrap in my direction. "May I congratulate you, Dor? Wonderful work, yesterday. It was all confirmed."

And how did his hat stay on in this gale? "What was?"

He waltzed asymmetrically about me, skirts swaying perilously. "Marconi attempted to receive signals, did he not?"

I nodded.

"Well did I know it! It was bedlam. They went mad, yammering and screeching and bawling. A din the likes of which you've never heard."

The fog, the confusion, and most of all, my failure.

"They were furious, Reverend. And I let Them go. I..." Shame flashed through me. "I cut the balloon. But They wouldn't do what I asked! They said They had her. They have my mother. I saw the coffin! *You're ours*, They said!"

Tears blinded me.

"I can't do it. I can't!"

"Now, Dor. Certainly you can. You *are* doing it, don't you see?"

I shook my head.

"That coffin—it wasn't an omen. That was just some glamour They cast. They're trying to lead you astray!"

"A glamour?"

"Take it as a compliment. They'd never attempt trickery if They didn't know you were on the right track."

"A compliment." I folded my arms tightly across my chest, as if that was the only way to keep my hammering heart inside the cage of my ribs.

"They're in for it. It's bad when someone generates signals, even as far away as Cornwall. But yesterday I finally understood: it all gets far worse for Them when someone tries to receive. And Marconi's reception system here is completely improvised. Kites and balloons! It simply isn't sensitive or reliable enough." He stopped waltzing, standing on tip-toe to place his hands on my shoulders. "That's your weapon, your bargaining chip, Dor— Marconi's attempts to receive the signals."

"It didn't work yesterday," I spat.

"Remember your knife. They don't like cold iron." The Reverend spun in a single graceful pirouette, then flung his hands into the air. "Oh, goodness, I nearly forgot. Very important. Don't let Them go until They've promised three times."

"Uh... three times?"

He waved his hand. "It's simply a thing, threes. They can't resist anything that comes in three."

"All right." Despite myself, his words set a warm glow of painful hope alight in my breast.

"And then, once you've made Them promise to let your mother go—in perpetuity, mind, They're mad for tricks—make Them promise liberty to you, *and* all your family, from now on and into the future until the world's end."

I was struck by another obstacle. "But Reverend! The house is on Their path!" Another impossible burden falling upon my shoulders. "Everybody says so, except Mother. And she's the one They've trapped..." I wanted to weep.

"One thing at a time, Dor," the Reverend said gently. "And I have a feeling..."

He lifted his eyes toward the Hill. I followed his gaze. The old, dark house perched on the Top above the slope of scree, shuddering in the wind.

"The matter of the house may take care of itself."

I forced myself to meet his eyes. "I hope so."

"I do too, child."

He twirled around and around, skirts spinning out like an inverted lily. With a flourish he came to a swaying stop, and stood on tiptoe to softly kiss my cheek.

The despair battering my body subsided.

Then the impossible, regal little figure set off down the road, skirts belling in the wind. He raised one hand without looking back, waving farewell. As he went, small, rectangular objects began to fly out of his hand toward me in a line, spindrifting through the air like autumn leaves. I caught one in my hand, then another, and another...

Jack of Spades, every one.

A dark-haired youth, well-meaning but unreliable, jealous and stubborn and quick. I started to laugh.

This was my day, as Nanny King had foreseen.

Marconi was high-strung that morning. His manner was still polite and unassuming. But beneath that he was a string on a violin, stretched and ready to sing, or snap. He and Kemp ensconced themselves in the hospital building for two hours, making arcane adjustments to their equipment, Kemp occasionally sallying outside to measure wire and check the kites.

At a little before eleven o'clock, Kemp gathered the men and myself in the lee of a knob of rock. "Sorry for the delay, gentlemen."

"Where's Mr. Paget?" I asked.

"Mr. Paget is too ill to be with us today," Kemp announced briskly.

"Poor fella," a man said. "Had a sick turn, did he?"

"Yes." Kemp looked nervously at the hospital building, where Marconi still lurked. "Now, as you know, we got a balloon up yesterday, but lost it in that blustery wind. Same with a kite, the day before. However, on the whole Mr. Marconi thinks our best bet is the kites."

"It's a right gusty gale today, sir," said one of the men. He was right. The wind could cut you in half.

Kemp nodded. "Nevertheless, we shall try it."

"Yessir, yessir," we all said.

"We have to try for a good height, and keep the kite there, more or less steady, for as long as possible. Some hours, even."

"How high?" I asked.

"At least four hundred feet."

I started to whistle, then, remembering the day before, suppressed it. The hired men made up for it, however, variously whistling, swearing, and rubbing their chafed hands through their gloves.

"Well, Mr. Kemp, we'll do our best," said the tall one. "We shall earn our pay today, b'ys!"

"When do we start?" I asked.

"Immediately. We expect signals to begin transmission in half an hour, and they will go on until this afternoon at regular intervals." He wagged his finger at me. "No sailing off with Mr. Marconi's equipment today, young man."

"Nossir," I said, hanging my head in a melodramatic show of sorrow. "Sorrysir."

Everyone laughed.

"Well, to work!"

At eleven precisely, flashes of parti-coloured light began stabbing at the corners of my eyes.

The station back in Cornwall had begun transmission.

The men took hold of a kite with two wires attached, each—according to the stalwart Kemp—five hundred and ten feet in length. Kemp stood in the leeward side of the kite sail, holding onto the frame.

We waited.

The flashes of light on the periphery of my vision became long, stabbing blades of shattered rainbow.

Marconi emerged, pocket watch in his hand. "Now, Mr. Kemp!"

Kemp released the kite, and the three men threw themselves onto the cord.

The wind was a long, lowering rush from the north, a great flattening pressure, and the kite bucked and pulled, hurting even the men's tough hands through the gloves.

"Sure, me hands are all rined out!" one complained cheerfully. They couldn't get the kite up as high as the one on the first day. But they were hard men, used to work, and clung doggedly to the cord.

I waited. As before, the light shimmers coalesced into an arc joining earth and heaven. And at the centre of my vision bloomed a black void, a flower of nothing.

The pulsing started in the rock beneath my feet. A spectral piano sang in the wind.

Oberon came and perched on my shoulder. "Do you hear it hear it?" he chirruped in my ear.

I nodded, peering between void and light, the small area of my vision that could still perceive the natural world.

There! Clustered up and down the cord, and all over the kite too! Diving around Marconi! Couldn't he sense Them? They were in pain and rage, stabbing down at him. He was speaking, but I couldn't hear his words over the pulsing, yammering cries of pain.

Let us go!

Every time he opened his mouth They dove inside, only to be spat out again by his breath. Every gesture of his hands, a miasma of sparkling beings swirled and sucked, pounding against him like waves against a towering cliff. *Let us go!*

"I will do it!" I said. "Only let my mother go!"

The arcing, pulsing jagged light soared high into the sky, raining down on me.

How? How? How?

The anguish in Their voices moved me, despite everything. "I will cut the cord," I said. "But you have to promise to let my mother go, and leave us in peace, forever!"

No! You're... ours... you're... ours...

"Fry, then!" I spat.

With a great wailing cry, the bits of light poured back onto the kite. The wind crashed and boomed; even the ground shook.

No, no, no! The note of the squealing went higher and higher. The shrieking rose until I clapped my hands to my ears and fell to my knees.

And then the cord of the kite, on its own, snapped in two.

The shrieks changed to laughter. The kite broke away, and sailed down Signal Hill, covered in shining multitudes.

THE CHANCE

You're... ours... you're... ours... you're... ours...

My mother would live forever in that hole beneath our cursed house, unless I bound the tricksy creatures. "Oberon!" I panted. "We have to find the kite!"

The men were too occupied by the operation of raising another kite to pay any attention to a barely useful errand boy. I left at a dead run, pushed by the wind, trying to outrun the pace of the growing distortion in my vision.

I spotted the white sail of the kite almost immediately. It lay on the rocks beneath Gibbet Hill, on the shore of Deadman's Pond.

Clare's wicked, mischievous bams ran through my head: criminals, the gibbet, barrel of nails, rolling down. The supposed bottomlessness of the pond.

But a bottomless pond was impossible. *This is science,* I knew my mother would say. *Ridiculous.* She, supremely confident, had no trouble reconciling her eldritch family history with science.

In a split minute my feet had carried me down from Cabot Tower—past the large expanse of frozen bog around George's Pond—to a small, weedy, haunted round of black water. Deadman's Pond.

The kite twitched in the wind like a dying animal. The air pulsed in time. Tiny, light-shattered beings crawled over the downed kite, coalescing, taking shape.

Diminutive people, they seemed now, like those I'd seen in the kitchen—dressed head to toe in grey, with red caps on their heads—twenty of them, maybe more. Half looked like men, dancing in one circle; sham women danced in another.

The soles of their shoes flashed under the slate-grey sky as they rompsed on the kite, victorious and mocking. They tripped to a tune shared between them and to which I was deaf. It had the same tempo, I realized, as the funeral march.

They were dancing to the music of my captive mother.

You're ours, you're ours, you're ours!

"Now's your chance!" Oberon cawed.

"To do what?" but my body was already skirting the edge of the pond. No time to think. Clutching my pocket knife, I flung myself forward and grasped the edge of the fallen kite. I used the iron blade to cut the frame from the sail. Then I flung the edge of the sail upward like I was spreading a sheet on a bed, sending the small dancers flying into the air with shrieks of rage.

They landed on the kite. And I rolled it up, swift as I could. I rolled it up, and pressed the iron blade of my knife to the mass with Them trapped inside of it, like I had my blade on the jugular of a murderer.

The kite thrashed and churned, firking and rolling. I hung on, knife jerking, the Little Strangers wriggling and shrieking and yammering inside. They didn't like to be bound, and They didn't like cold iron nor steel, no, not one bit.

"I'll let you go. Only free my mother!"

Black nothingness bled across my eyes. Yammering serpent and all, I was sucked into the roiling kite.

It was as I had dreamt before, darkness and stone. And Mother was there. She drank brackish water from a seashell as if it was the finest wine. She ate a living snail, crunching its shell. And all around her, babies mewled. Stolen and murdered, all these years, taken. All unknowing we had been paying a tribute—a toll—for the house was on Their path.

"Mother!" I cried out. "Mother! It's your Dor!"

She stopped, eyes shifting. She reached up with her hand and touched her left eye, and blinked.

"Don't believe what you see. They've got you, Mother."

She saw me, then. Her left eye lit on me, and took in her surroundings, the cave. Awareness dawning. Horror.

"I'll save you! Mother!"

But I was being pulled away. It was like being pulled backward through a drain, shredded through a sieve. I came back to myself, lying on a rolled-up mass of heavy, dirty cotton, knife clutched in fist, vast sail of the kite seething beneath me like a maggot-filled corpse.

I knew They weren't held merely by my arms around a kite, nor by the iron in my blade. For I could feel it too. The signals had Them in their grip. All the way from Cornwall, generated by some kind of hulking power station of Marconi's devising, the signals stabbed through the Strange Ones, torturing Them. And in such close proximity to Them, the signals jabbed at me. I could see the signals, and hear them: atmospheric noise, harmonics, electrical hash, clicking, and blasts.

"Let her go..." What had the Reverend said? "Promise to let my mother, and myself, and all my family alone, now and into the future, until the world's end!"

Such a screeching, bawling, frenzied caterwaul! I wondered the whole city wasn't transfixed by it.

"Promise!"

Free us... Their voices whispered and echoed, trees creaking in the wind, water hushing on a strange and distant shore.

"Let my mother go."

We relinquish her.

"And all my family for ever more!"

We relinquish you all.

"Again!"

We relinquish you all.

My lungs burned, my eyes blazed with spectral fire. "Forever!"

We relinquish you all.

The seething mass in my arms suddenly deflated. I heard laughter again, but not mocking, not triumphant.

It was gleeful.

Looking up, I thought I saw the air glowing high above me, vibrant swaths of red and green, purple and yellow light.

I closed my knife. "Did we do it?" I gasped to Oberon.

"I think so," he murbled. "I believe... we did. But something else has happened too."

"What is it?"

"I don't know." He cocked his head, looking up into the sky. "I don't know."

Silently, I gathered the kite up into a roll—empty, now, no longer writhing with power. I felt tired, tired in my mind and tired to the marrow of my bones.

Something called to me across the harbour. It was too hard, now, to stay split like this, body and spirit. It was time to rest.

But had I succeeded? Or was my mother still trapped?

Oberon flew ahead of me as I lugged the downed kite to the top of Signal Hill. Without him, I doubt I would have made it. I rode his wake like a goose on the slipstream of a fellow traveller.

The atmosphere on the summit was electric. The men still clung to the yawing kite, but Kemp—phlegmatic Kemp—had his arms in the air, and was dancing a jig. Marconi looked on, calmly triumphant.

"We did it!" Kemp shouted. "Three clicks! Three clicks!"

Oberon flew ahead, lighting over the doorway.

Marconi turned, disappearing into the old hospital. Dropping the kite sail in the shelter of the wall, I boldly followed him inside.

The warmth was heavenly after the howling wind. I stumbled up to the stove, rubbing my hands. The wire running through the window frame, attached to the wavering and unsteady aerial suspended by the kite, was attached itself to a strange mechanical device: two blocks of rich, red wood, with something like a bell, and a brass cylinder, and wires on top.

"That's the coherer," Marconi said, noting the direction of my gaze. "The tapper struck it." He stared into the wall, seeing something that wasn't there. "The tapper struck."

Then he turned his strange, intense eyes on me.

"Kemp heard it too. Three clicks. We shall listen again…" he consulted his pocket watch. "At ten minutes past one. Another signal should arrive then."

He seemed very calm for someone who had just changed the world.

"I am convinced," I said, intoning in my best English accent, "that the Martians interchanged thoughts without any physical intermediation."

His mouth quirked. *"War of the Worlds?"*

"H. G. Wells, yes, sir! Have you read it?"

"Of course. But it bears no relation to my work."

The wind roared outside, but in here the atmosphere was quiet, even homey. I let my eyes play over the array of wires and equipment on the battered old hospital table. "But it'd be exciting, wouldn't it, sir?"

He inclined his head. "To receive vibrations from other planets in outer space, older, wiser beings who could give us knowledge of the mystery of life? Certainly."

"But, hopefully, without voracious blood-sucking propensities."

He uttered a short, sharp laugh. "Science is discovering new things all the time. There are things we are just beginning to understand." He drifted over to the stove, and stood at my side. "There are more things in Heaven and Earth, Horatio, than are dreamt of in your philosophy."

I was thrilled to be noticed by him. This was how his charisma worked, I thought, or part of it. You just wanted him to pay attention to you; his regard seemed a great prize. He almost never smiled, too, that was another thing. It came off like a challenge, to make that man smile.

"Like two worlds," he said. He held up both forefingers, touching them tip to tip, then slid them alongside each other. "One inside the other."

I mimicked him, laying my fingers together like two stacked twigs. "Like two worlds..." My breath came short. Two worlds, alongside each other. Like the creatures of light alongside this new, revolutionary science. Like the world I walked in, along with everybody else most of the time, and the uncanny other world that had seized on my mother.

Trying for composure, I quoted Wells again. "With infinite complacency men went to and fro over this globe about their little affairs, serene in their assurance of their empire over matter."

A smile—a smile!—quirked his lips.

Swift as a snake, he gripped my fingers in his fist.

I gave an involuntary cry, trying to jerk my hands away, but his hold was strong. Nor could I pull my fingers apart.

"Well, *boy*," he said. "I've got you in Chinese handcuffs."

I stifled a desire to cry out again, and pulled so hard my knuckles cracked.

"What will you do now?" he said softly.

I glared. "Kick you in the shins, sir."

He smirked. "Oh, I don't think so." And then his free hand darted down.

His palm struck and left my fork in no more time than it took to draw a breath.

"Ah." He stared into my face. "I thought so. I must admit, your disguise is effective. I don't think the others suspect a thing."

Rage and shame washed through me. Willing myself to stop struggling, I let my arms and hands go limp. I sensed his grasp lightening, just the slightest bit.

In one convulsive movement I tore my fingers from his fist, and backed away from him, panting. "What does it matter to you?" I demanded.

"What's your name, young lady?"

My back was to the door, now. "What difference does it make? Would a *boy* have done better?"

"Come, now. I won't tell. Your secret is safe with me. What's your real name?" Oh, the laughter in his eyes!

"What odds?"

He smirked. "I am simply curious. I suppose too that you are not the *sister* of the ravishing Mary?"

I glared.

"Never mind. You are young. I must advise you, however, that attempts to impersonate the masculine will lead only to heartbreak and peril. It is a degeneracy not to be indulged. It would bring dishonour to your family."

His eyes narrowed, and his mouth made a moue of disgust.

"If you were a daughter of mine, young lady, I'd whip you." And he turned away.

How I loathed that phrase, *young lady.* I wanted to tell him! How I was unable to find any comfort or self-recognition in the idea of 'female'. How most other girls navigated it— or seemed to—but I simply didn't understand it, no matter how much I might want to. *Young lady* denoted limits, failure, imprisonment, watchfulness, miserable clothes, incomprehension, humiliation, and danger. I wanted to make him understand.

But I couldn't find the words. There were no words to describe my state.

And in any case, why should he care?

"They won't believe you!" I growled defiance at his back.

He caressed the Bell receiver. "Possibly. You may be right. They may not believe me. But I think they will."

My fork throbbed dully where he'd struck it. "Why should you tell? What does it *matter*, sir?"

"Matter?" He stared at me. "It will change the world!" He went to the window and leaned on the sill, gazing out. "If only the damn inker had been able to record..."

Suddenly I saw it. His accomplishment was on his mind now, not my impersonation. He'd confirmed his hunch about me, and was satisfied. He'd moved on.

"So, you did it." I tried to flatten the rage from my voice. "You received signals from... Pole Dew?"

"For all intents and purposes, yes. I did it."

"As far as the world will be concerned."

The vagueness in his eyes focused on me again. "I suppose it is rather like proposing to build a cathedral in a world which has never seen anything more grandiose than a log hut."

Slowly, I nodded.

It seemed we both had secrets, Marconi and I.

Just after one o'clock, Kemp came bustling into the building, cheeks red with cold.

I had a moment of agony, waiting for Marconi to expose me.

"Is the kite at height?" he asked Kemp, all business.

There was nothing on his mind but the signals.

Kemp nodded, rubbing his hands. "They're good men. It's bloody cold outside, and that wind keeps dropping and surging. Very gusty, sir."

I made to slip out of the room, but Marconi stopped me. "Stay here, *boy*." The emphasis was slight, but noticeable. I froze like a rabbit. "We could use your ears."

Turning back, I sidled over to the stove, eyes on him.

Silence filled the room. Nothing but the whistling, booming wind outside, the soft shifts in the wood stove, and Kemp's rasping breath.

Marconi had his watch in his hand, and his eyes didn't leave it.

My eyes went to the coherer. He'd said that the "tapper"—whatever that was—had struck when the first signals came in. Would it happen again now?

Marconi picked up the butterstamp receiver and put it to his ear, raising a finger. Kemp held his breath. I realized I was holding mine too.

Outside, Oberon let out a caw.

And the tapper struck.

Marconi stiffened. "Three clicks! Here!" and handed the thing to Kemp.

Kemp ground the receiver to his ear like he was trying to flatten it to his skull, his red face crinkling with concentration.

"I think... yes?"

"Give it to the boy!"

Startled, Kemp passed the receiver to me. I almost dropped the thing with shock. Marconi nodded at me impatiently.

I pressed the receiver to my ear.

It was a bit like listening to a phonograph recording—there was static, crackling interference, and a heaving sound, like a child's breath. The breath of poor Theo, the night before he died.

And then, I heard three clicks.

I snapped my head up, meeting Marconi's eyes.

Three more.

And again.

I nodded.

Marconi seized the receiver from me and pressed it to his ear. "It's definite. The boy could hear, and so can I." Taking out a notebook, he scribbled some notes. I leaned over. The note was: *Sigs at 12.30 1.10X.*

Was the X for me?

"Congratulations, sir," I said.

He scribbled some more notes, not looking up.

"I'll put a girdle round the earth in forty minutes!" I let my accent come out broad.

"What was that?"

"Shakespeare, sir. Puck from *A Midsummer Night's Dream.*"

"I'll put a girdle round the earth in forty minutes..." Marconi murmured. His eyes went vague on me again. "I'll put a girdle round the earth..." Back to his notes he went.

Kemp gave me the ghost of a smile, and sketched me a salute.

Shortly afterward, the recalcitrant wind died and the kite fell to earth. Kemp brought the men inside to warm themselves, and we were offered hot cocoa, the men with a dash of rum in theirs. They expressed congratulations. Marconi seemed pleased to receive their compliments. But how calm he was!

Not a word did he say about my subterfuge.

"Quite something to be part of this!" one of the men exclaimed.

"More glamourous than making barrels, anyway."

"Naar a bit!" said the third. "I'm a cooper and a cooper's son, and a cooper I shall remain."

Kemp made a gesture that he wanted to talk to me aside. I gulped, heart in mouth—had he, too, seen through me?

But it wasn't that at all.

"I want to thank you, boy, for corroborating the signals. I'm deaf as a haddock, you see. I could tell myself that I'd heard them, but... well, he'll be easier in his mind now, son."

"Th-th-thank you," I hackered. Then I tugged on the bill of my cap. It seemed a boy-like thing to do.

"We couldn't keep the antenna stable enough to use the Morse recorder, which would have inked the signals on a strip of paper, see. So there's no written proof. Just our ears."

And he shook my hand with vigour. I was so limp with relief that I almost forgot to squeeze back.

Shortly after two, the wind came up strong again, and the kite was raised for the final time that afternoon. I watched the men—much more merry, now, with some rum in them and knowing their hard work was almost over—haul on the line at Marconi's signal. The immense white kite sailed up, gleaming against the grey and scuddy clouds.

At twenty minutes past two—according to Kemp's watch—another set of signals was received.

Oberon glided to my shoulder. "They're bouncing," he said.

"They?" But I knew who he meant.

"Caw! In the airglow."

"What's that?"

"High up above the clouds, neither fully Earth nor fully space, where the atmosphere vibrates."

They were bouncing, pulling the signals in Their wake across the ocean. Trapped no more.

I left Signal Hill that day knowing I'd never see Marconi again.

The wind was fierce, and frigidly cold. With every step down the road, I felt myself flagging.

But I had one more task before home. I veered into the *Telegram*. To my delight, Murph was there.

"Look at you! How is my informant?" he said.

"A little the worse for wear."

"Shouldn't you be in school?"

He didn't know, I realized. He didn't know about Mother disappearing, and my broken head, and all. "Don't tell Mary, she'll have us beat all to pieces." I doffed my cap, smoothing the crease of my hair with my hand to cover the wound.

Murph stared in complete horror. "What have you done?"

"Cut my hair," I said, almost adding *idiot* before I stopped myself. "Don't you like it?"

Murph looked around, eyes wild. "God forgive me."

"Murph!" I shook his arm. "I did it, not you. And you know what else?"

His blue eyes, round with shock, looked into mine. "What?"

I leaned in and whispered, "I like it."

Murph moaned and hid his face in his hands.

"Stop it. I have things to tell you! More important than my hair, for the love of God."

He took his face from his hands. "Marconi?" he murmured.

"Yes. Oh, Murph, have I got a story for you."

I told him of overhearing Kemp and Marconi talking about signals from a place with a strange name, Pole Dew. And that Marconi had confirmed it with me.

"Poldhu!" he exclaimed, writing it down on his pad so I could see the spelling of it. "That's the name of the town in Cornwall where Marconi's built his beast of a station at the Lizard. Poldhu."

"And today, they did it. They received signals. And I heard them!"

"*You* heard them?" Murph exclaimed. Then he looked around the office, and leaned in, repeating his question more quietly. "You heard them?"

"He asked me to." I couldn't keep the pride from my voice. "Kemp is a bit deaf, you see, and Paget was ill, and the Morse code inker wasn't able to be used—something about the coherer, or something, not being sensitive enough. They used a modified Bell telephone receiver."

Murph seized a pencil and scribbled notes wildly. "What did they sound like?"

I thought. "There was this other noise all through it. Breathy, and scratchy. Sad."

"A sad noise?" He looked at me like I was a bedlamer.

My poor Theo. "Very faint. Like a dying child."

"Like a dying child..." He scribbled. "That's good. A quiver like an angel's breath ... low as the whisper of a dying child at first, but in half a minute gaining strength..." He looked up. "What exactly did you hear? I mean, aside from the breathy, scratchy, sad sounds?"

"Three clicks."

"Three clicks!"

"Over and over. Marconi heard them, then he passed the receiver to Kemp, who thought he heard it, but he wasn't sure. So he passed the receiver to me. I definitely heard three clicks, repeated."

"The letter S! Morse code..." More mad scribbling. "What ravishing music they made... Electrically charged kites whirling in the storm-tossed air over Signal Hill..."

I hesitated. "And Murph... he figured it out. That I'm..." Words stuck in my throat. "A girl, I mean."

"He did! How?"

I shook my head. "I don't know. But... he didn't tell the others."

"Well, good, then."

"You'd better not mention me in your article." It occurred to me that the knowledge of my subterfuge implicated Murph. "I'm sorry," I said miserably.

"Dor, me ducky! Don't give it another thought. Whether he thinks he knows anything or not doesn't signify now. He's done it! I'm going to telegraph the *New York Times*!" He sprang to his feet, embracing me. "Dor, you're a wonder!" And he rushed out the door in a frenzy, even forgetting his hat.

ROOTS OF THE HOUSE

Oberon flew near me all the rest of the way home. I was glad of it, for I felt faint and logy. He too seemed subdued. He'd fly ahead, then perch, wind ruffling his feathers, waiting for me to catch up before taking another swift dart ahead. The wind had driven almost everyone from the streets, and the few there were took no notice of us. We were like two ghosts.

This split self couldn't go on for much longer. It was time to bind my body and spirit together again.

I just hoped I could.

Crossing the Long Bridge I was forced to cling to the railing. The gale battered and pushed at me; I could almost lean my whole weight against the wind and be held up in defiance of gravity.

I made it down the Southside and up the Hundred Steps up to the Range—oh, how I longed to see Clare, and tell her everything!

And then that long straggle of a boardwalk leading up to the Top, the ledge to which my great-great-grandfather, during the Winter of the Rals, had hauled our house. Towed it across the harbour, up the Hill, and over the spring, backing it into the living rock of the Hill. *Grandfather said this house settled right in*, Grandmother had told me. *It just uncoiled. As if it had been waiting for him to bring it to its rightful place.*

I stumbled up the final dilapidated stairs of the Ratline, trudged along the side of the house. Oberon sliced through the wind over my head, perching on the still-unrepaired linney roof. The door hung open, as usual, heaving in the wind.

The clapboard creaked, loose tarpaper flapped. Cloud shredded and raced overhead, layer upon layer of purple and grey. Even the Hill itself seemed to shudder in the wind.

You're... ours... You're... ours... You're... ours...

I went through that sawing chaw of a door.

And there was a great, groaning sound, and I felt the roots of the house move.

I'd watched ships go into dry dock. Once, as a big schooner had been lifted, I'd heard this sound, like a trumpet of Heaven or Hell. The room shook, windows rattling. I grasped onto the doorframe.

Oberon cawed, three sharp alarms.

The house groaned again, and this time, I saw the cliff outside the linney shift away.

I screamed.

"Dor!" My father, a terrible note of panic in his deep voice.

Dishes slid in the sideboard. The house shuddered, timbers creaking and groaning. One of the kitchen chairs fell over, and I heard things sliding about on the floor above me.

"Father!" I leapt across the kitchen and up the stairs.

I was thrown to the side of the staircase, bashing my shoulder against the wall. The bedroom door was jerking open and closed, like an unseen hand had ahold of it; then I saw my father's familiar frame in the doorway. Two more steps and I was in his arms.

The house swayed.

There was nothing outside my bedroom window but sky.

I screamed again.

"Stay in the doorway!" Father gasped, bracing us.

The room tilted violently. The nightstand slid, coming up against the wall with a rattle, and the chamber pot under my bed—mercifully empty—went bowling across the floor. The bed slewed sideways, the chair fell over—

There was a great wrenching sound from the kitchen below, and a jerk that rattled my teeth.

With a noise as of a vast dragon uncoiling, slate scales shifting and clinking together, the house began to slide.

For a moment I was back up on the Hill in the silver thaw, sliding upside down and backwards toward a crash, everything jerking and juddering. Father braced himself against the doorframe; he held me so tight that I could scarcely breathe. The sound was a train, a ship in a storm, the opening of the gates of Hell. I think I screamed again. I wouldn't have been able to hear myself if I had.

There was another jolt, and I saw stars.

And then... silence.

WHICH AM I?

"Dor." My father blinked. "I thought I'd lost you."

We sagged together, huddled in the doorframe. Everything was crooked, slid to the front end of the house. But we were no longer moving.

"Where were you, my pet? I woke up and you were gone."

Tears pushed at my eyes and occluded my throat. "There was something I had to do."

Where was Mother? Had I failed? Had it all been for naught?

"Let me get a look at you..."

"Do you like my new rig-out?" I puffed out my chest, trying for a smile.

"Rather fine, Dor. Rather fine indeed."

"I stole them off of Clint. Well, Clare gave them to me." I dared a look up at him. "I like them." Marconi's words echoed in my head. *If you were a daughter of mine, young lady, I'd whip you.*

What he said next changed everything. "You are a marvellous child. Daughter or son, what odds. The best a man could ask for."

I began to cry in earnest. "Which am I? Which, Father?"

"Don't cry, little Dor. You've got both inside; both, you know."

How had my father known this about me, this feeling, deeper than words? I had never given him credit.

ON THE VERGE

"What do you say we go—very carefully, mind!—and find out where in hell this house has landed?"

I gulped. "What if we slide into the harbour?"

"Best get outside before that happens." Gingerly, he stepped out of the doorframe, never letting go of my hand. "With scrutility, now."

Ever so carefully, we tiptoed down the stairs to the kitchen.

All the furniture was tipped to the wall, and some dishes had smashed on the flagstones. "You stay there," he cautioned, leaving me at the foot of the stair. He moved smartly to the coal stove and looked all around it to see if any coals had jumped free. "It hasn't shifted, it's against the wall anyways," he said, relieved.

"Father!" I exclaimed. "The pump's gone!"

"Why, so it is." There was only a gaping hole in the flagstone floor where once it had stood.

"I'll check out the linney door, see where we are." Seeing his protest, I cut him off at the pass. "I'm lighter," I pointed out.

"Go carefully."

The linney floor groaned as I stepped on it. The damn door had slammed shut. I held my breath as I undid the latch.

It opened. There, right outside the door, was a smooth, flat place.

"Father? I think you want to come and take a look at this."

The entire house had slid down the Hill. We'd come up short on the verge of the Southside Road.

HAPPY FAMILY

"Taken down by a landslide."

We sat around the kitchen table, my parents and I. We were recovering from a grand scoff of food sent up by Mrs. Taylor. And they were arguing. Just like old times.

My father was taking the position that it was somehow Mother's fault that the house had shifted, since it had been her ancestor who'd built it. "We could have been killed. Crushed by a piano. For example!"

"But we weren't," she snapped. "Were we?"

"Or worse. If the thing had overturned... It's a miracle we survived. Miracle. Shoved off a ledge by the wind!"

That ledge now was bare. Beach rocks—which my great-great-grandfather had laid beneath the foundations—lay exposed, meandering across the ledge like an abandoned creek bed. And sticking out, just in front of the cliff, was the pump from the kitchen. Clear water poured out around it in a geyser of diamond crystals, surging forward, falling down the Hill like a rattle of pure white gems.

Behind the spring gaped a black, dank hole. My mother had been down there, I knew. They'd had her down there, bedazzled with glamour and spells.

But now all three of us were home.

The only damage was scrapes and dings on furniture slid to the front of the house, a couple of broken plates, one smashed window, a lack of a back wall in the root cellars where the cliff-face had been, and a gaping hole in the kitchen floor where the pump had stood.

And the portrait of my great-great-grandfather had been jolted off the wall, frame splintered.

"I'll miss that spring," my mother sighed, looking at the hole in the kitchen floor.

"We'll have to get plumbing in," Father agreed. And then he reached over and gently tousled my hair.

After he lifted his hand, my mother did the same. She had a speculative look when she gazed upon me.

Father hadn't told her a thing about the boy's clothes. Nor had he quizzed me farther about where I'd been. He told me that I'd been unconscious, in bed, for days. He'd never left my bedside that whole time.

"I had the doctor in twice," he said now, seeing my mother's troubled perusal of the stitches on my head.

"I only remember once," I said. "When he thought there was something wrong with my throat."

Father laughed, remembering the doctor's confusion about my husky timbre, then sobered. "I had him in a second time when you didn't wake again." To my surprise, he wrapped his arms around me. "Thought I'd lost you."

I stiffened a little at the unfamiliarity of a hug. Then I flung my arms around him and returned the embrace.

"He was at my side," I told my mother over his shoulder. "Whenever I woke up, he was always there."

Her look softened, and she reached around me and took my father's hand. We sat there in a knot, and smiled.

A happy family. How does one do that?

And then, there were the events of the past five days.

What did they know?

"Well, it'll be a wonder if I ever leave the house again," Mother said acerbically. "Since you can't even keep it anchored in place or keep your daughter from butchering her beautiful hair when I'm gone. And taking all those days off! It's a wonder you didn't lose your job." She began to rub at her left eye, then dropped her hand. Her eye was swollen, as if infected. "She could have been ki..." Trembling, she put her hand over her mouth.

"You're tired, my dear." Father's voice was kind.

"Yes," she admitted. "I think I need to put a poultice over this eye, and lie down. And you should get back to bed too, young lady." I shuddered at the phrase. "You need to rest," she protested, mistaking the source of my discomfort. "We're burnt to the socket, the two of us."

I trailed after her up the stairs and into her room. "Where were you, Mother? We had a search out, you know."

She nodded, sitting down on the edge of her bed. The red cardigan lay on the coverlet, and she took it up, turning it right-side out. "Strangest thing, losing this. I can't think how that came to happen."

"But where were you?"

Her gaze shifted out the window. "I can't say." She spoke slowly. "I can see the place in my mind. The inside, you know. I developed the notion that I was in one of those estates out in the country, for the house was very grand. A lovely couple. The woman seemed young, but strong, and her husband was very fair..."

She trailed off.

"What happened?"

"No trouble about the birth," she said firmly. Then her eyes went vague again. "They plied me with all kinds of dainties. And wine. I can't think what moved me to accept." Again her hand rose to her swollen left eye. "I remember the husband gave me an ointment. To rub on the baby, he said, a family recipe. But he cautioned me not to get any on myself; gave me gloves to wear. As if I wouldn't wash my hands! But then... I did touch this eye. Didn't I?"

She had. I'd seen it. Her left eye.

"I even thought I saw you, and heard your voice, Dor. Like a little ghost, or... Isn't that silly?"

"I saw you too."

She reached out and clasped my hand. "It's like a dream. I saw, or thought I saw, but only through this eye! The left one. The mansion was no mansion, but a dank cave, and the food and drink was... And they were... It was horrible. All chandeliers and diamonds, but it turned into rocks, and ancient filth, and ice. And then... I think... I got out. A landslide behind me. And I knew then... that the house had shifted, had slid down. And then... and then..."

I could see her struggle to remember, to make two worlds come together.

"And then I was at the Reverend's! He said he'd heard a hammering on his door, and found me dropped on his doorstep." She was remembering, and telling the memory to herself, for the first time. "A crow had found me, if you can believe that, wandering the Hill, and led me to him. The bird was quite concerned. Made a spectacular din, the Reverend said. He cannot tell a truth if he tries, that one." She shook her head. "I need to rest," she said, looking quite unlike her usual upright self.

But then she shuddered, and snapped upright.

"And so do you, young lady. Oh, look at that hair. I don't know what we'll do until it grows."

"I don't want it long. Not ever again," I retorted.

"Dor!"

"It's *my* hair."

"Watch your tone, you saucy flinter!"

Father yelled from upstairs. "Get to bed, the two of you!"

I obeyed.

They might not remember, but I did.

And I had the clothes under my bed, and the burn marks from the kite rope on my wrist, to prove it.

As I drifted into sleep, something nudged at the edges of my consciousness. Something not quite right.

No, it *was* right. Our house, now off the path, was at peace.

UNWORTHY

I spent a long time in bed. I woke only to eat. I had a lot of spent energy to make up for, I suppose. My body and spirit needed to come back together.

My dreams were vivid, more vivid than waking; they had to do with kites, and Marconi, and the Reverend and Oberon dancing on the rocks. The portrait of my great-great-grandfather came alive and he walked into my room, looming over me, telling me in no uncertain terms that it wasn't bad engineering that had caused the house to slide down the Hill, but my barbarous nature.

"But you put it in the wrong place. Somebody had to fix it."

He reared up, pale eyes glaring down at his miserable, unworthy descendant. He had a whip in his hand.

In my dreams I hunched, terrified of the blow. He would beat me; he would cut my tongue out. My jaw and neck and head ached continually. I scrunched my teeth together even as I slept.

That went on for a long time; I don't know exactly. Christmas came and went, a vague impression of church bells and a Christmas pudding all blue with fire.

All the time I couldn't rest, for where was Clare?

Why hadn't she come to visit me?

Did she hate me now?

She'd been the one to kiss me, up in her bedroom when I'd tried on Clint's clothes. But it was only her merry nature, I knew. She hadn't meant anything by it.

Then what of that time here in my house, when Father had come home and interrupted us? She'd hinted at wanting more, hadn't she?

I'd been about to kiss her when Father had come stumbling in. And after that... up here, in my room...

Nothing had happened that couldn't be explained away as playfulness.

I'd convinced myself that she wanted me, the way I wanted her.

But she saw me only as a friend.

And even if I was *only a friend,* surely, if she cared, she would have come to see me now and make sure I was all right.

So I re-imagined our last encounters, over and over, until I wore the memories into broken threads.

Darkness fell. I tumbled down into a despairing, dreamless state that lasted for a long while.

It was New Year's Eve when Murph and Mary came to call. It took that to rouse me from my miserable state.

They were all dressed up, Mary in a rose-coloured silk dress with a wrap-over bodice, lace about her throat and down the front over a crape underdress. Her hat was the size of a cartwheel, decorated with silken roses that she'd made herself. Murph was put quite in the shade, but he was clever enough in a gleaming top hat, black cutaway dress coat, white waistcoat, and boots so vigorously shone that they nearly blinded one.

They exclaimed of course over the new location of the house, and the manner in which it had arrived there, and the little that had had to be done to level it and ensure its security. A miracle, they said.

That's what everyone said.

When Mother complimented them on their appearance, they told us they were on their way out to the Casino Theatre for a performance by a touring American theatre company. And for the capper, Sir Cavendish Boyle had written a new song inspired by Newfoundland. The night before, it had been performed for the very first time by company star Daisy Foster; all St. John's was a-buzz with it.

Murph had come bearing copies of the *Evening Telegram*, printed crisply on their distinctive pink paper. Every edition contained pieces he'd written about Marconi, over twenty in all. He handed them to my father, but he winked at me as he did so. I knew he'd brought them for me. In my weakened state, this act of kindness almost sent me into tears.

"What's happened?" I asked, reaching for the papers with trembling hands. "What has Marconi been doing?"

"Let them sit down, Dorthea, for heaven's sake, before pestering them with questions. Mary, William, will you take tea in the parlour?"

I had to clamp down on my excitement while Mother served them tea and date cake sent up by Mrs. Taylor.

"I must tell her to cease and desist," she said, "although her baking is divine. She's been sending one of the brats up practically every day with meals and baking and I don't know what else. She even sent up a Christmas pudding, bless her."

My mind flung itself hungrily on this tidbit. So that's where the food with which my mother had been plying me had come from! Mrs. Taylor had been sending it.

Maybe Clare had been the one to deliver it...

But surely I would have known...

No, if Clare had wanted to see me, she would have! She hadn't bothered to come. Mrs. Taylor had sent one of the younger children. Despair seized me once more.

"We've been grateful," Mother went on inexorably. "But I'm quite capable of fending for myself in the food department at this point."

"She is doubtless motivated by a certain urgency to ensure your capable presence at her laying-in," Father said.

"Oh, my goodness, yes, she'll be coming along. William," my mother changed the delicate subject, "these are marvellous articles. I congratulate you. All of us are very proud."

"Thank you! And that is, perhaps, the end of the story as far as Newfoundland is concerned."

End of the story? "What do you mean?" I asked. Surely Marconi was going to stay here and set up a proper station, now that he'd gained his success?

"He left town on Christmas Eve. Hired a sleigh and went around town saying goodbye to every official in officialdom, then left St. John's in a private railway car provided by Reid himself."

I stared blankly. "Marconi *left*?"

"They let us out of the office early to see him off," Father affirmed.

"Marconi *left*, and you saw him *go*?" I felt outraged. Why hadn't Father told me? And how is it I'd not known Marconi was leaving? Not that I expected him to take any notice of me, a mere errand boy, but—

Mary gave a cough, looking at me meaningfully from beneath her eyelashes.

And I remembered. Neither Father nor Mother knew anything about my involvement with the whole grand experiment, and it had to stay that way. Desperately trying to stop the words bubbling up out of my throat, I shoved some cake into my gob.

"Goodness, Dorthea, don't eat like an animal!" Mother admonished.

"People came from miles away to see Marconi off," Murph said, covering for me.

"Weeping ladies," my mother said disapprovingly.

"Weeping newspaper reporters from all over the world too," Mary said.

"You know about the telegraph company, of course?"

"No, what?" I asked thickly through cake, earning a cluck from Mother.

"The nation is in a state of protracted outrage." Murph's eyes gleamed. "The *Telegram* has been snowed under by letters objecting to Anglo-American's threats."

"What threats?" I imagined, with some pleasure, Marconi at gunpoint.

"Their lawyers served notice that Anglo-American Telegraph Company would sue for damages if Marconi persisted in receiving telegraphic messages in Newfoundland so long as they hold the monopoly here," Mary clarified. "And now Canada's poached him. Premier Bond is incandescent with rage."

"He's going to Canada?" I felt a little outrage myself. "After all our government's done for him?"

Father shrugged. "He's a businessman, a man of industry. He'll go wherever he can continue his work."

"Sad thing is, the monopoly is over in less than three years," Mary pointed out.

"I suppose that's too long to wait," Mother said.

Remembering the way Marconi's eyes came into focus with an almost feral light whenever anything to do with the ether came up, I had to agree. I could not see that man waiting three whole years for some lousy monopoly to expire.

Three years was a long time. In three years, I'd be sixteen years old.

"They performed a re-enactment of the great experiment the other day," Murph was saying.

"Oh, yes, everybody who thought themselves fancy was there," Mary laughed. "Sir Robert Bond in top hat and frock coat, Governor Sir Cavendish Boyle naturally, and a murder of government officials, not to mention a swarm of ordinary onlookers, exposing themselves to the miserable weather on Signal Hill—"

"But Mary," I interrupted. "How could they have done it again? Surely they couldn't send or receive signals, with lawyers breathing down their necks?"

"Correct!" Murph affirmed.

"Guaranteed, half the people there will remember *hearing* signals," Mary laughed. "*Oh, I remember the day well! I was there when Signor Marconi transmitted* et cetera *and heard for myself the Morse signal flashing from Cornwall* et cetera*!*"

"I was covering the story," Murph said, with a lowering look. "Marconi practically asked Mary to marry him."

"Now, Murph," Mary soothed.

"He went down on one knee!"

"That dirty, salty dog!" came out of me before I knew I'd even opened my mouth.

Mother looked sideways at me. "Dor. Please. *Try* not to be vulgar."

"Do you think he knew?" Father inquired. "About the monopoly, I mean?"

Murph considered. "Oh, I would think so. He claimed to be astonished when the Anglo-American lawyer spoke to him, but later said he didn't believe the concession applied to *tests*... And a moment later still, protested that he'd modified his plans and set up a temporary installation with only balloons and kites."

"That's true," I pointed out. "I ..." Then I gulped, coming to a standstill, eyes darting over to my parents.

"Yes, but he didn't do that to mollify the telegraph company," Mary came in smoothly. "He did that because his receiving station in Cape Cod was blown flat."

"Anyway, congratulations have been pouring in. The Italian and Russian governments, the *London Times* and the *New York Herald*... This publicity is priceless, and he knows it." Murph twirled his mustache. "Because of the Anglo-American threats, he's an underdog, now. Everybody loves him. It's perfect!"

Marconi had left, then, as he'd arrived—with fanfare, good wishes, and having formed a real relationship with nobody at all. Was it due to that elusive quality in his personality? Or was this the way of the famous? To touch down, and mean something to others—many others—in a way you aren't entirely responsible for, yet must live with and manage?

In the end, Marconi wasn't the centre of my story. He, the great man, was a sidebar.

Nobody else really knew about it, except the Reverend and Oberon.

And Clare.

The portrait of my ancestor with its damaged frame sat atop the piano, awaiting repair. He glared at me. His painted arms went behind his back, as if he was clasping his hands. But I knew he held the whip.

Mother noticed my lowering mood, and said I looked pinched. Mary and Murph took their leave.

I trailed up the stairs back to bed, cold eyes boring into my back.

I lay down for what seemed an age, although it was probably mere minutes. I wasn't tired. I was in despair.

I tossed and turned. Underneath me burned a secret.

Clint Taylor's old clothes still lurked beneath my bed.

I pulled them out of the shadows.

Running my hands over the jacket, caressing the cap, the breeches, I realized I'd been holding them in the hopes of returning them to Clare in person.

If I could bear seeing the casual disregard she felt for me in her eyes.

There was something in the pocket. Sliding my hand inside, I grasped my pocket knife. And there was something else.

Something cool, smooth, and razor-thin came into my palm. A playing card.

I turned it over. No surprise there. Jack of Spades.

I began to smile.

Mary and Murph didn't know everything, but they knew about me being Jack. They'd even accepted it, accepted *me*, that way.

Perhaps they could tell me what to do about Clare...

I'd have to fly to catch them.

Hands trembling, I drew on the clothes. Old friends, sadly neglected, they seemed now. My bedroom window, in our new location, had a convenient hillock right outside; it was a simple matter to lower myself out the window and jump to the ground. I took to my scrapers and ran Over.

It was my first time outside since the day the house slid down the Hill. My legs felt weak. But oh—to breathe in the fresh, cold air!

Would Oberon help me now? As I rattled across the Long Bridge I scanned the sky, but saw no Stygian-feathered messenger in the sky. Only gulls, with empty yellow eyes. This was my knot to untie.

I managed to catch up with Murph and Mary on Duckworth Street, just as they were about to ascend the steps of the Casino. The theatre crowned the top floor of the Total Abstinence Society Hall, an imposing edifice, built—like practically everything—after the Great Fire, with grand arched windows and pediments. A good crowd clustered in the street, and more filed up the stairs to the entrance, but there was no mistaking Mary's hat.

I took off my cap and waved it in the air. "Murph! Mary!"

"Dor?" Murph exclaimed.

I sidled my way through the crowd. "Coming to the theatre with you."

"What!?"

"They'll never let a little girl in, but a disreputable maneen, now, he'll pass."

"I presume your parents have no idea you are here. They'll worry themselves sick," Mary fretted.

"They won't notice I'm gone," I said. "Please? I have to give these back soon," I plucked at the coat, "and it'll be the last time..."

"Oh, for..."

I gave Mary my best pleading look.

"Don't do that! It's not fair."

"There's no harm in it, Mary, is there?" Murph unexpectedly took my side. "I don't think there's anything unsuitable about the play..."

"Well." Her expression softened. "Let's see if we can get you a seat."

"Hurrah!" I leapt into the air.

I had never been inside a theatre. Mary had told me, from her thespian experiences, that it had five dressing rooms, two private boxes, four hundred opera chairs, three hundred gallery seats, and room for six hundred in the pit. The stage, she said, was nearly sixty feet wide. Surely even New York would be proud of such a theatre!

There was some kind of commotion up the stairway, so we drew ourselves against a wall in the foyer.

"Did you get the story to New York, Murph?" I asked.

"I did! They didn't believe me at first. Nor did my editor. But by God, they believe me now."

"He's been New York's main contact ever since." Mary drew his hand into the crook of her elbow.

The commotion up the stair increased, and a man came pushing down towards us. "Mary Kelly! Thank goodness you're here!"

"It's the manager," Murph murmured in my ear.

"What is it?" Mary asked.

"Terrible, simply terrible!" the manager lamented. "Miss Daisy Foster has fallen ill, a putrid sore throat. She can manage the play, but she assures me she can't possibly perform Sir Boyle's new song."

"No," Mary said. "Before you say more..."

"Please, Mary? You know Sir Cavendish. He'll be delighted, he loves you. He's in the theatre," the desperate man panted, "he's in his box right now! Half the house is here for the song, for really, *Mamzelle* is a dreadful play." He wrung his hands. "Please?"

"Oh, for—"

Murph took her hand. "Dor and I will be all right. Do it, Mary!"

I nodded, adding my voice to the chorus. "Please? It's been so long since I heard you sing."

At that her eyes softened. "Dor, you're a devil. All right. And now you can take my seat with Murph, you young imp." She turned to the manager. "Is there a costume? I assume you'll have me in some cruel mess of paste."

"Oh, thank you, thank you, Mary! You've saved the evening."

I remembered little enough of the play after, other than it was supposed to be a farcical comedy. The audience tittered politely, and Murph almost killed me by awaiting the crest of the laughter to fail, then saying loudly in a flat voice, "Ha ha, that's funny."

At the interval we found our way into the backstage frenzy to check on Mary's progress. She was surrounded by women with pins in their mouths, fitting her into the curvaceous Daisy Foster's gown of white, pink, and green—Newfoundland's tricolour, Irish verdure and Tudor rose—and having her twilight tresses piled on her head with costume jewellery wound through. She was holding a hand-written sheet and attempting to memorize the verses.

"Oh, Cavendish. It beggars belief. Pine clad hills? Where in Newfoundland are those? Hello, Murph, hello, Dor. Help me, Dor, be on book for me," and she thrust the sheet into my hands. "Tell me if I'm right. *When blinding storm gusts fret thy shores, and wild waves wash thy strands...* That's a mouthful. The whole front section will be covered with my spit. And what in Jesus' name are *rills*?"

"Two minutes, two minutes!" a woman sang out.

"Why did you talk me into this?"

"I didn't," Murph said in wounded tones. "It was Dor."

"Hey!" I glared.

"Well, it was."

An officious-looking woman in a black gown came up. "Sir Boyle has been informed of Miss Foster's replacement, and he's delighted, Mary," she purred. "He sends his felicitations. One minute, *one minute!*" she bellowed, disappearing at a flat run.

"You'd better get back to your seats," Mary said in despair, turning to the costumers. "Oh, goodness, can we leave that one out? My hair weighs twenty pounds already!"

Murph took me back to the pit. "She'll be wonderful," he said. I noticed his hands were twisting nervously together. "She'll be fine."

"She really will, you know," I said. "Nobody sings like Mary!"

He smiled. "You're right, Dor."

Was it my imagination, or was the room buzzing with even more anticipation than before the play? I craned my neck, looking for the Governor—there he was! Up in a private box.

I realized then that I still held Mary's lyric sheet in my hands. With a start I jumped up. How would she remember all those words? She'd only had a bare minute to memorize it...

And the lights in the theatre were extinguished, and the worried little man from the foyer came onto the stage.

WE LOVE THEE

"Ladies and gentlemen," the Casino Theatre manager announced, "I have the sorrow of conveying to you all that Miss Daisy Foster is not in voice this evening." His accent had totally changed. In the foyer he'd been a St. John's man; now he sounded like he'd just gotten off the boat from England. "She will not, therefore, be rendering the new tune by our beloved Governor, Sir Cavendish Boyle."

The audience murmured, ripples going across a pond.

"However, with great pleasure I introduce to the stage our own..." He paused dramatically. "Mary Kelly!"

Murph's hand reached out and clasped mine, almost breaking the bones. Under his breath, he was praying.

Mary emerged from the wings. Her tower of hair swayed perilously, glinting with a pandemonium of artificial jewels, and the robe was drawn so tightly about her torso I wondered how she was able to breathe, especially with all those pins I'd seen...

She took centre stage, and paused.

And looked straight at me and Murph, and smiled.

The orchestra began to play an unfamiliar tune. Mary opened her mouth. And the world turned to sunshine.

She'd sung to me when I was young, before everything went wrong in our house and she'd had to leave. That voice had been with me from the beginning of time.

It was a simple song the Governor had penned, singing the praises of each season, rising gradually to a straightforward chorus that alighted back down to earth.

We love thee, we love thee,
We love thee...

And then the appropriate adjective. *Smiling, frozen, windswept land.*

By the third verse the entire audience was singing along to the chorus, and by the time Mary got to the final verse, the place was on its feet, roaring like the sea.

God guard thee, Newfoundland!

Tumultuous applause.

"She took the roof off!" Murph said. "She took the roof off!" He dashed tears from his eyes, and applauded louder than anybody. "Brava! Brava!"

"Brava!" I yelled.

Mary curtseyed like a queen, and her tower of hair didn't even quiver.

"Miss Kelly rendered with exquisite feeling a new song robed in pink, white, and green. The audience took up the last refrain, and general appreciation was marked by unstinting applause. It now transpires that the song was composed by our popular and esteemed Governor, and the ode may be destined to become our colonial anthem, for we sorely lack one... My God, I'm turning into a hack."

"Yes. You've got the song robed, not me."

"Correct you are, Mary. Correct you are."

Murph and Mary were walking me back to the bridge. My feet dragged, for I knew that once home, I'd have to put off these clothes. Surely by now Clare's mother must have wondered what had become of them.

"Dor, there's something we have to tell you," Mary broke into my thoughts.

I looked up, heart sinking lower. It was never good when grownups said they had something to tell you. "What is it?"

"Murph and I... we're going to New York."

"Well, I assumed that." Suspicion grew. "When?"

"After New Year's Day."

"But that's... that's tomorrow!" My mind whirled. "Don't you have to get married first?"

"We're going to. We're not inviting our families. In fact, you're the only person we've told."

"You're *eloping*?" I couldn't believe my ears.

"We can't get our families involved," Mary waved her hands. "Between the two families, there's about two hundred of them, and..."

"And I've gotten a job with the *Times*," Murph said. "On the strength of my reporting for the Marconi story. So that's moved the timeline up a bit." He gripped my shoulder. "And I have you to thank for that, Dor."

Tears pushed at my throat and my eyes.

"I don't want you to go," I said. Then I shook my head. "I mean, congratulations. That's wonderful." I felt like I was going to my own funeral.

"Dor? We want you to come visit us."

I stared down at the ground, where the toe of my boot was occupied with trying to pry a cobblestone out of the street and kick it into next week.

"I mean it," Mary's voice came gently. "We're going to get settled, and as soon as you're old enough we'll send a ticket for you to come."

Old enough. How old was old enough? It would be years.

I nodded, unwilling to raise my head. I didn't want her to see my tears.

"That's a promise, Jack Kelly," Murph said, punching my shoulder.

That got a gulp and a smile out of me. "I'd like that," I whispered. I forced myself to meet their eyes. "You going to study singing, Mary? You brought the house down tonight. You really did."

"I am!" she declared. "Some day I will sing Bellini's *Norma* on the stage of La Scala! And then settle down in wedded bliss with Murph, of course."

"You'll need a stage name," I said.

"You're telling me. I am proud of my family name, but sadly, Mary Kelly won't do for La Scala. And no offense, Murph, but Mary Murphy is even worse."

"What about Marie something? That sounds suitably mysterious," Murph said.

"Marie. Marie de la something," she mused.

I looked over at the darkness of the hulking Southside Hills, the massive tor that had dominated my entire life. "Marie de la Roche!" I exclaimed.

"Marie de la Roche. Mary of the Rock. I like that."

As we moved away from the electric light of Water Street, stars blazed out in the winter sky. Murph and Mary walked hand in hand, pointing out the constellations: Ursa Major, the Great Bear; Orion, the Hunter; Machina Electrica, the Electricity Generator—just south of the Sea Monster—and Murph's favourite, Officina Typographica, the Printing Press. "Soon there will be one for a wireless telegraphy machine named Marconius Magna," he jested.

The image burned in our minds, and we walked in silence to the south end of the bridge.

"How will the world change now," I wondered, "if we can talk to each other any time at all? I could talk to you in New York just like we are standing here now!"

"Amazing to think on," Mary said. "Perhaps people will come to understand each other better. I hope it will be a force for good."

"It will certainly make my life easier," Murph said. "I'll be able to send reports anywhere in the world, instantly, wire or no wire. Boggles the mind."

"But it could make people worse, too," I said.

"How do you mean?"

I shook my head. All the telegraphy in the world wouldn't help me with my problem with Clare; she still didn't feel the things I felt. "People are people. New technology doesn't change what we are."

"Well, cheerio my deario, on that pleasant note... we bid you farewell." Mary pulled me into her, hugging me tight. "Don't change, Dor, and get all smart." She sounded like she was crying. "Promise me that. Hang on to the good things." She held me out at arm's length. "We'll see you in New York. That's *my* promise."

I nodded. "I can't wait," I said truthfully.

I stood and watched them walking Over, hand in hand, until I lost them in the dark.

The thought of living without them made my heart so heavy I thought it would fall out my body and onto the road like a stone. They were practically the only ones who seemed not to care that I was no young lady, but some mixed-up amalgam of boy and girl. In fact, they cheered me on. They prized me. They made me feel as though I was, in my awkward person, not annoying, not abominable, not even merely adequate, but grand.

But I'd get to New York some day. I would. The idea frightened me, and it also filled my body with thrilling, like electricity running through me from top of head through torso and down my thighs. The desire to see that great place left me panting, and I found myself gripping the rail of the bridge, swaying a little.

I'd get there. And I'd live there some day. Something awaited me, something I'd been feeling my way toward all my life, blind but sure as a meandering underground river.

CLARE

I hadn't asked Murph and Mary what I should do about Clare. I hadn't asked, because I no longer needed advice.

I wanted to see her, now, more than anything. I wouldn't be Dor, timid and unsure. No, tonight—for maybe the last time in a long while—I'd be who I wanted to be.

If she hadn't been to see me all these past days because she no longer cared for me— because she'd seen the abomination I was and was now disgusted—I had to find that out. I had to face it, head-on.

I ran into the night, up the Hundred Steps. It was late, and only the kitchen window was lit up inside the Taylors'. I crept around to the side of the house and peered in.

Mrs. Taylor sat knitting turned away from the window, stomach curved out like a bellying sail. Nanny King rocked by the stove. And sewing buttons onto one of her brother's shirts by the light of a lamp on the windowsill sat Clare!

She looked so lovely that my breath caught in my throat. The lamplight lit her white throat with a rosy glow; her eyes were downturned on her work, but her mouth was moving, red lips curving, and her mother gave out a great laugh at something her daughter had said.

Nan hitched in her rocking and looked right at the window, right at me—no—through me. That Nan, she saw everything...

With a shiver, I slid away into the shadows. This was madness. There was no way Dor's mysterious "cousin" could come calling at this time of night, not after weeks of invisibility. And in any case, what did I think I was going to say to Clare? I should just go home.

Then that electric feeling surged through me again. No. I didn't know what I would say or do, but I was going to see Clare Taylor this night!

Peeping around through the window again, I saw Nan looking down into her lap now, mashing her gums together with eyes closed.

I scratched at the windowpane.

Nobody responded. I scratched some more. Then gave three taps. Three taps, such as I had heard through Marconi's receiver. Three taps, such as Oberon used to wake me.

And Clare looked up; she saw me there. She gave a great start, clapping her hand to her mouth. And then she dropped her hand, and smiled.

Joy poured through me. Almost I wanted to laugh. I gestured that she should come outside.

Her cheeks flushed, a merry glint coming into her eyes. Rising, she threw a shawl over her head, then slid along the kitchen wall to the door.

Nan King looked up, and her black eyes blazed at me like twin stars in a new constellation.

She held me, transfixed, for a lost moment, and then, deliberately, she closed her eyes. I felt like something had taken hold of me—searched me through, like a beam from a lighthouse in the dead of night—and decided I was all right.

Clare stepped out into the night.

My joy became a kind of recklessness. I strode over to Clare Taylor, drawing her into the shadows under the rock of the Hill. By starlight she looked like a creature from a fairytale. I doffed my cap, smoothing my hand over my hair like I'd seen so many boys and men do.

She saw my boyish cut, and gasped.

"Do you like it?" I whispered with a grin.

She reached out and tucked a curl behind my ear, the touch of her fingers sending thrills down my body. "You looks some handsome, Dor!" she breathed. And then her words came out in a tumble. "Where have you been? I've been that worried. I didn't know if you was even alive! Your house fell down the hill, slid right down like a sled! It was horrible. I thought you was dead! I went down to your house about sixteen times, but your parents always said you was sleeping..."

"You came?" Joy surged through me.

"I've never baked so much in me life! I'm sick to death of it; I never wants to see our battered old cake pan ever again as long as I live, swear to God."

The food, the baking... "That was you?"

"Of course! Dor, of course I came!" Then she bit her lip. "But, Dor, why wouldn't you see me?"

"I was in bed... I didn't know you were there."

"In bed? For so long? Even... even over Christmas?" Her voice caught. Clare loved Christmas, I well knew. She treated it as her own personal holiday, generously shared with the world at large.

"I hit my head. I got a concussion..."

She gasped. "Are you all right?"

"I am now."

"Dor, I thought your parents had decided you couldn't see me any more..." Her voice choked with tears, "... and, and that they *knew*, and I'd never be allowed to see you again..."

"Knew what?" I was about to go on, say I didn't know, acting as though I was in a confusion.

Why? Because I couldn't believe it—no—was my Clare telling me that she... that she...?

There are moments in life when you think, *I'll always remember this; it's golden.* And you do, because it's sweet and hard and resplendent as rock candy—no, better—as treasure.

No, better than all that, because neither barley sugar nor gold will last. But the feeling when the queen of my life pulled me close, that moment when I kissed Clare Taylor's sweet mouth, and she kissed me back, would stay with me forever.

Forever and a day.

Nanny King passed away from this life on New Year's Day.

My parents and I went down to the Taylor house, bringing food and condolences in galore. Nan was laid out in the Taylor's front parlour. I'd never seen the room before, for they never used it except if the minister came to visit, or for times like now. When someone died.

The room was numerous with people. Everyone from up and down the Southside and even Over came to pay their respects; everybody spoke in low tones, saying what a shame she died on the first of the year, but what a good long life she had had! *Sorry for your troubles... sorry for your troubles... sorry for your troubles.*

As it grew darker the lights came on across the water.

Clare was kept busy, running back and forth with tea and arranging the offerings of food. I had wrapped up Clint's old clothes in a brown paper package, and I slid this to her when an opportunity presented itself. "I washed the shirt," I said. It was the least I could do.

"Thanks," she said, then thrilled me by dropping her eyes to my mouth and letting her gaze linger there for a long time, surrounded as we were by people. Her merry eyes came back up. "Made your knees weak, didn't I?"

"You know you did."

She pushed the package back into my hands. "Keep them. Mother won't ever notice."

"Clare, I can't—"

"Please? For me?" She put her mouth to my ear. "I wants you to have them. Our secret."

I stared at her, speechless with joy.

A stir at the door pulled us away from gazing foolishly into each other's eyes.

"Caw! Caw!"

It was the Reverend! With Oberon on his shoulder!

It was very strange to see him, here, in his tail coat and trousers. He processed through the room with his lop-sided, stiff-legged gait, not even glancing at me, and the crowd made way for him. He marched over to the coffin, and placed his hand on Nanny's brow. The room fell into silence. He bowed his head and seemed to pray.

Then he nodded, a single, decisive nod. Oberon spread his wings and cried out.

"She's gone to her reward," Mrs. Taylor breathed, awed. "I felt her spirit leave the body. They've seen Mother on her way."

Her husband, oddly tender, put his arm around her, and the room filled with hushed and wondering talk.

Turning, the Reverend lurched slowly across the carpet. When he got to me, Oberon rolled marbles in his throat, that tender sound. The Reverend stopped, stretching to his full four-foot-eleven, and put a hand on my shoulder.

"Good job," he whispered. "They're happy, now. In fact," and he leaned even closer, speaking so quietly I could hardly hear, "They can't wait for it to happen again. They're *bouncing!*"

"Bouncing?"

He raised a finger. "I don't exactly have it figured. But I suspect there was some part of the Hertzian waves, a different spectrum, that Marconi needed to be using. He had no way to know this. But They did. And They burst open his frequencies until the signal could be received. And this, they rode. From Signal Hill to Cornwall and back again." He looked about, ensuring that only Clare was overhearing us. "Quicker than forty minutes," he chuckled. "Faster than anybody could imagine."

I stroked Oberon's head with a finger, gazing into his bright eyes. Something told me we would not be speaking Crow to each other anymore, and sadness touched my heart.

"Was it worth it?" the Reverend asked.

Our eyes met, and I saw, to my surprise, that a tear trembled in the Reverend's. "Worth it?" I repeated. "Oh, yes. All of it."

EPILOGUE

It took more than three days to write this.

But then, you already know that.

Tomorrow our quarantine lifts.

I will venture into the streets to buy some food, and I will make you the best damn meal of which I am capable. We will eat it sitting up at our rickety table, with candles and linens scrounged from church sales. I will wear my favourite suit, complete with that tie you say you like the best.

For you are alive! You are alive.

And then, for you insist, I will read this to you.

You gave me the answer to the puzzle of the Ship of Theseus. *Ship!* you exclaimed. *It's just a word. Parts of the ship are replaced over time, sure. The identity of the ship, little by little, changes.*

But it is the same ship—or house, or person—as long as we keep telling the stories.

Do the stories have to be true?

Yes.

Do they have to agree on the facts?

No.

Facts matter. But sometimes they aren't the only way to the truth.

The influenza epidemic is subsiding. It tore across a famine-weakened, war-ravaged globe like a Great Fire. What utter destruction our people have wrought. Carrying our warfare sunward, like Wells's insatiable aliens.

Nobody knows how many died around the world. So many countries were involved in the War; they reflexively censor the news. Murph—in contact with other journalists around the globe—suspects unbelievable, obscene numbers of victims have succumbed, as many as fifty million, maybe more. But he and Mary are safe. Most of our friends are safe. It's a miracle. Everybody says so.

Within a year of his experiments in Newfoundland, Marconi established reliable communication with ships over two thousand miles away. Radio is an accepted fact, now, and it has changed the world, for good and bad. We have survived a terrible Great War, you and I, a war that used radio to help kill millions of people.

I wish I could claim credit for tricking the tortured beings into freeing my mother. And in a way, I did. But if They hadn't learned how to bounce off the higher levels of the atmosphere, I doubt anything I tried would have worked. And in the end, it was the shifting of the house that mattered most, and how that occurred will never be clear in my mind.

The throbbing ache of homesickness that I felt after leaving St. John's was unexpected. It was a physical pain. It has dulled over the years. Or perhaps I've simply become inured to it.

This body is, in superficial respects, the same body as that of the thirteen-year-old who first felt a thrill when pulling on boy's breeches. But the body has grown up, now, and has found a place in this great city. The filthy urchin is friend to a number of brilliant artists, refugees from war and from life. The urchin's work is published, excoriated, debated, and celebrated in a magazine of the best new work being produced. And that magazine is published by women who wear men's clothing. One of them wears lipstick and gauzy dresses, too, but only as the mood takes her, or when she needs to charm wealthy patrons into funding the magazine. Often enough, it works.

You and I live among people who aren't afraid to be themselves, all philosophizing about ships aside.

The sensuous feel of words in the mouth, in the body— the look of words on the page—the raw, the true, the personal— wild erasures of boundaries between art and life—this is my work.

I write my parents' love of old poetry—the echo of the cliff I grew up under, singing back to the skies—the tidal bore, swelling the river twice a day—the inspired breath of Christmas strangers— the rote of the sea—the sighing chaw of the house, trying to suck us under. *You're ours. You're ours. You're ours.*

Critics call my poems a reckless and dangerous devotion to irrationality and intuition. Oh, yes, please, in the face of the great slaughter let us be rational!

What am I? An abomination.

I am also an artist, an exile, an emergency kitchen volunteer, and a survivor. What runs through it, for me, is a shimmering crescent stretching from our bleeding earth to the tumult of the wounded skies. Sawtoothed, glistering, with an impossible void at the centre. What other people call *reality* is the merest fragment, glimpsed between the jagged-edged dance of falling stars, and the light-sucking hole.

I first saw it that December, when I was still a child. It has never left me, nor those glimmering creatures of home.

It is dawn. Your fever has broken. Your Jack lies next to you. And as I fall into sleep, the image comes through with the clarity of a sudden strong radio signal breaking through static: the tall, bald hill and the gleam of a kite, white against a colourless sky, and the rough hands of the wind, pulling me into the air.

ACKNOWLEDGEMENTS

Nobody does this alone. Many people and works have aided me with this book.

Without Marnie, *Urchin* would literally not exist. She asked for "historical, set in Newfoundland, for younger readers, with fairies." I hope this satisfies the bill! Your work as a publisher and editor bring life and delight to so many of us, for which I am profoundly grateful. Thank you, too, to Veselina Tomova for the design, and to the whole crew at Running the Goat.

Essential research includes Marc Raboy's *Marconi: The Man who Networked the World*; Barbara Rieti's *Strange Terrain* (again, and I am sure not for the last time); Paul O'Neill's *The Oldest City* and *A Seaport Legacy: The Story of St. John's, Newfoundland*—those familiar with these quixotic historical tomes will recognize aspects of real-life characters in this novel! Helen Porter's *Below the Bridge* once again proved invaluable to me, as did a long and utterly delightful phone call. Katharine Briggs's *An Encyclopedia of Fairies* was essential help. G.M. Story's article "Building a St. John's Victorian House" confirmed many things I thought I already knew about the house I grew up in, and the older one down the road, while also delivering fascinating facts of which I was completely ignorant; I thieved merrily to build the fictional house in this book. G. M. Story (also known as Dad) comes in for thanks again along with Herbert Halpert for the fabulous *Christmas Mumming in Newfoundland*. *The Dictionary of Newfoundland English* (Story, Kirwan, Widdowson) is not only a word-hoard, but illuminates the light and shadow of the lives of our forebears on the island, and I am very grateful to it and for all the work an army of people put into it. Any mistakes are mine, not anybody else's!

I quote H.G. Wells's *War of the Worlds*, and one of the poetic letters of John Donne, as well as his poem "Song" (more often known as "Go and Catch a Falling Star"), and bits from Shakespeare's *A Midsummer Night's Dream, Hamlet,* and *The Tempest.* I am grateful to Heritage Newfoundland and Labrador for their excellent online articles, as well as MUN's online archives of the *Evening Telegram,* from which I stole liberally in composing Murph's articles.

I have moved the "Ode to Newfoundland"'s initial performance almost a year earlier, and given the (second) performance to Mary. I also built on the controversy over whether Marconi did actually hear those three clicks. Some say he could not have done so; this article from the *Guardian* perhaps explains it best: https://www.theguardian.com/education/2001/dec/11/highereducation.news. I used this kernel of doubt to build an idea that the Little Strangers actually, in the end, aided and abetted Marconi's transmissions by bouncing off the then-undiscovered ionosphere. Please also note that the Marconi depicted here is a fictional version of the real person.

And, of course, then there are the people who helped me write the damn thing. Joe Davies and Janette Platana were my earliest readers, and pushed me to make it better with their incisive comments and editorial feedback; they didn't always agree, which helped me even more. Big thank yous to my first younger readers, Zoey and Kristian, for giving me substantive feedback, and making me feel that this might actually work. To Lindsay, thank you for believing in this book, and reading it so closely and with much intelligence and wit. JoAnne,

I don't believe I would have gotten through the first draft without you—for your compassionate heart and incisive wisdom, I am always grateful. To my brother Lachlan, keeper of the remaining tomes from our father's library, gratitude and love. To Simon, for constant encouragement and reflection, much love and respect. Love and gratitude to my mother— for being able to see Them, and for being at all times who she was—a brilliant flare against the dark. And also to my father, for his love of language, and of home, and for making me know in my bones that books matter. Big love to Charlie Petch, for not only reading the book, but also for having Dor's back, and helping me articulate my genderqueerness; I will always be grateful for your kind, clear-eyed thoughts and support. Gratitude, too, to Colleen Quigley and Jessie Chisholm for reading for historical accuracy (again, any mistakes are mine, not theirs!). I was very lucky to be able to approach Gerry Penney with bizarre questions about plumbing and electricity on the Southside Road in 1901, which he answered with great good humour for months on end; news of his passing left me gutted, and my sincere condolences go out to his loved ones. Melvin Baker helped me tremendously as well with articles, historical lore, and a good talk on the phone. Love always and gratitude to my Aunty Ann, who told me that Great-grandfather White was the Inspector of Lighthouses, and that Marconi actually came over to the house for tea! Bill Coultas provided some valuable perspectives on the Southside Road and old stories about his relatives and mine. And I'd be remiss not to mention everybody who weighed in on an epic Facebook thread that also serves as a list for a kitchen party in heaven: Colleen Quigley, Benjamin van Veen, Dale Jarvis, Amy Bowring (to whom I owe the "hoop and scarf evolutions" —WHAT ARE THEY???), Heather Squires, Ruth Lawrence, Alison Butler, Geoff Younghusband, Alison Carter, David Somers, Philip Hiscock, Alanna Wicks, Christopher Darlington, Annemarie Christie, and Neachel Keeping.

If anyone is curious, the New York publishers mentioned near the end of the book are Margaret Anderson and Jane Heap; they helmed *The Little Review*, and were fascinating, brilliant people who attracted likewise fascinating artists to them, so far ahead of their time that we are still catching up.

If you've never had someone in your life who has your back, I highly recommend it. Finally, as always, deep gratitude, respect, and love to Ryan. You are my coming home.

Photo: Wade Eardley

Kate Story is a genderqueer writer and theatre artist from
St. John's, Newfoundland and Labrador. Uncanny occurrences
were not unheard-of when Kate was growing up in the house
on the Southside Road built by Kate's great-great-grandfather.

Having fled to the mainland at sixteen, Kate keeps coming
home to see family, present the occasional performance work,
and get the occasional fit of the shudders. Kate lives
in Peterborough/Nogojiwanong, Ontario, where the shudders
are fuel for the writing and performance work.

Previous novels include *Blasted, Wrecked Upon This Shore,
This Insubstantial Pageant*, and YA fantasy duo *Antilia*. Next
year sees the publication of Kate's collected short fiction *Ferry
Back the Gifts*.

This book was designed by Veselina Tomova of Vis-à-vis Graphics,
St. John's, NL,
and printed in Canada.

978-1-927917435

Running the Goat, Books & Broadsides is grateful to Newfoundland and
Labrador's Department of Tourism, Culture, Industry and Innovation
for support of its publishing activities through the province's Publishers
Assistance Program; to the Canadian Department of Heritage and
Multiculturalism for support through the Canada Book Fund; and to the
Canada Council for the Arts for support through its Literary Publishing
Projects Program.

Canada Council   Conseil des arts
for the Arts   du Canada

Funded by the Government of Canada
Financé par le gouvernement du Canada | Canada

Running the Goat
Books & Broadsides Inc.
General Delivery/54 Cove Road
Tors Cove, Newfoundland and Labrador A0A 4A0

www.runningthegoat.com